CONTENTS

Preface

WHEN "Manager Qiao Assumes Office" appeared in the *Worker's Daily* in 1979, the author Jiang Zilong, the head of a workshop in a large heavy machinery plant in Tianjin, was a relatively obscure amateur writer who had been publishing fiction since 1965. The story was immensely popular and thus marked a turning-point in Jiang Zilong's literary career. It was broadcast over the radio and adapted for television. Almost overnight Manager Qiao entered the ranks of Chinese folk heroes, and his creator became something of a celebrity.

Slogans welcoming Manager Qiao were pasted up by some workers in their factories, while others bought copies of the story and gave them to their managers to read. An anecdote, quite authentic, tells how a certain vice-minister of a certain ministry telephoned Jiang Zilong's editors to ascertain who the model for Manager Qiao was in order to promote him. Yet the story was regarded as controversial, and some critics had misgivings about the socialism of Manager Qiao's peremptory methods. The *Tianjin Daily* launched a full-page condemnation of the story. Fortunately Jiang Zilong had strong nerves. Angered by the attack, many people wrote letters to the paper supporting Jiang Zilong, while some individuals even went to protest in person. Opinion remained divided, and Jiang Zilong was asked by the director of his plant to give up writing altogether.

Then a forum of writers and editors was held in Beijing to discuss "Manager Qiao Assumes Office", which Jiang Zilong attended. While certain weaknesses in the story were pointed out, Jiang Zilong was finally vindicated, praised and encouraged to write more. Moreover, the story went on to win the first prize in the first-class awards section of the 1979 National Short Story Competition.

Industry is notoriously difficult to write about even in China, where literature about factories and workers abounds. In the West such writing is rare. While reports carried in English-language publications are packed with facts and figures concerning the problems and progress of Chinese industry, they are often hard going for the foreign layman. Jiang Zilong's talent lies in his ability to communicate vividly what it feels like to be a worker, manager, Party secretary or bureau chief at a time when China's modernization means being flexible and not rigid, discarding archaic, useless practices and experimenting with new techniques.

China aims to quadruple production by the end of this century, and for that an annual growth rate of 7.2 per cent must be maintained. This cannot be achieved without modernizing the economy. According to an article in the magazine *Red Flag*, there were 382,000 industrial enterprises in China by 1981. Many of these do not run at full capacity and some have already closed down. Only a few are technologically advanced by international standards, while most meet only the standards of the 1960s or even the 1950s. The Chinese labour force lacks sufficient education with too few skilled workers, technicians, engineers and competent managerial staff. It is against this backdrop that Jiang Zilong writes.

He knows the industrial scene intimately, for he has been attached to Tianjin Heavy Machinery Plant since 1958, except for a five-year stint in the navy. He said, "I've been a worker, a foreman, a secretary to a manager and now I'm head of a workshop. I've also studied how enterprises are run in Hungary, Yugoslavia, Japan, the United States and the Soviet Union. I know much more about industry than literature." He has witnessed the developments and setbacks from the disastrous Great Leap Forward of 1958, the economic recovery, and the chaos of the "cultural revolution" to the present drive for modernization.

"Manager Qiao Assumes Office" was the result of Jiang Zilong's systematic study of economics, bureaucracy and politics. "It was inspired by my political sense. I don't really regard it as a work of literature. I paid little attention to style." His characters accurately voice the thoughts and feelings of millions of Chinese workers, and Qiao Guangpu embodies the kind of qualities they wish their managers to have: energy, expertise, confidence, resourcefulness, boldness and vision. Jiang Zilong remarked, "Whether you like it or not, only people like Qiao can achieve anything in our society today. I've visited many factories, and those that are efficient have managers like Qiao."

Jiang Zilong draws heavily on his experiences and acquaintances for his plots and characters. Qiao Guangpu was modelled on five managers he knew. In 1979, when Manager Qiao made everyone in his plant sit exams to separate the skilled and capable from the untrained and incompetent, such ideas were still new. Those who failed were demoted to a service team until they improved their levels. Now 60 per cent of Chinese factories have such service teams. Also debatable were rewards or penalties for good or bad work. Only in the summer of 1982 did Premier Zhao Ziyang at a National Conference on the Reorganization of Industrial Enterprises stress officially the policy of rewarding the hardworking and penalizing the lazy. This was further emphasized at the 12th Party Congress in September 1982 by the Minister in Charge of the State Economic Commission, Zhang Jinfu.

The city of Xiangfan in Hubei Province made the front page of the *People's Daily*, cited as a successful example of rapid industrial growth in China. Among the measures taken there was the removal of 21 incompetent leading cadres from their posts, while 38 engineers and technicians were promoted to be directors and factory leaders. Also more than 400 factory directors and high officials were rotated through training sessions in business management and related subjects. In Fuxin, Liaoning Province, however, 78 industrial enterprises continue to suffer financial losses, mainly because of mismanagement of lack of responsibility by the leadership. According to the *Liaoning Daily*, serious steps are being taken. Leaders of these unprofitable enterprises have been advised to resign if they feel they cannot improve the situation. Those leaders, including directors and secretaries, who do not resign, will be removed and demoted if their enterprises still show deficits by the end of 1982. The city government will also award and promote those managerial

staff who turn their enterprises from losing into prof-
itable concerns.

When people remark on his foresight in predicting
trends in industry, Jiang Zilong explains that he is
merely describing existing situations which he tries to
record truthfully. As head of a workshop with nine
hundred men under him, he himself was confronted
with seven slackers who refused to mend their ways.
Finally he removed them from their jobs and formed
them into a service team to clean the lavatories and
showers and do other menial chores. Furious, the men
complained to their Party secretary, who went to talk to
Jiang Zilong. "I told him, if you don't agree, then
dismiss me. If you want me to lead this workshop, then
don't interfere." The Party secretary decided to turn a
blind eye to the whole affair, thus giving Jiang Zilong
his tacit support. The young workers therefore had no
backing. Their personal lives were also affected, for
like Du Ping in "Manager Qiao Assumes Office", who
is ditched by his girlfriend, these young men found
themselves in similar predicaments. After about six
months, when their attitudes had changed, they returned
to their old work.

It is interesting to note that the 60 million young
workers aged under 35 account for 60 per cent of the
total industrial work force in China. An article in *Red
Flag* analyzing this force stated that 20 per cent are
advanced workers; 50 per cent make high demands on
themselves; 25 per cent fulfil their production quotas
but lack proper motivation; and 5 per cent lead
meaningless lives and work in a slapdash manner. It
also stated that less than 5 in every 1,000 actually vio-
late rules and discipline.

"Manager Qiao Assumes Office" and its sequel "More About Manager Qiao", like all Jiang Zilong's writing, introduce readers to the realities of Chinese factories. It's a warts-and-all portrait. Qiao Guang-pu is confronted with the importance of connections (*guanxi*), something to which he is not naturally inclin-ed. Ji Shen, however, excels at this, having helped some high cadres in difficulty during the "cultural rev-olution". Now they are back in power, they owe him some favours. There is the "iron rice bowl", which guarantees job security: a person will normally receive his salary or wage and cannot be sacked, even if he is lazy or unfit for the work. But this is changing. Some leaders hesitate to make decisions or take the initiative for fear of incurring political risks.

There was the problem, uncommon today, of un-qualified persons ordering expensive yet useless foreign equipment, thereby wasting precious foreign currency. A recent report in the Shanghai *World Economic Herald* pointed out that in 1978 the wrong decision was made to import 22 unnecessary sets of equipment, squandering 12 billion dollars of China's foreign exchange. The projects also needed 55,000 million yuan of domestic investment which could not be met. Thus the whole foreign currency situation worsened. Ji Shen, who indulges in this, is described by Jiang Zilong as "a country moneybags shopping in Shanghai in the old days", who wants everything he sees, the more expensive the better.

Manager Qiao makes this anguished reply when he is asked how he spends his time: "Forty per cent on pro-duction, fifty per cent on wrangles and ten per cent on slanders." To which Huo Dadao, the bureau chief, comments: "You should spend eighty per cent of your time on production and the rest on research." Unfortunately it is not an ideal world.

Though he presents many of the negative aspects that impede China's modernization, Jiang Zilong also describes the positive forces that are combatting them. There are responsible and far-sighted leaders like Huo Dadao, who supports and encourages Manager Qiao with these words: "Modernization doesn't mean technique alone. You'll have to offend some people. Of course, it's safest to do nothing, but that's criminal. . . . If you want to achieve something, demand a free rein. We're racing against time." The minister also asks Qiao to be bolder and experiment with new methods. At all levels from the top down, men and women are using their imagination and initiative to overcome the problems. Jiang Zilong's stories chronicle the changes in the industrial scene and inspire Chinese workers to strive for a better future. While analyzing and criticizing, Jiang Zilong also points to solutions. His tone is optimistic not defeatist.

In "More About Manager Qiao" for example, Qiao starts to introduce ideas new to China, but well established abroad, such as modern selling methods to compete with foreign products on the world market, setting up a sales department, advertising products, printing attractive brochures for home and foreign consumption, meeting orders promptly, servicing machines, supplying spare parts and doing market research. It may be an uphill struggle, but reading Jiang Zilong's stories one is convinced Chinese workers will make it to the top.

His characters are realistic. Manager Qiao is not a

shining plastic hero of the type manufactured *ad nauseam* during the "cultural revolution". He emerges as credible, a man with fine qualities and certain weaknesses. One failing is his quick temper. He is not the easiest of men to work with, nor the most understanding of husbands, of which latter fact he is cheerfully unaware.

His stories often contain interesting glimpses of Chinese life. There is, for example, a delightful scene at the home of Tie Jian, the chief of the Municipal Economic Commission. From a poor peasant background, Tie has risen to become a leading cadre. Readers see how the extended family system works in China, as Tie's relatives and fellow villagers descend on him to seek his help. Though he cannot meet their demands, he must, out of politeness, at least offer them some hospitality. His home is like a country inn full of peasants consuming bowls of noodles, which they feel he can easily afford on his high salary, while his wife, like the innkeeper, bustles about providing food and drink day and night.

"Pages from a Factory Secretary's Diary", in terms of writing, is a more polished piece of work, yet paradoxically Jiang Zilong finished the basic draft in only one night. The language is terse, the style ironic. Before he wrote it, Jiang Zilong had been reading the essays of Lu Xun, and perhaps something of their economic prose stuck. In the form of a diary kept by Wei, secretary to the new manager Jin Fengchi, the story describes how Jin revives the enthusiasm of his workers and increases production in his factory. A somewhat jaded observer, Wei has watched three managers come and go in the space of four years, all victims of

Luo, the ruthless Assistant Manager. Wei, believing that he has seen it all, takes nothing to heart any more. That is until Manager Jin arrives, for he soon shakes Wei out of his lethargy. Jin establishes his authority over Luo and shows his concern for the workers' welfare, winning their support. His unorthodox methods, however, bring him into increasing conflict with Liu, the Party secretary. A decent man, Liu is, as Wei notes, "too old-fashioned and too inflexible", whose ideas pre-date those of 1958. The times have changed, but Liu has not. While not actually breaking any rules, Jin is prepared to bend them to the limit. When the question of the bonuses arises, Jin must either offend Liu or his workers, and he chooses the former.

Like Qiao, Jin is a believable character. Though he cares for the interests of his men, he ignores the needs of his family. As a result of his neglect, his home is the opposite of domestic bliss. Jiang Zilong explained that the model for Jin was a friend of his. "He's a Party member and his factory is well run. He knows the problems of the bureaucracy and the importance of connections, so he has found his way of dealing with the system as it stands now. He's totally selfless and does everything for socialism, but he does it his way. For example, bonuses were supposed to be equivalent to two and a half months' pay maximum, but he stretched it to three and a half months. He gets results and his factory is one of the best. He's trusted by the workers and production keeps going up."

One night he visited Jiang Zilong's home and sat drinking and grousing about some problems. After he left, Jiang Zilong decided to write about him and the story took shape within a few hours. When it was published, some managers were rather angry, suspecting Jiang Zilong had written about them, and one complained to the authorities. Workers, however, appreciated Jin's methods and wrote many letters to that effect. As one said, "If we can't have Qiao, Jin will do."

Chinese writers and intellectuals particularly like the literary style of "Pages from a Factory Secretary's Diary". Workers tend to prefer the stories about Manager Qiao. Young people find the novelette "All the Colours of the Rainbow" most appealing because it deals specifically with their lives and problems. The novelette won an important literary prize and has since been adapted for television and as a feature film. Its main characters Liu Sijia, the driver, and Xie Jing, his deputy team leader, have both been disillusioned and scarred by the political upheavals of the past years, though Xie Jing still cherishes socialist ideals.

In Liu, the bright peasant boy from Cangxian county who leaves his village primary school to study at middle school in Tianjin, there is a strong identification with Jiang Zilong's own childhood experiences. The parallel is too close to be mere chance. Sneered at because of his thick country accent, bullied by the city-born schoolchildren, Liu is finally goaded into hitting back. Because of the "cultural revolution" he loses the chance to go to university or be trained as an electrician. Doomed to be a driver, he knows he is more talented than many of his mates and some of the cadres in responsible positions. Naturally he feels deeply frustrated and grows increasingly cynical, which is expressed in his taunting the plant's leaders at every opportunity.

Xie Jing rose to political stardom during the years

of chaos, becoming the deputy head of the plant's public relations section. She was also the protegée of the Party secretary Zhu Tongkang. Realizing she has wasted much precious time, she decides to start again from the bottom up and asks for a transfer to the transportation team. To begin with, the drivers regard her with dislike and suspicion, suggesting that she is a stooge sent by the leaders to spy on them. Xie Jing faces their jeers and brickbats and through her hard work, determination and courage eventually wins their respect. She quietly exerts a good influence on those around her, especially on Liu and his girlfriend Ye Fang.

Stylish clothes and becoming hairstyles were frowned on during the "cultural revolution" and people dared not wear them. When Xie Jing joins the transportation team, she is told bluntly by Ye Fang, the girl driver, "Politics is your job, isn't it? All political workers are dull, just like your clothes, and difficult to get on with." So Xie Jing learns to dress fashionably. After all, why shouldn't a young woman Party member look attractive? But this and the fact that she starts to smoke shocks her old boss Zhu. He blames himself for having sent her to join the drivers, who have visibly corrupted a promising young Party cadre. Xie Jing senses his disappointment in her and is angered by it, because she has done nothing wrong. The awkward meeting of these two deftly illustrates the generation gap that sometimes exists. Zhu admits to himself that all young people baffle him. Xie Jing is like a stranger, grown out of her dependence on him and now thinking for herself.

Jiang Zilong had wanted to write the novelette for some time, but had never found quite the right angle.

Then one day by chance while out shopping he met a political cadre in his workshop with her boyfriend. At work she had always worn her baggy old green army uniform, but this day she was smartly dressed in a western-style suit. She seemed very embarrassed by their encounter, and Jiang Zilong was surprised to find her transformed into a beautiful girl. Reflecting on this, he found the title and theme for his novelette. Life should be as rich, colourful and varied as all the colours of the rainbow.

Humour and irony feature prominently in Jiang Zilong's stories. When he ridicules, and those whom he mocks are the arrogant and ignorant, he aims his shafts with deadly accuracy. His victims wriggle with embarrassment or simply gape in astonishment, as does Hu, the woman head of the organization department who resents the introduction of new ideas. Manager Qiao throws her off balance with his opening shot: "Hu, do you think the Monkey King can join the Party?" Hu is not amused, but Chinese readers delight in such irreverence. When Qiao encounters the hapless and careless Du Ping wheeling his barrow with cement pouring from one of the sacks, he asks, "Isn't your barrow like an ox running and urinating at the same time?" Jiang Zilong's language is earthy and colloquial.

One basic weakness is that his stories suffer from hasty writing and lack careful editing, understandable in a man who works full-time in his plant. His leader was suspicious that perhaps he wrote on the sly during working hours. In fact, Jiang Zilong only writes in his spare time on his one day off a week, rising early in the morning and working until late at night. Then he sets aside his manuscript until the next free moment. Such a regime requires dedication and stamina. Although there are periods when he writes nothing, once he starts he tries to continue until his story is completed.

He explained, "When I write, something strange happens to me. I don't stop to eat or drink. I only write. When I begin a story I try to write it at one go, but that isn't always possible. If I'm interrupted I have to start all over again. A certain mood grips me, but I can't really define it. It's like seasoning in food or air in a room, something I can't do without. I think over the short stories carefully, and only when I've found the ending do I start to write. I have the gist in my mind, even some details and dialogue. But with a novelette I search for a good beginning and then write without knowing the ending.

"I don't think a writer should impose himself on his characters. They should be natural and have their own logic and dynamic. I don't like to add sensation or indulge in lengthy descriptions and details. Nor do I like to preach or appear to be giving advice. But perhaps there is a philosophical flavour to some of the stories. Sometimes I feel I cannot be a writer and then suddenly a character or dialogue will occur to me.

"Before I begin a story I have a feeling of agony usually. I feel nervous during that period when my ideas are incubating. Once I wrote the draft of a bad novelette over a period of a few days. It was a terrifying and depressing experience. With short stories the suffering is less."

Jiang Zilong does not pay any attention to the demands of his readers and editors. "If you bother about them, you'll end up producing rubbish, drained of everything you wanted to say." But his popularity is such that people are always eager to read more of his work. So far he has written seven novelettes, more than thirty short stories, fifteen articles and a book of reportage. Since 1979, he has won several major literary prizes.

After the success of "Manager Qiao Assumes Office", Jiang Zilong was given five months' leave from his plant to study at a literary institute run by the Chinese Writers' Association. In 1981 he spent four months in Yugoslavia and in the autumn of 1982 he visited the United States with a delegation of writers. Increasingly his writing clashed with his duties in the plant, so he was invited to become a professional writer. Jiang Zilong himself has suggested that he would like to live and work in his plant as a writer. One thing is certain. He will not cut himself off from workers and factory life.

Patricia Wilson

November, 1982

All the Colours of the Rainbow

IN a big world like this, wonders never cease. That's what makes life so complicated.

Let's have a look at the entrance to the No. 5 Iron and Steel Plant one spring morning in the early eighties.

This modern plant built in the seventies was virtually surrounded by a free market — a result of the boom in the countryside. At the foot of its front wall, there were baskets, carts and stalls displaying millet, lentils, turnips, Chinese cabbage and all manner of merchandise. The pedlars' shouts woke up this city of iron and steel and drowned the roaring of the furnaces. The workers in the plant's living quarters no longer relied on alarm clocks because the hucksters' shouts always got them up in time for the morning shift. And housewives could take their pick of snacks, fresh vegetables, live fish and shrimps. So long as you had money you could buy whatever you fancied. Inside the plant production had slumped, while the peasants outside were doing a roaring trade. They had surrounded the state-run iron and steel plant, and could make as much in one day selling jelly-fish as a worker's weekly pay. However, the workers were glad to give their cash to those pedlars, even though their wares were expensive. It was better than having nothing to buy with their money. Though the plant's output was low, the workers were not short of money, for their purchasing power had gradually risen.

Economic laws, like a humorous, clever magician, have
played this trick on us in recent years so that we are
forced to acknowledge their existence.

There was a commotion in front of the plant's main
gate, the centre of the market. Apart from vegetables,
flapjacks, fritters, roasted peanuts and boiled beans
were being sold. Business in this little square was particularly good before it was time to clock in. The
plant's security section had made a rule that no one
should block the entrance. A way must be kept clear
for trucks and cars. But eager to sell their wares the
peasants edged forward, and as a result the passage
kept narrowing. Prices also kept changing. Whoever
knew how to manipulate them could make a small
fortune.

But today a tall young man had attracted most of the
customers. He did not look like a dusty, dirty peasant
from the country or a greasy costermonger. He had
clean hands, a clean face, shining eyes, and wore a large
gauze mask over his mouth. With his white over-
sleeves, white apron and white cap, he appeared like a
first-class chef of a big hotel, graceful and elegant. His
appearance alone made him stand out at the market.
He had an assistant of about his own age but very
different from him, a burly fellow with big hands and
big feet. The flatness of his long, lean face was somewhat redeemed by the large sun-glasses perched on his
nose. The tufts of hair sprouting from his ears were
partly covered by the long hair over his temples. He
looked a tough customer in a cream-coloured cardigan
and a tight pair of light brown trousers. He sauntered
about till he found an ideal spot just in front of the

plant's entrance. But a peasant of fifty was selling eggs there.

"How much a catty?" he came up to him and demanded in a harsh voice.

The man looked up and was dismayed to see such a fellow towering above him. What foul luck, he thought, meeting a customer like this first thing in the morning. Yet he couldn't afford to offend him. He had to be careful. With a smile he replied, "Want some eggs? One yuan a catty."

"Too expensive!" Flat Face reached out, picked up two eggs in each hand and began rolling them round like an old man playing with two walnuts. "Fresh? Cheating people with rotten eggs!" While speaking, he fixed his eyes on the peasant. When the latter turned to attend to his other customers, he slipped the eggs into his trouser pockets. With a whistle, he then picked up another four eggs and rolled them around in his hands.

A middle-aged woman behind him was startled to see all this. She was on the point of denouncing him but his truculent air made her think better of it. Why ask for trouble?

However, the thief would not leave the peasant in peace. With a jerk of his aggressive chin he roared, "Look there, don't you see the notice issued by our plant's security section? No one should block the entrance. Get moving quick!"

The peasant smiled wrily and nodded. "It's quite far from the gate, and I'm not in the way of traffic or anyone."

"Quit that! Make it snappy! Buzz off!"

The young man with the white mask and apron stepped over to intervene. "He Shun," he said, "let him

stay here. We'll set up our pitch just beside him. Anyone who wants to have pancakes with eggs can buy eggs
from him and pancakes from us. That's killing two
birds with one stone. We'll all do better business."
With that he parked his bike and on each side of it
drove into the ground two posts, on which he balanced
a board. On this he placed a pan, some millet flour, a
slice and brush. So the little pancake stall began
business.

He Shun put up a white sunshade of the type used
by the traffic police in summer. But now it was chilly
spring and the sun had not yet risen, so what use was
a sunshade? First, it could keep away mist and dust,
second, which was more important, it was eye-catching.
He had also tied a twelve-foot bamboo pole to the bike's
handle bars and on this hung a wooden board with the
big character: Muslim.

With his strident voice, accustomed to slanging
matches, He Shun started bellowing, "Hey! Come and
buy! Pancakes and fritters! Piping-hot and tasty! Good
and cheap! Ten *fen* a pair instead of twelve! We're not
out to make a profit but to do our mates a good turn.
Come and have a taste if you don't believe me. One
taste and you'll be hooked!"

"Stop yelling, He Shun! Take the money and put on
your mask and cap. Take off your glasses and behave
yourself. Don't look as if you're spoiling for a fight."
The young man in white took from his basket a four-
speaker stereo recorder which he put on a little stool by
his feet. As soon as he switched it on a rousing tune
filled the air. At once the noisy market quieted down.
People turned their heads to look in this direction, some
even came over.

He Shun was delighted. "Super! How clever of you to have brought it. Me, I'd stand here simply to listen to the music." Looking over the cassettes he added regretfully, "Hell! Why did you only bring these? Bring Deng Lijun and Li Guyi next time! Their songs are really terrific! We'd do better business for sure!"

"Get away! What do you know? Get on with your work!" The young man's voice was not high but held a note of authority which subdued He Shun.

"OK." Chuckling he fished out the four eggs from his pockets. "Sijia, make me four pancakes with these eggs first. I can't work on an empty stomach."

Soon a crowd had gathered round the white sunshade, some to buy, some to watch, some to listen to the music. With a man like He Shun taking their cash, the customers stood in an orderly queue. Seeing so many people there, He Shun's spirits rose and he cried his wares more loudly, his head moving now right, now left. The pancakes were delicious and the price was two *fen* cheaper than elsewhere. The young cook was so clean and deft, all the other stall holders envied his brisk business. The workers of the plant came and bought his pancakes. For ten *fen* they could buy a snack and watch the fun, for these two men, Liu Sijia and He Shun, were drivers in their transportation team. Although they drew their wages from the state, yet they had started this small business on the side. What would the plant say about this? There were other workers who traded outside, but always on the sly. Now these two dare-devils had set up a stall at the entrance of the plant, deliberately drawing attention to it.

Customers tried to strike up a conversation with them.

Liu said little, but He Shun rattled away while counting his takings.

"You're doing fine. In just one morning you can rake in eight or ten yuan, can't you?" someone asked.

"There's no bonus now, so we have to do something to raise a little extra cash," He Shun replied righteously.

"Did you get permission from the plant?"

"What if we didn't? Who's in charge these days? Only cash and bonuses count! Take it while you can. Whoever earns most is smart."

"Have you got a license?"

"Of course. My old man's license. True Muslim."

"You're paid by the plant and do business in your spare time. So you've two incomes, eh?"

"Take it while you can, I told you. When eight deities crossed the sea, each had his own ways and means. Those who have guts have more than they can swallow; those without guts starve to death. In the United States, a university student can wash dishes in a restaurant after school; a turner can drive a taxi after his shift. Our peasant brothers can come to town to make a little money by selling their produce. Why should we workers, their big brothers, starve to death? Why can't we make a couple of extra yuan selling our skills?"

"But if everybody did this, wouldn't things be topsyturvy?"

"Go to hell! Aren't they that way? Piss off if you aren't buying! Stop making trouble here!" Realizing the weakness of his argument, He Shun reverted to type.

"How can a pedlar curse people?"

"So what? You bastard!" He Shun was ready to fight.

"He Shun, what are you up to?" Liu Sijia snapped without even looking up.

He Shun was silent at once. He behaved to others like a thug, but to Liu like a slave. What a queer pair!

The cassette came to an end with a click. Liu changed it and started a Spanish melody *Drift, Little Boat*. Keeping time with the music, he clinked the pan with his small slice. Then, while kneading the dough on the board, he cried, "Pancakes and fritters! Piping-hot! Think before you buy. My pancakes can fill your stomach, sharpen your wits. . . ."

He seemed to be talking to himself.

The little stall beneath the white sunshade had attracted a crowd. People are curious by nature. A man falling off his bike always draws the crowds, not to mention this strange pair with their foreign music. The way leading to the plant was blocked. Those workers who had come on foot stopped to look; those on bikes craned to peep too. The pancake stall had stirred up the whole market. Workers or staff members of the plant who had eaten the pancakes spread the news till very soon the whole plant was talking about it. The workers did not care whether it was legal or not. So long as the pancakes were good and cheap, they would buy them. But the more sophisticated cadres only glanced at the stall from a distance. Some were too timid even to do this, saying to themselves, "That young fellow's looking for trouble again!"

Quite a number of people did not know whether it was right or wrong, but they felt worried. Cadres of the political and security sections were afraid to intervene, let alone break up the stall and confiscate its takings. They were not afraid of He Shun, only uncertain what action to take, since they had no arguments to prove that this was wrong. There were no official directives on how to deal with such matters, so those in charge said nothing. Besides, nowadays, the economic policies were very flexible. Who knew what was allowed? The government policy should be consistent. If something was legal for peasants, why not for workers? Most cadres were used to doing as they were told and following instructions from above. They disliked taking any responsibility themselves. In the absence of instructions, they did not know what to do. While the situation kept changing in the plant and the rules remained inflexibly rigid, the two young men had availed themselves of a loophole.

It was nearly time to clock in for the morning shift and more workers were arriving. This further boosted Liu Sijia's business, and his buddies bought four or five of his pancakes and fritters, some even as many as twenty to keep for lunch. This was also a show of solidarity and support.

A bicycle bell rang urgently in the distance and kept ringing until a bright red Phoenix bike nearly bumped into the stall. He Shun, standing up to swear, saw that the rider had put one foot on the ground to steady the bike while remaining seated on it. His taunt cheek muscles relaxed in a broad smile. "Ye Fang," he said ingratiatingly. "Have a pancake! As many as you want. I'll treat you."

Ye Fang ignored him but glared at Liu Sijia.

Liu did not raise his head. Instead he said as politely as a real businessman, "Please keep away, Ye Fang. Don't disturb us."

Ye Fang snorted. She was a very pretty girl, though

perhaps dressed a little too gaudily. Her glossy black hair was carefully dressed in a chignon in which she had stuck a flashing golden hairpin. Goodness knows how much time she had spent on that coiffure! From her ears dangled green earrings. She was wearing a light blue western-style suit, so well tailored that it revealed her graceful figure. She looked unconventional, uninhibited, and smelt of some strange, pungent scent. Gripping Liu's sleeve, she said, "What on earth are you doing this for? Have you no sense of shame!"

"We're not robbing anyone," Liu replied politely, "not breaking any law. What's there to be ashamed of?"

"Don't give me that talk! Are you broke or something?"

"We're not doing this to make money but to do our mates a good turn."

"Nonsense! Pack up and go! I'll give you all the money you could earn in a day."

Liu turned towards her abruptly, his cheek muscles twitching, looking daggers at her. In a low voice he said grimly, "Ten yuan a day, three hundred a month, three thousand six hundred a year. Can you afford that? Leave us alone and don't interfere!"

Ye Fang tried to catch his eye, to force him to tell the truth. But Liu turned back to his pancakes, ignoring her. No matter how she pleaded, he seemed to hear nothing. This was harder to bear than being told off or taunted. She felt wronged. Who had ever rebuffed her? When had she asked for any favours? She had never knuckled under to anyone. But now she was like a wild horse broken in by Liu Sijia. For him, she was willing to sacrifice everything, to put up with any insults, any injustice, if only he would love her. But he blew hot and cold towards her and never showed his true feelings. Take this pancakes and fritters business for example. It was not a simple matter, yet he had not said a word to her about it, showing that she had no place in his heart. Angry and embarrassed at being put on the spot, she pedalled away in a huff.

There was hooting now from a black car which could not get into the plant because of the crowd. The angry driver kept honking the horn. Zhu Tongkang, the Party secretary of the iron and steel plant, looked at his watch. There were only ten minutes to go till the morning shift. Frowning, he complained, "The head office has time and again told the security section to issue a notice forbidding stall holders to block the entrance. They just don't bother!"

"That isn't a peasant's stall!" the driver fumed. "Two of our men are selling pancakes!"

"Who?"

"Liu Sijia and He Shun."

"Oh! Have they got any customers?"

"A lot!"

Just then He Shun, holding up a pancake and a fritter, shouted deliberately towards the car, "Steaming hot! Ten *fen* for a pancake and a fritter! Nice and cheap! Two *fen* cheaper than elsewhere! Tasty and delicious!"

In exasperation Zhu waved his hand and said, "Reverse! Go to the back door!"

2

Once in his office Zhu Tongkang received several phone calls from workshop Party branch secretaries asking the

Party committee's opinion about Liu and He's pancake stall and informing him of the workers' reactions to it. Liu Sijia again! He had stirred up the whole plant once more!

In spite of all the years he had spent on political and ideological work, Zhu was finding it harder and harder to deal with people. Nowadays the workers seemed unfathomable and difficult to handle. Their class origins were much simpler than before, but their minds had become ten times, a hundred times, more complex. This complexity was most confusing! He had tried hard to understand them and figure out what made them tick, but it was no use. Since wages had been raised and bonuses issued, ideological work should have been easier. But on the contrary, things were getting out of hand. As Party secretary of the plant for twenty years, he ought to have complete control of the situation, like a senior lecturer able to recite his textbook. Besides, there was no sword at his back, no whip over his head. His position was secured. But he knew only too well that he was unable to cope with his task. Small fry like Liu Sijia were standing in his way. . . .

Was Liu really after money? Surely he wasn't short of cash? Everybody knew that two years before he already had the coveted "seven machines": a television, recorder, record-player, camera, washing-machine, calculator and refrigerator. He was the first to wear fashionable sun-glasses, which he had discarded when others followed suit. It was he again who had started sporting jeans, but once they were in vogue he no longer wore them. Instead, he dressed in a Chinese tunic suit or a western suit with a tie, looking like a scholar. And now he had fitted himself out like a stall holder. A good actor! But a headache to Zhu! The young workers, especially those who liked to be smart and in fashion, admired him or even worshipped him. His words carried more weight than those of the plant's Youth League secretary. But he never said anything to support the Youth League. Instead he kept picking fault with its secretary.

However, he had never made any big mistakes or broken any laws. He always found loopholes in the regulations and policies, so that it was difficult to catch him out. Once the security section had suspected him of being a gang leader. Otherwise how could a young worker afford to buy all those consumer goods? How could a fellow like He Shun, who would fight at the drop of a hat, do whatever he said? If Liu were not a cunning ring leader, he could never control a hooligan like him. In fact Liu must be the craftier of the two, for ever since He Shun had ganged up with him, though he remained a trouble-maker, he had avoided any entanglements with the police. This showed he had learned some sense. But had he changed for the better or the worse? Was this change the result of Liu's craftiness or his good influence? The security section suspected the worst of them, although their thorough investigation of Liu's activities disclosed nothing illegal. Nor had he any connections with other gangs. Whatever way you looked at it, Liu seemed a shady-looking character, yet they could not pin any thing on him. The management therefore did not understand him. It was natural then that Zhu was powerless to deal with him.

For the Party secretary to be no match for an ordinary young worker reflected very badly on Zhu. With regard to seniority, position, power, experience and age,

Liu was not up to him. But these two men, each so different, had become opponents. Liu's sale of pancakes had shaken the whole plant. When had Zhu's words or decisions ever aroused so much interest? Now the young man had placed him in a dilemma. He had long before heard that some workers were privately doing business. Some did it in their spare time; others simply took French leave. This way they earned much more than their wages. A man who took a week off, forfeiting his pay, could make more than two months' wages. Anyone could figure that out. Was it illegal? It definitely would have been in the past. But now the management turned a blind eye. To be frank, they had no idea what to do about it. They did not even know how to keep the plant solvent. Economic laws determined people's ideas and actions. Zhu could not keep up with all the many changes. When uncertain as to the legality of an action, and so long as no one complained, he would gladly ignore it. In a leading cadre, irresolution and fear were fatal weaknesses, which would render him helpless, unable to take the initiative. But this time he resolved not to let Liu get off scot-free, not when he had set up a pancake stall, put up a white sunshade and played a tape recorder right under the noses of all the workers! It was a challenge to him, to the Party committee! He found it hard to contain his indignation.

But Liu was not afraid of Zhu's fury. On the contrary, it was his aim to annoy him. It was very common nowadays for youngsters to bait or ridicule old cadres. Liu knew that Zhu would not dare to punish him, because he was only following the example of many others including some leading cadres.

Zhu was really between the devil and the deep blue sea. Young people were unpredictable nowadays. Anything could happen. What could Zhu do? If he took no action that was tantamount to accepting it as legal. If others followed suit, there would be chaos. Worse still, Liu would have scored over the Party secretary, and he would have admitted publicly that he was powerless. Things could not go on like this. He must do something! But what?

He picked up the receiver and asked to be put through to reception.

"Who's speaking? Old Zhang? Would you have a look outside? Has Liu Sijia of the transportation team packed up his pancake stall?"

"Yes, he has. They came in just as the bell was ringing."

Doing business during work hours was a different matter. Liu would not give Zhu that handle against him. This young fellow was slick, cunning and glib. Though Zhu did not know what to make of him, he would never admit it. Once he had gone to the transportation team and happened to meet He Shun, who had just been transferred to the plant. "Old man," He Shun teased him, mistaking Zhu for a pedicab driver, "how can your three wheels compete with our four?" Seeing his driver make fun of the Party secretary, Tian Guofu, the head of the team, felt very agitated. The young man was asking for trouble! Tian's face darkened and he snapped, "He Shun! Stop playing the fool! Show some sense of respect. This is Zhu, our Party secretary!"

Zhu had been very annoyed.

Then Liu had come up and said with a smile, "Old Tian, no praise can be better than taking Old Zhu for a pedicab driver. That means he's just like a worker, simple, honest and friendly. Comrade Zhu, am I right?"

What could Zhu say to this? He had to nod. A serious man, he did not like the relaxed way Liu talked to him. People might call him flabby, and not decisive (a few years earlier when cadres had been classified as soft, slack or lazy, he had been put in the first category), but no one could deny his good qualities. In all the years of political turbulence he had stuck to his principles and not let himself be corrupted by his power. He treated the workers well. Perhaps that was why Liu dared talk to him in such an off-hand way. The younger generation treated everybody alike. To them, money, social status and power were nothing. No matter whom they talked to, their manner was casual. Zhu took exception to this, though he did not believe in social stratification. He felt nettled when a worker called him "Old Zhu" instead of "Secretary Zhu", but he took care to hide this. What was even worse was Liu's attitude towards Tian, his team leader.

Liu had turned and thrown an arm round Tian's shoulder. "Old Tian," the young fellow in his twenties had said to his boss of fifty, patting his shoulder, "you're not very smart today. Usually you call us brothers, join in our binges, never lay down the law, just let us do as we like. But with the Party secretary here, you're standing on your dignity, putting on a disgusting act! You can't fool a cadre of the old school like Zhu."

He spoke as if only for Tian's ears but pitched his voice high, meaning Zhu to hear every word. Tian turned pale with indignation and stammered, "You, you...." But he could not go on. To spare him further embarrassment, Zhu pretended to have heard nothing.

How dare Liu make fun of his superior as if Tian were his junior! And why didn't Tian discipline him?

Zhu rang up the transportation team. He waited a long time but no one answered. He was forced to send for the head of the team.

"Shall I ask for the team leader or the deputy?" Zhu's secretary asked.

Tian was not much use. Besides, Liu would never listen to him. So what was the point of sending for him? The deputy team leader was only a girl, a newcomer. Was she able to deal with Liu?

"Ask Xie Jing to come. . . ." Zhu answered hesitantly.

The secretary knew what was preying on Zhu's mind. As the Party secretary was an easy-going, good-natured man, the staff liked to keep him informed of new developments.

"Secretary Zhu, I hear Xie Jing's ganged up with those young drivers now."

Zhu's heart missed a beat. "Oh . . . how?"

"When she first arrived, they baited her. But now she's in league with them, drinking, smoking and even wearing fashionable clothes like them."

"What? She's learned to drink and smoke! Impossible! Ask her to come here right away!" He glanced at a pile of documents on his desk and plumped down on a sofa, in no mood to read or sign anything. His ears were itching, a sign he felt irritated. According to western medicine, this was due to nerves; but Chinese traditional doctors said it was caused by anger which inflamed his ears. Anyone in a leading position was bound to be angry at times. So it seemed his ears would itch until the day he retired. He took out a match and began cleaning them, first the left then the right.

If what the secretary said was true, this would be a worse blow to Zhu than Liu's selling pancakes. Liu could make him furious without distressing him, because Zhu had no personal feelings for him. Xie Jing was another matter. If she had made a mistake, he would be bitterly distressed because she was his protégée, whom he had discovered and trained himself. How could she side with Liu?

Zhu sat back, resting his head on the armchair. The sparse white hair revealed his shining, smooth crown. Narrowing his eyes, he drew on his cigarette, smoke floating round his head like clouds round a snow-capped mountain. From this armchair he had talked many times with Xie Jing. For an old man, a veteran Party member, it was a pleasure to talk with such a girl and could even help to clarify his thinking. Because she herself was so pure, so transparent, and she would tell him all her innermost thoughts. This was rare in such a complex society. She would write down what was in her mind and hand it to her Party branch every day, but not to ingratiate herself or show her loyalty to the Party. Each report she wrote was a genuine self-appraisal. In her eyes, the Party secretary was the Party, the father to whom she owed her political life. And her political life meant more to her than her personal one. The day that she joined the Party, she had wept with gratitude and a sense of shame. The Party, to her, was so noble and great yet she had joined its ranks so easily. She felt guilty because she had done nothing for the Party and felt unworthy to be a Communist. Zhu had stroked her hair, his eyes wet too, because he himself had once felt the same. Her innocence was touching and admirable, enabling others to see their sordid faults and strive to overcome them. Zhu had said many times that if everybody were like her, the world would be a better place. He wanted her to retain her innocence yet hoped she would soon be mature enough to understand this world and the meaning of life. Yet her naivety was dangerous, as it meant she could be used by others. However, his position prevented him from telling her the truth about the world. Besides, he did not want to weaken her love for the Party. She had asked him: What is maturity? What is sophistication? Does maturity make you sophisticated? He had not been satisfied with his own answers. For a long time he appeared to her as the embodiment of the Party, and he protected her like a real father. Under his aegis she was promoted from secretary to deputy head of the Public Relations Department. In his view, Xie Jing was a talented model girl. After the fall of the "gang of four", as a veteran revolutionary he was promoted and gained more prestige. But Xie Jing, a new cadre who had emerged during the "cultural revolution" and had been doing propaganda work, was no longer considered a promising young hopeful. She was cold-shouldered everywhere. The sweet smile disappeared from her face for good. She seemed to have grown ten years older and matured all of a sudden. She volunteered to work on the shop floor. Zhu did all he could to console her, saying that she had not been admitted into the Party because she had been a "cultural revolution" activist, nor had she had anything to do with the "gang of four", so nobody would dismiss her. She had been naive in the past, but was now fearfully stubborn. Fearing she might have a nervous breakdown, he finally consented. Since she was not familiar with the work on the shop floor and might be bullied, he sent her to the transportation team. All she needed to do was look after the loading and unloading of fifty-odd trucks. Zhu wanted her to be the deputy Party branch secretary, but she would not hear of it, resolving not to have any more to do with politics. She had lived on politics but now, young as she was, she was fed up with it. Since Tian was not very capable, Zhu agreed to appoint her deputy team leader. Had that decision been right or wrong? Zhu rather regretted it. How could a girl reform the transportation team? He had ruined her character, sending her to work with all those hooligans.

3

IT would soon be time to begin the day's work. Xie Jing drove her lorry down the country road and returned to the garage through the back entrance of the plant. None of the regular drivers had turned up yet. Exhausted, she rested her elbows on the steering-wheel. Anyway there was still time before the bell. It was hard even for a strong young man to work such long hours every day, let alone a girl like her. For almost a whole year now, she had practised driving from six to eight every morning, after which she would return the lorry to its driver. Again at five in the afternoon when the workers knocked off and went home, she got into the cabin and drove till eight. She worked fifteen or sixteen hours a day! How could she stand that?

However, she managed. One has to pay for learning a skill, she told herself, practice makes perfect. If as deputy team leader of the transportation team she knew nothing about lorries that would be ridiculous, and the drivers would play tricks on her as though she were a child.

She would never forget how she had been treated the first day she came to the team. Two years ago now. That day, Party Secretary Zhu himself rang up Tian Guofu, the head of the transportation team, and asked him to go to the Party committee's office. Xie Jing had a good impression of the man, though production dispatchers nicknamed him "Aunt Tian" because he was irresolute, incapable and irresponsible. He never lost his temper, never spoke without a smile on his lips. He was a veteran middle-ranking cadre who got along with everybody and never discriminated against young cadres. Naturally they thought highly of him. Xie Jing, of course, was delighted to work with him, and she was also grateful to the Party secretary for his thoughtful decision and concern.

On hearing of her appointment, Tian was all smiles. Gripping her hand he said eagerly, "I'm so glad to have you working with us! The very person we need. I'm sure our team will turn over a new leaf with you in charge. We welcome you!"

Xie Jing blushed. She said earnestly though rather shyly, "Old Tian, I'm really a greenhorn. But I'm sure you'll help me. Take me as an apprentice."

"Oh, come off it! I've no technical know-how myself and can't drive a lorry. Cadres who can drive won't stay long in our team anyway. You're young and clever and we really expect a lot from you."

Tian nodded as Secretary Zhu explained what her work was to be and then took Xie Jing to his team.

It was very warm for late spring, unusually muggy. The sun was not strong, and the sky looked hazy as if there would be a storm. Under the tall poplar tree in front of the garage of the transportation team, stood a dozen or so drivers, both men and women, dubiously looking their new boss up and down. They all recognized her as the former deputy head of the Public Relations Department but none of them bothered to greet her.   An awkward silence reigned.   Xie Jing blushed, not knowing what to do.

Tian's pasty, usually amiable face lengthened as he put on a show of gravity.   Like an actor on a stage, he announced, "Well, mates, this is our new deputy team leader appointed by the Party committee. She's a well-known, most promising young middle-ranking cadre. You all know her name anyway...."

The drivers roared with laughter, making Xie Jing feel even more uncomfortable.

Acting or not, Tian kept a straight face, which only caused further laughter.   "I can tell by your laughter," he went on, "that you're all pleased to have her with us. So I don't have to say any more.   Anyway, in future, cooperate well with Deputy Team Leader Xie, and I'm sure we'll do an even better job."

Another peal of laughter.

"Chief Tian," someone shouted, "you've got a good sense of humour!"

Tian winked meaningfully at the drivers.   He seemed to be on very good terms with them.   He would casually pick a cigarette out of a driver's pocket, and the driver would light it for him.   Xie Jing admired him for being on such a friendly footing with them. Now they began commenting on her, some in low voices, others loudly regardless of her presence.

"She was sitting pretty up there, why come down to the garage?"

"Most likely she had to. Her lot used to hammer people in political movements. Climbed up when the 'gang of four' was in power. But that doesn't work now. So they come down to keep a low profile. . . ." The speaker was a driver with a flat face.

It was like being doused with cold water. Xie Jing turned pale and lowered her head. She had thought that once she was out of the administrative office, she would have left politics for good and would hear no more gossip or rumours. But she had jumped out of the frying-pan into the fire. Though the cadres in that office did talk behind each other's backs, at least they did it in a round about way, which was not too embarrassing. Since they were all in the same boat, they couldn't go too far. But these workers were different: sharp-tongued, outspoken and scathing. She had thought the team might hold a party to welcome her, or greet her with applause or at least some show of politeness. Maybe they would invite her to say a few words. It was very common for a cadre going to a new post to express his determination to do his work well. And in fact she had prepared a short speech. Now all these formalities had been omitted. Far from welcoming her the drivers were eyeing her antagonistically, making crude jokes about her.

"What can she do? She's only fit to light our cigarettes and brew tea for us."

The drivers laughed among themselves.

"Mind you, that slip of a girl has strong backing at the top. She's Zhu's favourite, once was his private secretary."

"She had an easy life up there while we sweated out our guts down here. And now she's been sent to bloody control us. We'll still have to slave away. Where the hell can we take our case?"

The swearer was the man with a flat face.

But there was a driver in his forties squatting outside the crowd smoking without a word. He was completely bald, his big head shining brightly. But strangely he had a short stiff growth of beard from his cheeks down to his neck. The engraved wooden pipe in his hand was as large as a hand-grenade. Fed up with all the talking he sprang to his feet and said with a slight stammer, "Oh, come off it, will you? You can't be too hard on a newcomer! Why bully the girl?"

"Big Head Sun," the driver with a flat face retorted, "you're really a bootlicker! You've lost no time currying favour with the new boss."

"Are you looking for trouble, He Shun?" Sun grabbed at the young man. Everybody laughed. Some tried to stop him, others joked, "Haven't you got your hand-grenade? Bash his head in!"

This set off another peal of laughter.

Enraged, Xie Jing trembled all over. However, she gritted her teeth and held back her tears.

What was strange was that Tian, the head of the team, seemed to have heard nothing. He had been off laughing and talking with some of the others. Now seeing that they might soon come to blows, he stepped over and said, "Stop it! A joke is a joke. You've gone too far! What will the new deputy team leader think? Get cracking! One more trip and we'll call it a day!"

Big Head Sun and some older drivers got into their lorries and drove off. But He Shun's group did not move. They turned a deaf ear to what Tian had said and went on fooling about.

"All drivers are like this," Tian whispered to Xie Jing. "They're frank and full of foul language. But they're a good lot. Don't take it to heart. You'll manage fine with them once you get to know them."

So he had heard everything. Xie Jing felt upset that he had pretended not to. Lowering her head, she said nothing. Seeing this, Tian left her to "have a chat with the workers".

With Tian and the less obstreperous drivers gone, all the rest gathered round Xie Jing to fire questions at her. Some were rude while others feigned politeness. They seemed to want to swallow her up. To deal her a head-on blow at this first encounter, to make her leave in disgust and not come back. That was what they hoped for. The transportation team was theirs, and they had the say there. Not knowing the ropes, Tian did not dare to offend them. So they did whatever they liked and enjoyed themselves. Now the Party committee had sent their young favourite to the garage, to wedge the door open and make them all toe the line. In future, Xie Jing would report even the least little goings-on to the Party committee. That would be terrible! No, they mustn't let her get a foothold there.

All this was master-minded by Liu Sijia. Hiding himself in a lorry some distance away, he watched his buddies making fun of the new woman team leader. He appeared lost in thought, his face a mask. He was a dark horse who had a hand in everything, good or bad, that went on in the team. An excellent driver, his safety record had reached a million kilometres. But at the same time he was a trouble-maker, the ringleader of the other trouble-makers. He had staged this farce to make a fool of this up-and-coming young cadre, favoured by the Party committee. But he took no pleasure in seeing Xie Jing's desperation. Indeed, the whole performance got on his nerves, striking him as futile and contemptible.

Xie Jing had never been treated like this in her life. Her face flushed, she felt weak and isolated. She could neither clear herself, nor lose her temper. Worse still, it had been a great effort to hold back tears. "Are they working class?" she thought. "A mob of hooligans, that's what they are! How can I stay here with all these hooligans?" She felt upset and disgusted. She had wanted to make a success of this new job, had come here from the best motives, only to find herself dropped into a dust-bin! Though she had been in this plant for six years, she had never really understood it.

"Stop bullying an honest girl, you bastards!" Ye Fang, a girl driver, could not stomach this and came over, a cigarette in her hand. Putting an arm round Xie Jing's neck, out of a sense of fair play she consoled her, "Don't be afraid, you don't have to be polite to this scum."

She fished out a filter-tipped cigarette from her pocket and offered it to Xie Jing. "Do you smoke?"

Xie Jing shook her head, embarrassed, then looked up curiously at the girl who had the guts to come to her rescue like this. She was a beauty! She seemed to have been carved out of jade. She wore an embroidered silk blouse, a western-style skirt and high-heeled white leather shoes. No wonder her colleagues called her a "fashion model" in a half-admiring, half-contemptuous way. She looked very smart. Other girls, if they dressed up like this, might feel awkward and look garish. But on slim, graceful Ye Fang these clothes looked quite natural, and the colours suited her. Indeed, they set off her beauty. She looked as though she had been born to wear fashionable clothes and to dress differently from the common herd. A progressive orthodox girl like Xie Jing would normally never have so much as glanced at her. But today she felt that compared with smart, elegant Ye Fang she herself was provincial, dowdy. She especially admired her extrovert character.

Chuckling, Ye Fang, her arm still round Xie Jing's shoulder, whispered to her, "The work here is different from office work in that administration building. First, you must learn to swear and fight. Otherwise you will get bullied."

"Come off it, stop buttering her up." Blinking, a man turned on Ye Fang. "Little Ye, why curry favour with the deputy team leader? Want to join the Party, eh? Or get promoted?"

Exhaling a ring of smoke, Ye said in a proud, provocative way, "Yes, I'm currying favour with the deputy team leader. I want to join the Party and get an official post, so as to give you a hell of a time!"

The drivers guffawed heartily as if they enjoyed being abused by a pretty girl.

"What a shameless wretch! Why offer a cigarette to a nonsmoker? Buttering her up for all you're worth," He Shun said and then stretched out his hand towards

Ye Fang. "Well, you've got good cigarettes, eh? May I have one?"

Ye turned away and ignored him. He Shun was not thin-skinned. Though given the cold shoulder, he kept pestering her. He tried to grip her arm and snatch the cigarette. But before he could do this, his own arm was punched hard. "Hey!" he cried affectedly. "That hurts! What a bitch!"

Ye Fang took out her packet of cigarettes and tossed them contemptuously on the ground, saying, "You shameless bum! Have the whole packet, I hope they choke you."

"Kicking or swearing, all signs of love!" The drivers cheerfully jostled one another to pick up the cigarettes.

Ye Fang chuckled and said to Xie Jing, "What can you do with such wretches?"

She lit herself a cigarette and again urged Xie Jing to smoke, "Have a try. It'll buck you up."

Blushing deeply, Xie Jing shook her head. "Oh no! I dare not smoke."

Ye pursed her lips and said, "You're too prim. Everyone in our line must learn to smoke and drink. You're a girl of a single colour."

"What do you mean by a 'single colour'," Xie Jing asked in amazement.

Ye Fang chortled, "Red! Politics is your job, isn't it? All political workers are dull, just like your clothes, and difficult to get on with. Grass only lasts till autumn and human life is short. Why not have a taste of all the enjoyment you can?"

Xie Jing could not agree with such a theory of living for enjoyment. But this was not the right time to argue with her. She had to keep a low profile at the moment.

However, Ye's remark about clothes had made an impression on her. After all she was a girl and loved beautiful things. She wanted to dress herself up but was afraid of criticism. It was not worth spoiling one's reputation over such trivial matters. She admired Ye for her strong personality and disregard of what others thought. But she herself had too many inhibitions.

As Ye led Xie Jing towards the locker room, Liu Sijia suddenly started the lorry and pulled up in front of them. Poking out his head, he said matter-of-factly, "Deputy Head of the Public Relations Department, you've never ridden in a lorry, have you? Since you've come to this team, you'd better get to know the life here. Come on! I'll give you a ride."

Ye's face darkened. Jumping on to the running-board, she fixed her eyes on Liu's and asked softly, her head close to his, "What are you up to, Sijia? It's her first day here, and you want to take her out?"

With a set face, Liu retorted, "Why should it worry you?"

"This is Liu Sijia?" Xie Jing raised her head and saw the cold glint in his eyes. Instead of calling her by name, he had addressed her by her former title. That showed he did not regard her as his new deputy team leader. And he was really rubbing it in. She had never seen him before. But the young driver in front of her was totally different from what she had imagined. His hair was not long and he had no beard. His clothes were plain. He looked pale, calm and honest. He seemed to be a man with a mind of his own, a strong character.

"Well? Afraid?" Liu asked. "Comrade Xie Jing, if you haven't the guts to ride in a lorry, how can you be the deputy leader of the transportation team? Afraid of an accident? Don't worry! I don't hold my life so cheap. I wouldn't risk it."

Xie Jing had no idea what he was up to. They didn't know each other and there shouldn't be any bad feeling between them. He did not appear to be like He Shun, so why should he make a fool of her just for fun? Anyway, having no choice, she got into the cabin.

"I'll go with you!" said Ye Fang. As she was about to climb in too, she was pulled back by He Shun. He had one cigarette clamped between his lips, another two stuck behind his ears.

"Jealous, eh?" He Shun said, winking at her. "Well, I'll go and keep an eye on him for you."

"Oh shit! You'd better stuff a cigarette up your ass as well." Having cursed him, she laughed. The lorry shot past her, churning up a cloud of dust.

Once out of the entrance gate, the lorry raced down the road to the suburbs. It was getting dark. A north-westerly wind sprang up and in no time blew hard, darkening the sky. As usual in the north, the wind carried sand with it. Heading into the wind, the lorry shot on. In the cabin, one could hear the roaring wind outside. Xie Jing was wedged in between Liu Sijia and He Shun. Liu seemed pinned to his seat, keeping the wheel under control. He Shun leaned against her, putting all his weight on her. To avoid him, she sat with her body inclined towards Liu. She was suffocated by the stench of He Shun's sweat and cigarette and found this male smell unbearable. She kept her mouth shut, not uttering one word. She had never before sat as close to young men as this. It was disgusting, and she felt very nervous. However, she couldn't show her un-easiness. She had to make an effort to keep calm.

Though the wind blew into the cabin, she was wet with sweat.

"What's your idea anyway, coming to work in our team?" He Shun asked. "It must be wonderful just to sit in an office with a cup of tea in your hand and an electric fan to keep you cool! Most people who want a job like yours can't get it. So why should you come and sweat here? What appeals to you about our transportation team?"

Liu picked up where he left off. "You don't understand. She's using her brains to get ahead. When politics was in fashion several years back, she got a political job. Now when they're pushing technical skills, she comes down to pick up some technical know-how. Those kind of people grab all the best jobs. This world is made for them. And we're damn slaves all our lives!"

Xie Jing kept silent, pretending not to have caught his meaning. What could she say? Could she have a heart-to-heart talk with the two of them? Explain what was on her mind? Though she had been a cadre for several years, she was shy and rather tongue-tied. When she had first joined this plant, she had been assigned to work in the laboratory of the open-hearth furnace workshop. She could have become a good laboratory technician, but her superior kept asking her to write up materials and criticism articles. When the Party secretary came to this shop to get some actual practical experience, he was struck by her ability and transferred her to the head office to be a secretary. That hadn't been her fault, had it? All transfers in fact were decided by the plant management. Besides, she was always willing to go where she was needed. What she had believed had now been proved wrong. The things she had thought important had turned out to be valueless, or even empty talk, harmful fallacies. Her mind seemed a vacuum. Ignorant and incapable, that was what she was. She had wasted many years of her time. So she wanted to go to the grass-roots and learn something really useful. What was wrong with that? Why should she be treated like this? The drivers thought that she was in disgrace. What nonsense! Those who had made mistakes would never go to a workshop. It was understandable that people still smarting from the persecution of the "gang of four" had grudges against those working in political departments. But why should they take it out on her? After all, she was a victim herself. In a way, she had suffered more. She had wasted her youth and her life, and now she had no skill whatsoever. If the staff members were to be cut, she would be the first to go. Maybe she would have to be gate-keeper or a street-cleaner. Worse still, she had been hoodwinked, used as a tool by others. Now in her twenties, she must find a new set of values and start all over again. She must learn something really useful. Was that wrong? Xie Jing made a great effort to overcome her sense of regret. She blamed herself for coming down in such a hurry. It was naive, not carefully thought out.

The wind was blowing harder. It was difficult to tell the sky from the earth. Sand and grit pelted noisily against the cabin. Now the lorry had reached the lime depot far out in the suburbs. The place was smothered with white lime, so that the workers had to put down their hat flaps and cover their faces. Liu pulled up in the teeth of the wind. Instantly the lorry was swallowed up by white powder. He Shun did not get off, but stretched out and handed a requisition slip to a depot worker, who was wondering if the driver was out of his mind to fetch lime in such weather.

Knocking at the windscreen, he shouted, "It's too windy! Half the lime in your lorry will be gone by the time you get back to your plant."

He Shun shouted back, "What can we do? We obey our orders, like donkeys pulling a millstone. What our chief says goes!"

"Your chief must be blind! It's raining sand now!"

"Aha, our chief's suffering from pink-eye. Even if it rained knives, he would never know. Anyway we're the ones who have to sweat it out." Then turning to Xie Jing, he continued, "Well, deputy team leader, don't just sit and watch. As the saying goes, a new broom sweeps clean. You'd better make sure the work is done properly. It's so windy that they may be too lazy to shovel enough lime on. Or they may botch the job and dirty the cabin."

Xie Jing knew he was trying to make a fool of her. But if she remained in the cabin, they would certainly laugh at her and say she was afraid of hard work and getting dirty. In fact she didn't mind roughing it, but she could not swallow an insult. Gritting her teeth, she jumped down from the cabin. The wind was so strong that she almost fell, having landed unsteadily. She heard the laughter of Liu and He Sun from the cabin. With one hand on the hood, she stood erect in the fierce wind. She was immediately engulfed by lime. Her eyes smarted, her mouth and nostrils filled with white powder, making it hard to breathe. There was a hot stinging feeling in her throat. Hastily she closed her eyes and shut her mouth. Before long, her hair and clothes were covered with lime, her ears and nose clogged with it. Impossible to tell whether this was a woman or a man. A worker who was shovelling lime on to the lorry led her out of the wind and dusted her down. He was surprised to find that she was a girl.

"Are you a new driver at the iron and steel plant?" he asked.

She nodded.

"He Shun's really a loafer! Makes his apprentice see to the work while he himself sits comfortably in the cabin."

"You don't have to come down actually," said another. "We won't make a mess of the loading."

The words were simple but touching, her eyes moistened. That warm-hearted worker went on complaining though it had nothing to do with him, "The heads of your plant are fools. With such a wind, half your lime will be blown away on the way. It's not only a waste of money but means polluting the air. Besides, people on the road will call you names."

After a moment's reflection Xie Jing said, "In that case, you'd better stop loading."

"But we've already loaded quite a lot."

"Unload it. Why let it be blown away by the wind? I'm sorry to have put you to so much trouble. Thank you anyway."

"It's all right with us. But what will your boss say when you go back empty-handed?"

"It doesn't matter. I'll talk it over with him."

"Very well. You're smart. Just get in and ask He Shun to tip the truck. And we'll rake off the rest of it." He gave the requisition slip back to her.

She got into the cabin. But how should she persuade them? In name she was the deputy team leader; but in fact she was not even an apprentice. They wouldn't listen to her. Her nerves on edge, she had to face the ordeal. Bracing up, she said politely, "Master Liu, please tip the truck and unload the lime."

"What?" Liu fixed his inquisitive eyes on her. "Unload?"

"It's too windy. It would be blown away on the way back. That would be a waste. Besides, people would swear at us."

"Is this an order from the deputy team leader?"

Xie Jing blushed. However, she put her foot down and said, "I'm consulting you, aren't I?"

"What if the administrative office criticizes us for delaying the plant's production?"

"I'll answer for that of course." Her voice was sweet and mild, but held a stubborn note.

Liu had never expected Xie Jing to be so bold and decisive. His chin twitched, and an unusual expression appeared on his face. He Shun, not sizing up the situation, bellowed, "Who do you think you are? You've just arrived yet you're throwing your weight around. Go on, mates, load!"

Without looking at He Shun, Liu started the engine and tipped all the lime off the truck. He Shun shot him a glance, somewhat puzzled. This reckless rascal misunderstood. He thought it was Xie's position that intimidated Liu. How absurd for an uncontrollable young fellow to let himself be twisted round a girl's finger! He must settle scores for his friend. He stood up, indicating that Xie Jing should sit in the middle.

"I'm covered with lime, I'd better sit on the side," she said, squeezing into the seat.

"That won't do! When the lorry turns, you'll be thrown out. Who'll be responsible for that?"

Xie Jing looked out of the windscreen, ignoring him. When the lorry had left the depot, to break the awkward silence He Shun said, "Xie Jing, if you really want to stay in the transportation team, you'll have to learn how to drive."

That was true. Xie Jing turned to him, asking, "Do you think I can?"

"I can teach you, if you take me as your instructor."

Being on guard, Xie Jing did not give him a positive answer. Instead she said, "Anyway I'll have to start from scratch. You're all my instructors."

Seeing she was rising to the bait, He Shun continued smugly, "Then you'll have to abide by our rules. I bet you don't know, do you? First, you must learn how to light the cigarette for your instructor. He has to hold the steering-wheel and can't easily strike a match. That's where the apprentice must help. Like this...." He fished out a cigarette and put it into Liu's mouth, then struck a match and lit it. Next, he put one into his own mouth. "Have a try," he urged, "let's see if you're qualified to be an apprentice."

Xie Jing was very angry and looked away again.

"Get on with it! Are you shy or too self-important?" With that, He squeezed against her. There was almost no room for her on the seat and soon she would fall off. Squaring her shoulders, she faced up to him and said, "Where are your manners?"

"Manners? Ha! Ha!" He lit his cigarette and, after

drawing on it, blew the smoke in her face. "Don't put on that act! No one in our line has manners. As the saying goes: All drivers, boatmen, innkeepers and porters should be killed even if they've committed no crime. And drivers top the list. To be frank, lighting cigarettes for instructors is the simplest thing to do. There are many other things you'll have to learn. A girl who wants to learn to drive will have to pay for it."

While speaking, He Shun put his arm round her shoulder. At once she jumped with a shout which sounded more like a wail, "Stop the lorry!"

Instead, Liu put on speed. Ripping open the door, she cried, "If you don't stop, I'll jump off!"

In dismay, Liu braked and the lorry screeched to a halt. Xie Jing leapt down and, heading into the wind, walked off without turning her head. Liu was flabbergasted. "Never mind her," He Shun snapped. "Let's go!"

The lorry flashed past Xie Jing. She could no longer control herself. Tears which had long been held back streamed down her cheeks. But the wind drowned her sobbing. She did not bother to wipe off her tears and let them roll down to relieve her frustration and anger. While weeping like this, she trudged on in the gale.

The weather here has its own rule. If the wind starts at sunrise, it drops when the sun sets. If it rises at dusk, it abates when the sun comes up the next morning. Now it was getting dark, and the wind grew fiercer. There was not a soul on the road. Xie Jing had her heart in her mouth and was shivering. She had no idea how far it was to the plant or how long it would take her to get there.

4

"Wake up, Xie Jing! Secretary Zhu wants to see you right now." Tian Guofu rapped on the windscreen, a briefcase in his hand.

"What is it?" Xie Jing looked up from the wheel. Having rubbed her eyes, she noticed a cryptic smile on Tian's face.

"I just met the secretary of the head office at the front gate. He asked me to tell you that Zhu wants to see you — it's urgent."

Xie Jing looked at her watch: it was twenty past eight. So Tian was late again, for he still had his brief-case in his hand.

Noticing her raised eyebrows, Tian explained as though to himself, "There was such a long queue in the clinic, I waited for twenty minutes to get registered. Xie Jing, you'd better hurry." Then he turned and went into his office.

Xie Jing sat motionless. She had been here for two years now and never gone to the administration build-ing except on urgent business. In the first place, she did not want the drivers to suspect that she told on them to the Party secretary. Old Tian, in particular, knew that she and Zhu had been on good terms and was afraid she might say bad things about him. Indeed, he was not at all pleased at having the Party secretary's favourite working with him. Only since coming here had Xie Jing realized that her relationship with Zhu counted against her. She deliberately avoided him. Secondly, she did not want to go back to that building, did not even like to see it or those junior cadres with much the same background as hers who were still working there. But Zhu was the person she most dreaded meeting. He had helped her, cared about her, and she was grateful to him. But now she found it hard to express any more gratitude, for she was paying the price for his protection. Was Zhu to blame? The best way was to avoid him. But today he wanted to see her! What for? Tian must know but would not tell her.

Having taken out the key from the ignition, she jumped off and went to find Ye Fang, whose lorry she had been driving. She pushed open the locker-room door and found Ye smoking. Why did this carefree girl look so worried today? She snatched the cigarette from her and trod it underfoot. "Ye Fang," she said speaking as a friend, "if you smoke too much, your lips will turn black and your face sallow. Do remember that. Well, what's upset you?"

"Xie Jing," Ye blurted out, "do you know that Liu was selling pancakes this morning?"

"Selling pancakes?" Xie Jing was taken aback.

"Yes! He and He Shun set up a stall and sold pancakes! What a disgrace!"

Xie Jing's obvious surprise made Ye feel better. She had been afraid that Liu might have told Xie Jing about it but not her.

"The bell's gone. Is he still selling?"

"Oh no. They stopped before work began. Now they are counting the money. Liu doesn't want a cent and has given it all to He Shun. What's he after?"

"Well. . . ." Xie Jing's heart missed a beat. She felt there was more to this than just earning some money on the side.

"Xie Jing," someone called outside, "Zhu just rang. He wants you to go and see him right away."

"I know." With that, she walked out of the locker room. Now she knew why Zhu wanted to see her. Actually Old Tian should have gone to see to such things, since he was the head of the team. But she had to go as the Party secretary had sent for her. Still she felt easier in her mind, knowing that he would not be asking about her progress or her own future plans. The riddle now was Liu Sijia. He did not want the money they had earned. What was his motive then? She ought to sound him out before going to see Zhu. But she knew she would get no answer for the time being. She had no choice but to go to the Party secretary. She could deal with the problem later. But why was Ye Fang so upset? She loved Liu and made no secret of it. This time, he had obviously hurt her feelings. This pretty girl had only been to a primary school. She loved fine clothes and liked to use abusive language, so many people misjudged her. Xie Jing had despised her once and found her disgusting; but it was Ye who had come to her help when she was in difficulty. Xie Jing appreciated her candour and sense of justice, and they had become good friends. She even thought that Ye and Liu would make a fine couple and would have liked to help bring off the match. But Liu neither accepted nor refused the proposal. No one knew what was in his mind.

That first evening, before Xie Jing had trudged very far in the wind, she was exhausted. There was not a building in sight, she was all alone in a world of wind and darkness. Sand and grit stung her face. She dragged on, thirsty and hungry. If not driven on by fear, she would have lain down on the roadside. Just then she saw two yellow beams coming towards her. Just my luck, she told herself. If only it had been a car from behind, she might have asked for a lift. Then, to her surprise, a lorry pulled up beside her. The door opened and out came Ye Fang!

"Xie Jing, come on in!"

She helped Xie Jing into the cabin. Seeing the way she was covered with dust, Ye felt genuinely sorry for this newly appointed deputy team leader.

"What a dirty trick to play, the bastards!" she cursed. "I'll sort them out. Oh yes, they're gambling at Yellow Bridge Restaurant tonight. Let's go and make He Shun treat us."

Turning off the cabin light, Ye Fang opened the throttle and the lorry drove off. Leaning back on the seat, Xie Jing rested and calmed down. However, she was dying for a cup of tea, her body aching all over. She had never expected Ye Fang of all people to come to her rescue. She was really a warm, kind-hearted girl. She loved Liu Sijia, but when he bullied others she would intervene. She had been jealous when he drove off with Xie Jing; but on learning that he had left her out in the wilds, instead of being pleased she had gone to help her. Xie Jing's heart began to warm. When battling against the wind, she had resolved to go to the Party committee first thing the next morning to resign. She would not stay in that transportation team! But now she had changed her mind. She determined to stay. There were good people around. Even the so-called "fashion model" was good-natured and ready to help others, let alone old drivers like Big Head Sun. She suddenly felt she was not alone after all.

She gazed at Ye Fang with gratitude, her interest

aroused by the other girl's skill in driving. How had she learned to drive? Had she been bullied too at the beginning? Insulted by her "instructor"?

"Master Ye," she asked, "who was your driving instructor?"

"Oh please! Don't call me that. Call me Ye. Big Head Sun was my instructor."

"What's his real name?"

"Sun Xuewu."

"Did he take advantage of you when you learned from him?"

"Never. Big Head Sun looks a terror. But at heart, he's a real fine fellow. He flares up quickly, but soon gets over it. He never bullies his apprentices. It's those young wretches who always want to take advantage of girls. Better watch out."

"Did you have to light cigarettes for your instructor?"

Ye smiled and said, "That's nothing."

"When did you learn to smoke?"

"When I came here to learn to drive. It's an occupational disease. Wherever you go, you meet people who smoke. The reek of tobacco is awful if you don't smoke."

"You want one now? I'll light it for you."

Xie Jing lit a cigarette for her, which put her in a good humour. Taking advantage of this, Xie Jing asked a question which had been on her mind, "Ye, I've never offended any of the team. Why should Liu Sijia and He Shun hate me?"

Having never worried about questions like this, Ye Fang answered matter-of-factly, "Don't be narrow-minded! They don't hold anything against you. Why should they hate you? Just because you're doing so well, better than us, they're envious. That's the trouble with men. They always want to take advantage of girls."

"Well...." Xie Jing was not entirely convinced. However, the first half of the answer was worth considering. As they were chatting, they entered the town. Instead of going back to the plant, Ye turned west and stopped the lorry at the gate of the Yellow Bridge Restaurant not very far from the plant.

"Look, those loafers are enjoying a hearty meal," Ye Fang said, pursing her lips towards them.

The restaurant was brightly lit. Through the large glass windows, Xie Jing saw Liu, He Shun and two other young drivers sitting round a big table. The two young drivers each holding one of He Shun's ears shouted, "Why don't you give in? Hurry up!"

The racket they made could be heard even in the street.

Ye eagerly gripped Xie Jing's arm, wanting to jump off. "Quick! Let's have some fun too and a bite to eat."

Xie Jing was disgusted to see such a scene. Besides, how could any decent girl share a table in a restaurant with such rowdies? What if word of this got out?

"You go ahead!" she said to Ye Fang. "I'll wait for you here."

"That won't do! Since we've caught them eating, we must go in and have a share. They must pay for what they've done to you. Otherwise, they'll think they can get away with anything."

"No, really! I don't drink!"

"You can eat something then."

"Look at me! I'm covered with dust. How can I go to a restaurant like this?"

"That's the whole idea! Let He Shun see you. And we can fine him by making him treat us."

"No. I'm not going in."

Ye Fang's face darkened. "Do you think we're beneath you a Party member? Honestly, you won't get on in this team if you put on airs. You mustn't blame me for not warning you." She whirled round and entered the restaurant.

Xie Jing was in a dilemma. It was very awkward waiting in the cabin. And she could hardly up and leave without saying goodbye to Ye Fang. She saw her walk casually into the restaurant, sit down by Liu, pick up his cup and take a gulp from it. Ingratiatingly, He Shun offered her a dish. She took it without the least hesitation. It was obvious that she had not had her supper yet. She must be starving the way she was wolfing the food. Looking at her, Xie Jing felt her stomach begin to rumble. She wished she could go in and eat something too. Even some water would quench her thirst. But she hadn't the guts.

Meanwhile, in the restaurant, everyone's attention had focused on Ye Fang. Her buddies were apparently currying favour with her by offering her dishes and drink. Other customers looked at her too. She just drank and ate, talked and laughed, ignoring the other tables. When she had eaten enough, He Shun put a cigarette into her mouth and lit it. Having had a deep pull on the cigarette, she raised her head and pointed her chin towards the lorry outside. She was probably talking about Xie Jing. Xie Jing hastily turned her head away.

"Comrade Party member, do you dare to drink this wine from a loafer's cup?" Surprised, Xie Jing turned her head and saw Liu Sijia standing beside the cabin, proffering a beer to her. She had no clue what he was up to. It would be very rude if she turned down the offer, which might embarrass him. These people set great store by being matey. Refusing him would put his back up. Xie Jing had never before drunk so much as a sip of alcohol. She was terribly thirsty now. She took the glass and sipped. It was cool and refreshing. She downed the whole glass in one go. She felt very comfortable, but slightly dizzy.

"Another glass?"

Xie Jing shook her head. "No, thank you."

"Well, not bad. If you want to command others, you must first be in command of yourself."

She looked at this eccentric young man, puzzled. She could not catch his meaning.

"Dignity, the qualification for leadership is not bestowed by others, much less by the Party committee. Some people may be good at playing at politics. But they are no longer trusted. If you want to keep up with the rat race in this society, apart from being good at political manoeuvring, you must also have strong nerves. Deputy team leader, I hope your nerves are strong." As he flung those words at Xie Jing, she smelt the reek of alcohol.

"Don't worry about my nerves. I've never tried to harm anyone. Why say such cutting things?"

Liu sneered. "You can't call them cutting. Surely someone like you involved in politics ought to know this. A man's strength is shown through his words.

People who don't speak their minds are no better than animals."

Xie Jing found it difficult to talk to this young man, who kept putting her on the defensive and making her tense. Her head swimming, she looked away, ignoring him. But she sensed he was still eyeing her like a male chauvinist.

Ye Fang came out of the restaurant and said sulkily to Liu, "So you strike up a chat with her under the pretext of bringing her some beer, eh? What are you talking about?"

Instead of replying, Liu got on to the running-board. "You go ahead with your meal," he turned and said. "I'll drive this lorry to the plant then come back."

"You're taking her to the plant?" Ye asked, grabbing hold of his jacket. "You don't seem to know your own mind! You hated her just a moment ago and mixed alcohol in the beer. Now you've made her drunk and want to take her back. What are you really up to?"

Though dizzy, Xie Jing's mind was clear. In dismay she braced herself to get off the lorry. But Liu pushed Ye Fang aside and got into the driver's seat. Ye Fang went to the other door and got in too. She sat between Liu and Xie Jing. Liu, ignoring her, started the engine and the lorry, as if drunk, shot forward unsteadily in the teeth of the wind.

Unable to control her frustration, Ye Fang suddenly pounded Liu's shoulder with her fists like a maniac. Then she wept leaning on his shoulder.

Liu sat erect, his eyes on the road in front, his hands tightly gripping the steering-wheel.

"Are you crazy or something?" he asked. "You

should learn from our deputy team leader. All those involved in politics are inscrutable. No matter what happens, she doesn't turn a hair, not like you, blowing hot and cold in turn."

"Tell me, what's behind all this? Why do you want to take her to the plant?"

"It was He Shun who mixed alcohol in the beer. You saw that, didn't you? I'm taking her back because you've drunk too much. What if you had an accident?"

All of a sudden, Ye Fang showered Liu with kisses, regardless of Xie Jing sitting beside them. She thought there was no harm in letting Xie Jing see this, to let her know how much she loved him. Then Xie Jing wouldn't poach on her preserve.

Unfortunately Xie Jing did not see this. Overcome by drink and exhaustion, she had fallen sound asleep.

5

Xie Jing had a strange feeling when she started up the stairs of the office building which had been so familiar to her. Anything altered? No. Nothing had changed. The rooms with odd numbers were the administrative offices: 201, the head office; 203, the meeting-room; then the offices of the managers, Production Department, Supply Department and so on. The rooms with even numbers belonged to political departments such as the Party committee's office in 202, the Organization Department in 204, then the offices of the Militia, Security, and Public Relations. The Party secretary, Zhu Tongkang, worked in 212. Nothing had changed. Even the brown wooden plaques on each door were there, the names on them written by her. That was the first time she had shown her talent for calligraphy. The spittoons in the corridor remained in the same places. Everything was the same except her feelings. Two years before when she left this building, she had felt lacking in self-confidence. Now she knew how to drive and was a deputy team leader both in name and reality. Life was full, and walking along this corridor her steps were steady and forceful. Strangely, when she had worked here before she had not felt that this building belonged partly to her. Now she had left it, yet she felt qualified to have a say in its administration.

She was somewhat worked up when she opened the door of the Party secretary's office. She saw the old man's head above the sofa, his silky white hair like a baby's unable to cover his shining head. Even his taut veins could be clearly seen. A mixed feeling of respect, gratitude and vague resentment filled her heart. She called softly, "Old Zhu, you want to see me?"

"Ah, Little Xie, sit down, sit down!" Zhu, who had been lost in thought, made haste to greet her. He was agitated. He had a special feeling for this girl. As Party secretary, he was concerned about her. Besides, he had a fatherly affection for her, a feeling which had grown stronger when he was disappointed by his own children. Pleased, he looked up and scrutinized her. Was there any change in her after so long a time down in the garage? Looking closely his heart sank. His face darkened too, and his cordiality vanished. He resumed his usual serious air and appeared stern and aloof.

Xie Jing was nonplussed by the changes in his expression. She looked at her clothes. No wonder! How could she have entered this office in such a suit!

One day after work the previous month, Ye Fang, who had nothing to do, accompanied Xie Jing while she practised driving. When they were back in the locker room after a ride, a strange idea suddenly occurred to Xie Jing. She wanted to try on Ye Fang's western suit to see if it suited her. When she put it on, she could not recognize her reflection in the mirror. As the saying goes: "A good saddle makes a handsome horse, a smart dress brings out a girl's beauty." It was quite true. Xie Jing had never realized that she was pretty. She was somewhat embarrassed, but inwardly very pleased. Ye Fang urged her to have a suit like that made. Though she did not commit herself, she began to think about it. Finally, she made herself a silvery-grey suit in the western style. At first, she dared not wear it in the plant, only when she got home. But gradually she grew bolder and wore it even to work. She stopped going by bus for fear of attracting too much attention and giving rise to gossip. So she rode a bicycle to and from the plant. By now she had got used to wearing this suit. That morning she was late up and began her driving practice without changing. Then she was pressed to go to see Zhu and, in a hurry, forgot to change into her blue working clothes. A Communist, a middle-ranking cadre wearing a smart western suit to work? What would others think of her? Xie Jing felt uneasy and flushed. But she could not defend herself. That would only have made things worse. She knew very well what the reaction would be in this office building. What was done was done. There was no need for regret and nothing wrong about wearing a western suit. She collected herself and appeared confident and firm, the little mole by one lip slightly red. She assumed a serious expression so that the Party secretary would not ask any personal questions. Not wanting to talk about herself to her former, respected leader, she took the initiative to ask, "Secretary Zhu, what did you want me for?"

Zhu, instead of answering, asked casually, "How have you been doing at the garage this last two years?"

Her reaction was annoyance. "If you want to talk about Liu Sijia selling pancakes, just out with it!" she thought. "Why should you talk about me? Seeing me in this suit, you instantly frowned and closed your eyes. Obviously you don't like it. Is there any need to make a show of your care, concern and regret?" She made an effort not to reveal her impatience. Looking very grave, she asked calmly as if they were on the same footing, "What do you want to know about?"

A good question! What did he want to know? He knew everything. What was the point of asking her? His heart sank. Now he realized that he had committed a serious error. In the Party committee, he was the man who was in charge of all cadres in this plant. But ever since Xie Jing had gone to work in the transportation team, he had not once inquired about her. Though he had heard the gossip that Xie Jing did nothing because she was so engrossed in driving that she never attended meeting in the office building, he was too busy to talk to her. A promising young cadre had now turned out like this. Who was to blame? Was his influence as her Party secretary too weak? Or was Liu Sijia's corrupting influence too strong? Nowadays, all young people baffled him. He could not understand his own son, nor Liu Sijia. Now even Xie Jing had become a riddle too.

He lit a cigarette and abruptly offered her one, saying, "Have a cigarette!"

"No thanks. I don't feel like it."

"I heard you smoke now. Do you?"

He dared not look at her, annoyed with himself for asking such a question.

"Yes, I do, but I'm not an addict. I don't smoke much."

Her answer was unaffected and polite, sensible and to the point.

He resented the way she spoke to him as though they were equals. Nevertheless, he had to lump it. He wanted to have a good talk to her. In the past she had always come to him whenever she had a problem. But that was ancient history. Though she was still his subordinate, her mentality was utterly different from his. In her eyes, he was no longer the embodiment of the Party, a father figure. She had changed and matured, though as a girl, she was somewhat shy, aloof and curious. He had wanted her to grow up faster. But now that she had really matured, he found her a formidable stranger. There was a gap between them, and they could not confide in each other as before. He hoped to end this talk as soon as possible.

"Liu Sijia and He Shun from your team set up a stall selling pancakes this morning. Did you know?"

"I've heard."

"Workers with wages are not allowed to go into trade like that. You must deal with them severely. There's already been a lot of talk."

"Tell me how to deal with them."

"You'd better submit your proposals first."

"But based on what? It there any government regulation dealing with these things?"

"Well.... Go and ask the Security Department."

"I did just now, and there aren't any clear regulations. What if Liu refuses to be penalized?"

"You can bring him to his senses, can't you?"

"What if he turns a deaf ear?"

"So you think there's no way, eh?"

"Of course there's a way. But it's up to the Party committee. It's the Party committee that should make a decision. What is the real quota of our plant this year? How many workers have nothing to do? How long can you keep paying wages? Will there still be any bonus? When can we change the present situation? Can't workers do a little business on the side? What if such things happen? As Party secretary, you ought to know the answers to these questions and explain them to the workers. But now, you people at the top are confused while those below are worrying about their future. What's the point of just making an example of Liu Sijia for selling pancakes?"

Zhu was stumped. He had no answers to these questions.

"According to the plant's regulations, a worker who has left his post without permission for half a year will be sacked. But a worker of the No. 2 Workshop has been away for a whole year and gone into trading. The Party committee has done nothing about it. No punishment. No sacking. Now what do you think I should do about Liu Sijia? Then there's the problem of our canteen. It serves nothing but steamed buns and porridge for breakfast. And pancakes at the snack bars are cold and covered with dust. The workers say Liu Sijia has done a good thing!"

"Want to put in a good word for him, eh?"

"I'm just telling you the truth."

"Little Xie, don't forget what you are."

"I'm a Party member!"

They could not go on fencing like this. Zhu was the first to capitulate with a sigh. It was difficult to cope with youngsters nowadays and with young cadres too. They had their own views or rather prejudices. They would just answer back no matter who you were. Old people whose mental processes were a bit slower were simply unable to cope. Zhu regretted having sent for Xie Jing. He should have called Old Tian in, and that would have been simpler. Tian might not lift a finger, but at least he would never embarrass a superior. He would just nod and promise to do as the Party secretary said. But now his most trusted subordinate no longer listened to him.

Xie Jing had not meant to speak to the Party secretary like this. She respected him and felt guilty about hurting his feelings. But she could not control her emotion! She had been cold-shouldered for two years in the transportation team, partly because she had been Zhu's secretary. She could not help getting her own back by pouring out these grievances to her former protector, on whose account she had suffered. But was this fair?

Nowadays, when a stalemate occurs, older people usually compromise and climb down, whether in society or in their own families. Zhu changed the subject and tried to be more cordial. But he no longer felt his old genuine concern for younger cadres.

"Little Xie, I hear you're engrossed in learning driving every day, aren't you?"

"I've been learning for over a year now. I can drive cars and trucks, not coaches. There'll be another test tomorrow. I've passed all the rest already. If I pass tomorrow's test, I'll be given a driver's licence."

"That's not your job. You're a cadre, not a driver!"

"A cadre in the transportation team who knows nothing about driving might as well be blind and deaf!"

"If you find the work there too much for you, the Party committee could transfer you somewhere else. People are badly needed in our offices up here." He was thinking he might change her back if he had her under his eyes every day. He genuinely wanted to take this chance to get her out of that garage.

"Never!" Xie Jing was firm in her resolve never to leave the transportation team. She was determined to change her white learner's licence for a red driver's licence. It shocked her that the Party secretary should make such a proposal. Did he really not understand why she wanted to learn to drive? For two years he had not even asked how she was getting along. It was precisely because she had sweated it out for those two years that she could now hold up her head when she entered this building. She was confident, capable and knew what she was doing instead of blindly following other people as she had done in the past. She took nothing on trust now, but judged by her own experience. This had changed her whole outlook on life.

It was the rule in this plant that there must be one cadre on night duty in each unit. Since Xie Jing's transfer to the transportation team, she had taken on this job virtually *in toto* for Tian always had health problems or something to do at home. On the third night after her arrival, she was woken up at two o'clock by a phone call. No. 1 Workshop urgently needed oxy-sodium, and the manager on night duty wanted her to send a truck for some immediately.

She opened the register of the drivers' names to find someone who lived nearby. The closest was He Shun! Their paths were bound to cross! What could she do? She set off by bike through the silence of the night, feeling very nervous. Suddenly a dog chased after her, scaring her almost out of her wits. She pedalled frantically to He Shun's home, and braced herself to knock at the door. It seemed ages before he came to open the door, wearing only his underpants. Stretching his arms, he yawned and stared at her with drowsy eyes.

"Oh hell!" he muttered. "It's warm and comfortable in bed. If you don't want any sleep, OK. But why wake me up at this hour of the night?"

"No. 1 Workshop has run out of oxy-sodium. Please take them some."

"What has this got to do with me? It's your cadres' concern. I'm not going!"

"Of course, the cadres of the Production Department are to blame for bad planning. But now they're desperate. We can't let their production come to a standstill. Please help them out!"

"Help them out? Who'll help me out?"

"You'll be on overtime pay. And if you like you can have a day off for this."

"I don't want either."

"What do you want then?"

"A girl to sleep with."

Without a word, Xie Jing whirled round and mounted her bike. He Shun roared with laughter and shouted, "Hurry up! The manager's waiting to bawl you out!"

Xie Jing was too angry to be scared. Nearing the office she heard the telephone ringing so shrilly that it sent shivers down her spine. With a trembling hand, she picked up the receiver.

"Why haven't you sent a truck?" the manager bellowed. "What! Who are you? If what you say cuts no ice, what are you doing on night duty? If production's held up, will you take the blame? Go and get Tian Guofu at once!"

"The truck will be there very soon," Xie Jing said in a low voice.

She knew it would be more difficult to get Tian than a driver. She cycled back to He Shun's home. This time, instead of joking, he flew into a rage.

"What the hell have you come back for?"

"What do you think?" She took a firm stand and answered with assurance, "If you didn't know that No. 1 Workshop needs material urgently, no one could blame you even if the sky fell. Now that I've come and told you how urgent this is, I've done my part. If you refuse to go, I'll have to report you to the manager. If our plant's quota for this month is not fulfilled because of this delay, if we can't hand in a profit and issue bonuses, you, and you alone, will have to answer for it!"

"Ha! Ha! Want to call my bluff, eh? You can't scare me, I tell you!"

Inwardly though, he was dismayed. Why had this

soft-hearted girl team leader suddenly become so tough? He could make fun of her or bully her, but he didn't want to have his wages docked or lose his bonus; and if she reported him to the management he might be penalized. He stepped out of the dark doorway and bore down on her.

Xie Jing told herself: Don't back down! Stick it out! See what he can do.

"I didn't refuse to go. But on certain conditions."

"I agree to your conditions and tomorrow I'll tell the head office and let everyone know about them."

"Bah, don't try to scare me. Do you think I'm a coward?"

"Why should I try to scare you? You've got guts, haven't you? You're not afraid of anything!"

Instead of backing away, she moved forward, her voice raised. "How about this? Ask your parents and sisters to get up and listen to your conditions. Then let's find out what they think. Then we won't have to stir up the whole plant. How about that?"

"For Heaven's sake, cut it out!" He Shun caved in. Giving her a nudge, he said, "You go ahead! I'll get dressed and be there in no time."

"Let's go together." She was afraid he might play another trick.

Without a word, he followed her to the plant and got into his lorry.

Back in her office, she felt wide awake. Acting tough had paid off tonight. Luckily it had been too dark for him to see her expression. In broad daylight she could not have coped with such a situation. But things could not go on like this. Tian and Xie, as cadres, were asked to be on night duty, but neither of them could drive. Whenever something urgent cropped up, they had to go and get a driver. That held things up. The drivers should take it in turns to be on night duty. But what she said carried no weight. Who was willing to work at night? She thought of Big Head Sun who might take the lead. These days, old drivers like Sun had been very polite to her; but the younger ones had grown more and more difficult. They simply would not listen to her. Yet they made up the majority of the team. And they were the ones who caused the most trouble. In just a few days in the garage, she had heard and seen a great deal. There were not many drivers but the team had problems galore. If there was a profit to be made on a trip, everybody wanted to go; if it was a tough job, such as transporting lime or cement, no one wanted to go. Although there were altogether fifty lorries, sometimes only four were in operation. All the rest, according to the drivers, needed repairing. When a little screw was missing, the driver claimed that his lorry must be overhauled. What could the cadres do? Knowing nothing about motor vehicles, they let themselves be bamboozled. And having no control over the drivers, they passed on their lies to their superiors. If these were seen through by one of the managers, they would be taken to task. Sandwiched in the middle, they caught it from both sides. It was not that the administration of the transportation team needed improving, there was in fact no administration at all. The drivers threw parties and accepted bribes — anything could happen.

Xie Jing was frustrated, realizing the problems but quite unable to cope. She consoled herself: If the team leader doesn't worry, why should you care? But no! Tian was getting on in age and had a high salary. He would retire in a couple of years so that his son might get a job in this plant. But you want to do a good job here. You made a bad start in the plant and can't afford another slip. You must learn some real skill, like attending a school you must go up one grade, even two grades in one year, so as to catch up with the others and make up for the five years wasted in the office block. It would be a shame to be kept down like a poor student. You are still young, and can't go on expecting to get preferential treatment. . . .

All of a sudden, she caught sight of a packet half filled with some poor-quality cigarettes on the window-sill of the office. She took one out and put it between her lips, then struck a match, lit it and inhaled. It tasted so acrid that she chucked it away and rinsed her mouth with water. After gargling several times, she still could not get rid of that disgusting smell. She had to brush her teeth and then suck a sweet before finally eliminating it. Smoking was worse than taking bitter herbal medicine, she concluded. But how could she stay on in this place with everybody around smoking? It was a matter of will-power. So she resolved to learn to smoke. Frowning, she tried again, giving up in disgust. Once more she had to rinse her mouth with water. She kept this up until the drivers came to work. Deliberately holding a cigarette, she went to see Ye Fang, who hugged her, giggling.

"With your two fingers raised like that, you've given the game away. You seem to be holding poison instead of a cigarette."

"Ye, from today on I want to be your apprentice."

"To learn smoking?"

"No. Driving!"

"Driving?"

"Won't you teach me?"

". . . I will, of course."

"Promise?"

6

Was this a meeting? Yes and no.

Yes, because it *was* a special gathering. It was in the men's locker room shortly after the morning bell. The chairman, neither appointed nor elected, was Liu Sijia, the real boss of the transportation team. It was open to anybody. He Shun and some other young drivers were of course there.

No, because it really did not seem like a meeting. No notice had been issued, there was no agenda, no list of speakers either. Those attending it did not think of it as a meeting.

Nevertheless, those men who were inactive in formal meetings, study groups or discussions willingly attended special meetings like this. They spoke up freely and eagerly aired their views. News on the grapevine, hearsay, all kinds of strange tales and criminal cases were discussed. Sometimes they talked at great length about one subject, even swearing or coming to blows. And it was always Liu Sijia who made the conclusion and ended the meeting.

Today their topic was selling pancakes.

"What a bright idea! No one need worry about wedding expenses! There is a marriage bureau, and now we can start a financial aid committee for marriages. Make Liu the director. Whoever wants money for his wedding can come and be his assistant. Let's make a list of applicants. He Shun's at the top of the list."

"But his wife's not born yet. Put him at the end. Liu should be the first."

"But he doesn't want a cent!"

At the moment what was preying on He's mind was the money they had earned that morning. They had just counted it and the profit came to thirty-seven yuan and forty cents. Liu gave all of it to He Shun, who was surprised, delighted and somewhat embarrassed. Of course, the more money that rolled in the better. But it was Liu Sijia who had done most of the work. Besides, Liu was his good friend. It was unfair to grab all the money himself. And it would cause talk. Again he produced the money from his pocket and put it on a stool. "Sijia," he said, "that won't do! If you don't take it I won't either. You're always good to your mates, and I don't want to be a money-grubber. Business is business. Let's go halves."

Liu said nothing, squatting in front of an electric ring, his eyes fixed on the slices of sweet potato in the pan of boiling water over the fire. He picked up a slice with some chopsticks and tasted it, then smacked his lips and took a handful of corn flour and dropped it in the water, stirring it with his chopsticks. He had done this so often that he was a dab hand at it. Soon the gruel was ready, neither too thick nor watery. Some greedy youngsters helped themselves to it. Not that townsfolk thought much of it, but Liu seemed to find it delicious. The young drivers considered him a gastronomic expert, as he had been to many Tianjin restaurants and sampled all kinds of western food. But what he loved most was this gruel made of sweet potato and corn flour, which was popular in his hometown. He never ate fritters or pancakes for breakfast, only a big bowl of gruel.

Having downed it, he wiped his mouth and asked with a glance at the cash on the stool, "Are you serious?"

"Of course. . . ." He Shun sounded slightly less determined than he had a moment ago, but he could not go back on his word.

"Well, that's fine." Liu looked into He's eyes, making it impossible for him to recant. "But you must tell outsiders that you take all the pancake money, because we're using your father's trading licence. Then if the Party committee ask any questions or take the case to court, we'll be in the right. You can say your father's unwell and needs money, so you're helping him in your spare time. As for me, I like frying pancakes, and doing my friends a good turn."

He Shun nodded repeatedly. The others approved, "Right. That's a good idea!"

But what He Shun wanted to know was who would get the cash. "Well. . . . What about the money?"

"Don't worry. I won't take it either. Big Head Sun is in a fix. It's been half a year since his wife came from the country to have treatment for her stomach cancer — it's terminal. So he's heavily in debt. Besides he's got four kids in the countryside. We ought to help a mate out. . . ."

He Shun jumped to his feet, snatched the money on the stool and stuffed it into his pocket. "What do you mean? You want to give it to him? Nothing doing! I'd rather throw it away than give it to that bumpkin!"

Liu's face darkened. However, he did not raise his voice. "I'm a bumpkin too. All our ancestors were peasants. You were born in this big city but your people were peasants too. If you don't like the idea, fair enough, take the money. The rest of us will have a whip-round to help Sun out."

The others nodded in approval.

He Shun couldn't bear to lose that money.

"If he can't tide over, he can put in an application for a subsidy."

"You know how it is. Last month he asked for twenty yuan. The application travelled from office to office to get the approvals, and finally he was given fifteen yuan. If he applies again this month, do you think he'll get anything? At present, the plant can't even afford to buy gloves and soap. This month's pay is in arrears. How can we rely on the plant? The managers are too busy to care about him. As a peasant, his wife can only be reimbursed half her medical expenses. He's been working for more than twenty years and never complains about anything. How can we do nothing when he's in such trouble? If I start a whip-round, I'm sure everyone will chip in. But we haven't had a bonus for several months, and I can't ask people to fork out part of their wages. So I thought of selling pancakes. If the plant lets it ride, fine. If they want to see me about it, I've got a lot to say to them. Honestly, He Shun, I used your father's licence and you gave me a hand. Naturally you're entitled to what you've earned. Your father can at most earn five yuan in one morning. Why not give Big Head Sun thirty yuan, and you keep the rest — seven yuan forty. How about that? You can look on it as a gift to me."

"You've got a point. As a friend, I can't let you down." Gritting his teeth, He Shun fished out the stack of cash and threw it on the stool, saying, "I won't take a cent of it. Give it all to Big Head Sun."

"Great! A friend in need! But pocket it for the time being. When you go out, make a detour to take it to the hospital."

"Not me! I'm no errand boy. Why should I humble myself in front of him? I don't even do that with my parents."

"What a fool you are, He Shun!" Liu explained smiling. "You'll be doing him a favour. Isn't that alright? You always bully him. Now you're sending him cash when he's in a fix. He may even bow to show his gratitude. It's an errand everybody would like to run."

He Shun smiled and put the money into his pocket.

"One thing, though. Don't tell him this comes from selling pancakes, or he'll be afraid to accept it. Just say you collected it from your mates, and you can have all the credit. Take my word for it, I won't let you down. If the higher-ups forbid it, then forget it. If they don't, I'm going to sell pancakes for a month. Of course we won't make as much as we did today. But no matter how much it is, you and Sun can go halves. I won't take a cent."

Liu's words warmed the others' hearts. Someone said, "Sijia, look out! The Party committee just phoned to summon Xie Jing. Probably about your selling pancakes."

"Don't worry. I won't talk to anyone except Zhu. That's what I'm hoping for." Turning to the man who checked on work attendance, he continued, "Don't mark Big Head Sun absent. Otherwise his pay will be docked and he'll be done for."

The man countered, "But what can I do? It's not like last year. Now Xie Jing's learned to drive and knows everything that goes on in our team. Nothing escapes her eyes. And she's strict. If she finds out, I'll be in trouble."

"Give me the attendance record. If there's trouble, I'll take the blame."

"That's not a bad idea. But take care! Xie Jing goes by a chart which is so well worked out, she keeps tabs on everybody in our team. Don't let her catch you out."

Liu kept quiet. He knew that chart of Xie Jing's. What surprised him was her growing prestige. There were even people who were afraid of her, and thought he must be too. Since she was deputy team leader while he was a driver, he ought to listen to her. But his attitude towards her was ambivalent. Sometimes he made trouble for her; sometimes he admired and helped her. The way she ran the team was based, partly, on his ideas. He had not foreseen that these might boomerang against him.

The meeting ended. Liu Sijia was really a somebody. The trouble-makers were afraid of him while honest people respected him. In fact, the workers all thought highly of him. Sometimes he was reasonable, at others unreasonable. He could behave better or worse than anyone else. The stricter the authorities,

the more he resisted them, but he never bullied honest
straightforward people and helped them most of all.
He was especially good to those from the countryside,
because he himself had been brought up in a village.

When he was in the fourth form of primary school,
his family had moved to Tianjin from Cangxian
County. Though the best pupil in his new class, he was
often bullied. His classmates laughed at his clothes,
imitated his countrified accent and called him "Little
Bumpkin". Seeing he was so good at his lessons, the
teacher made him class monitor. Every time the teacher came into the classroom, he would shout, "Stand
up!" and the whole class would stand up to show their
respect. But his thick local accent made "stand up"
sound like "cicada". So he was nicknamed "Cicada".
Whether in the school grounds or in the streets, his classmates would keep calling him "Cicada". This made
him too embarrassed to open his mouth. So after class
he kept to himself and steered clear of his classmates.
In the village school, he had been clever and lively, a
model pupil. His grandparents had high hopes for
him, wanting him to go to university, and in order to
give him a good start they sent him back to his parents
in Tianjin. But in the city this star village pupil found
himself kicked in the teeth. A small outcast, he developed an inferiority complex. But the more he tried
to keep out of the way, the more he was bullied, for
city boys despise weaklings. One day he had just left
the school gate when a classmate, the son of a battalion
commander, kicked him viciously from behind. He was
thinly clad and the kick landed on the small of his back,
hurting so badly that he rolled on the ground while

other boys booed him, calling out his nickname. Not wanting more people to mock him, he gritted his teeth and pulled himself to his feet, then limped off and washed his face at the tap at the end of his lane to remove the traces of tears.

He longed from that day to go back to his village school. But he could not go like this, he must first avenge himself. When still very small, he had heard many stories about heroes from his grandfather. Cangxian had produced many heroes, he was told, and each household had swords and cudgels. After the autumn harvest, the old man would teach some youngsters the martial arts. But strangely, Liu Sijia, his own grandchild, had turned out a weakling. After Liberation, his father went to Tianjin to learn electrical engineering and later became an electrician. He was cited as a model worker and then married a technician who had been through university. When mentioning them, the villagers would raise their thumbs in admiration. How could such a couple give birth to a spineless son? After school the following day, he kicked that battalion commander's son four times and knocked out one of his teeth. When he had been kicked, he had not said a word to his teacher. But now the commander's wife came to school to complain bitterly. Liu Sijia did not defend himself and wrote a self-criticism. And he could no longer serve as a monitor.

He changed. He looked at his teachers and classmates with hostile eyes. He worked hard to remain a top student so as not to give the teachers a handle against him. After class, he would not take the least attack lying down. When his classmates called him

"Little Bumpkin", he would shout back curses in the Cangxian dialect. Once out of the school gate, he would punch them. He was strong, agile and thirsting for revenge. When it came to blows, he would never scream or cry but just fought with all his might. His eyes red, he looked a terror. City boys might have a sharp tongue, but after a few fights they were scared of him. That son of the battalion commander knuckled under to him and did whatever he was told, not daring to complain to his parents or teachers. Liu fought all the boys who had ever bullied him. They called him "Country Bully" and feared him more than their teachers. He found the Tianjin dialect disgusting and Cangxian's rather uncouth, so he determined to learn standard Chinese from his mother. To him, it was refined and civilized, the language used by newscasters. By the time he started middle school, he could speak standard Chinese fairly well and was always more smartly turned out than the Tianjin boys. His classmates began to call him "Little Beijing". When the "cultural revolution" started, he was naturally elected to be a leader of a rebel group. To cope with fights, he went to his hometown and persuaded his grandfather to teach him his martial arts. He stayed there for three months. When his parents learned this later, they locked him up for fear he might cause trouble outside and trained him to be an electrician. At that time, work in factories had been disrupted by the so-called "revolution". Every morning, his father would go and clock in, then come home to teach his son how to make tape-recorders and television sets. Gradually his interest in electrical engineering grew. Every day he ran to an electrical appliance store to buy cheap rejects. He learned to make a refrigerator and a gramophone by dismantling and then reassembling them. Sometimes, he went to second-hand shops to buy used machines to cannibalize. His parents gave him as much money as he needed for electrical engineering. Since all universities and colleges were closed then, they could only hope that he would become a good electrician.

When he left middle school however in 1972, he was assigned to be a driver in the No. 5 Iron and Steel Plant. He spent a good part of his wages on electrical appliances, and made his own tape-recorder, camera, sewing-machine, TV set, calculator, washing-machine and radio. Most of them were better designed and made than those on the market. He used stainless steel to make his Latinized trade-mark "Cang Xian". No one except his parents knew what this meant, and he kept it a secret. Therefore many people believed that all these home-made electronic devices of his were imports.

He really was an oddball. He and He Shun appeared to be great friends. And He Shun did regard him as his trusted friend. But at heart, Liu despised him and sometimes played tricks on him just for fun. He liked Ye Fang's beauty, honesty and shrewdness. However, he objected to the fact that she was a Tianjin girl, superficial, rough and lacking in feminine charm. He found Xie Jing serious, with firm convictions for all her gentle manner. He liked that. Besides, her handwriting was superb. Nevertheless, he was jealous of her. A girl without any skill, she was in a position to supervise others. He had an instinctive aversion to such people. Especially as she had once been Zhu's secretary. At times he even looked down upon himself. The odds were against him. He had missed university, missed becoming an electrician, was doomed to a life of driving — a bleak prospect. When feeling blue, he would go to a restaurant or mess around with He Shun and his mates. But sometimes he felt himself smarter than those cadres. He knew the plant's problems and had thought up many solutions, only he could not put them into practice. He would neither thrust himself forward nor humbly confide in those higher-ups. Team Leader Tian was slick, nursing his health and holding on to his position and power. Unable to accomplish anything, he was liable to spoil everything. Apart from official airs, he had nothing. As for the Party secretary, you could not say he was a bad man, but did he understand this plant and its workers? How much did he know about business management? Then there was Xie Jing. What did she know? Even Big Head Sun would make a better team leader. But she had been given this post, a young girl put in control of older drivers. Non-professionals were in charge of professionals. Luckily this young cadre had a good head on her shoulders after all those years of political work. Those endlessly changing political campaigns had confused people's minds and created a rift, a credibility gap between management and workers. In such circumstances, the workers liked Liu Sijia's matey way of helping the weak and those in difficulties. They no longer believed in "class struggle" or "supreme instructions", only in brotherhood. Liu Sijia was so good at his job that no one could find any fault with him. This won the admiration of the old workers, gave him a special position in the transportation team. He was a functionary without a title, the *de facto* team leader.

7

"Xie Jing's back!" The drivers gathered in front of the garage as they had done when she had first come two years before, expecting some excitement. They all knew that the Party secretary had had a talk to her about Liu Sijia's selling pancakes. Now what would she do? It was no joke! If she did nothing, how could she answer to the Party committee? If she took action, would those two knuckle under? There might be a big fight. Some people were worried for her, others for Liu Sijia. Others just wanted to watch the fun.

As soon as she saw the crowd, Xie Jing knew what was in their minds. She glanced at them as if nothing had happened. Most of them were trouble-makers. There was not a single old driver, all of whom had gone out on errands. Liu Sijia was not there either. He might have gone off to work too. Xie Jing was pleased. That was what she had expected. He would simply do his job so that no one could fault him. He was not going to quarrel or show any sign of panic.

"Where's Liu Sijia?" she asked on purpose.

"Sure enough, the first person she wants is Liu Sijia." The drivers gathered round her. One of them replied, "He's gone out in his lorry."

"Why don't you get on with your work?"

They did not know what to say.

Xie Jing was puzzled. Why hadn't Tian protested against their slacking. She remembered seeing him a little after eight o'clock. Had he left again?

Ye Fang came up and said to her, "Xie Jing, Old Tian's heart is playing up again, so he's gone home. He asked me to tell you."

Someone in the crowd commented, "The old fox! Sensing trouble, he's bolted!"

Ye Fang stood beside her, very depressed. She was still upset about Liu's selling pancakes, and worried for him too. Though a lively girl, she had not seen much of the world. She was eager to know how the Party committee had reacted, but could not bring herself to ask with so many people around. The drivers, though embarrassed by Xie Jing's question, were reluctant to leave before seeing how she handled the business. However, none of them would break the ice. They looked at Xie Jing and waited.

He Shun was really a muddle-headed idiot! He had got up earlier than usual to fry pancakes, and now he was actually snoring at the foot of a high wall!

This made Xie Jing furious. It seemed she would have to give this bum a lesson or his buddies would not go to work. Taking Ye Fang with her, she strode towards him and shouted, "He Shun!"

He Shun, sound asleep, did not stir. Ye Fang gave him a kick. Then, rubbing his eyes, he scrambled to his feet and asked, "What's up?"

Very calmly Xie Jing demanded coldly, "Why aren't you at work?"

"The others all went for petrol. Why should I have to fetch lime?" He sounded indignant, ready for a fight.

"First, fetching lime is also our work. Someone must do it. Why shouldn't you be sent? Secondly, yesterday when you went to get petrol you smoked in the oil depot. That was very dangerous. It's being enlarged and the whole place is in a mess. One small spark could have started a fire. The man in charge reported it to the police, and the police notified me. Now you must write a self-criticism and promise not to smoke again in the oil depot. Otherwise you'll not be allowed in there. You'll have to take on the job of fetching all the lime, cement and oxy-sodium."

"What are you talking about? You want to give all that dirty, hard work to me? You can't bully me like that. Nothing doing!"

"Fine. Give me your key, and I'll go and fetch lime. When I come back, you tell me whether this counts as absence without permission or whether you're on strike."

Xie Jing held out her hand. But He Shun backed away, not wanting to surrender the key. She stepped forward and said evenly, "The head office is worried because we have too many workers and don't know how to pay them. They will be only too glad if someone quits work and doesn't want his wages."

This reasonable argument silenced He Shun. If he capitulated, he would lose face in front of all these people. If not, there would be trouble. Xie Jing was able to drive now and had struck roots in the team. She could easily call his bluff. Worse still, there was the problem of the pancakes. He hoped she would not bring it up. As Liu Sijia had said, if no one from above came to ask about it, they could sell again the next day. Then all the money would be his. Weighing the pros and cons, he forced a smile and tried to smooth things over. "Well, well, a finger can't match a fist. You're a cadre while I'm a driver. If I don't listen to you, I'll get myself in trouble."

Was this firebrand going to take it lying down? Those who had wanted to watch the fun were surprised and disappointed. How quickly the whole confrontation had ended. And why didn't she bring up the matter of selling pancakes?

As He Shun was about to go, Xie Jing called out, "Just a minute, write up your self-criticism after you come back with the lime. This afternoon you can go with the rest to get petrol."

Give her an inch, she'll take a mile, He Shun thought, shaking his head. He smacked his lips and piped up, "When a wall is tottering, everybody gives it a push. But have you people in charge ever realized my good points? In the past, I used to fight. Couldn't do without a set-to every three days. That was meat and drink to me. But do I fight any more? I reckon I'm qualified to join the Party."

His smug look disgusted Ye Fang. "You long ago qualified to join the Kuomintang Party," she snapped.

The drivers smiled wryly, and He Shun laughed sheepishly as he got into his lorry and drove off. Seeing this, the other drivers made for their lorries too. But Xie Jing stopped them.

"Just a minute, comrades. Since it's already late, I might as well say something else. . . ."

The drivers turned and looked at her in surprise.

"These days, I must say, we've been rather slack. Perhaps you think our plant's going to be readjusted, and we don't have much work to do. You've had no bonus for months, and can't be sure now even of your pay. Discipline is as lax as in the hard years of the early sixties. But I assure you no matter what happens, you'll get your wages, not a cent less. Our transportation team will have more work to do. The head office wants us to take on the job of transporting materials for other units to earn a bit of money for our plant in the period of readjustment. It's counting on us to help tide over the present difficulties. So we mustn't slack off. On the contrary, the rules and regulations of our team must be strictly carried out. The bonus system will be restored this month."

The drivers looked at one another. This was really a piece of good news. Everyone was delighted. As workers, none of them wanted their team to fold up. So long as there was work, there would be money. What surprised them was that this slip of a girl was so calm and spoke as if she had powerful backing. The team leader had sneaked away when things looked bleak. But she had the guts to go ahead without any hesitation. "We'll have to watch our step in future," they said to themselves. "It's all very well to earn more to please the folks at home, but that extra money won't be easy to earn. We'll have to work hard. This deputy team leader never loses her temper and is thoroughly reliable. It's no good crossing her — she knows what she's doing."

Xie Jing produced a piece of paper, spread it out and held it up, saying, "A few months ago, I found this crumpled up on the office floor. I picked it up and found it was a diagram. Here it is! I had a good look at it and studied it, and I came to the conclusion that it's very well worked out. Today I'll pin it up so all of you can have a look at it. You can discuss it and suggest improvements. Then in future we'll run our team according to this diagram. But I still don't know who drew it."

The drivers craned to look. None of them knew who

had drawn the diagram, and some of them could not make head or tail of it.

"I've already told the chief engineer about this," Xie Jing went on, "and he's decided to give whoever drew this a fifty-yuan award from the technical innovation fund. Please help me find out who it is and tell him to collect the award."

This was really interesting. At first, the drivers were puzzled, then they began making animated guesses.

Xie Jing folded up the diagram and said, "Now get moving. I'll paste this up here and you can have a good look at it during the midday break."

As the drivers left, Xie Jing hugged Ye Fang and said, "You don't look very well today. I'll go with you. Let me drive and you can have a rest."

Ye Fang was delighted for she wanted to tell her something.

Xie Jing started the engine and asked, "Do you have any idea who drew that diagram?"

Ye Fang shook her head.

Xie Jing looked at her and suddenly pitied her. Poor girl! She did not even recognize the writing of the man she loved. At least she should know what was in his mind. But what did she know about him? Who else in this team could have drawn such a diagram? You love him but don't understand him. Why do you love him? Because of those electronic devices of his?

8

As Xie Jing had foreseen, Liu Sijia did not come to claim the diagram and get the award. He kept silent as if it had nothing to do with him. Xie Jing had already learned of their meeting that morning in the locker room, for some of the drivers now confided in her.

After consulting the chief engineer and manager, Xie Jing had amended that diagram by making a few corrections and adding some new ideas. Then she re-drew and annotated it in her fine calligraphy. Finally she added the heading: Standards for Checking the Work of the Transportation Team. This stirred up the whole team, and no one was more surprised than Liu Sijia. At first, standing in the crowd of spectators, he had felt elated. But after a closer look, he was shocked. It was not his critical diagram but a constructive one giving carefully worked out guide-lines for improving both the team's work and management. His own diagram had only served as a basis for this better and more scientific chart. So the award should be given to Xie Jing, not him. Why should she do such a thing? To encourage him or mock him? He was all at sea. What kind of person was Xie Jing? She not only had the guts to amend his diagram but had done it well.

When she had first arrived, she started learning to drive and at the same time began to tighten up the team's management. He was not sure whether she was only making a show or resolved to stay in this team. Once at a meeting, he stealthily drew a diagram and threw it on the office floor when the meeting came to an end. He did it deliberately to see how Xie Jing would react. The diagram made it clear where the problems in this team lay. If she really meant to do a good job, she could start by tackling those problems. If she just tried to keep a low profile or meant to use her experience at the garage to win promotion and go back to the head office, then she would throw it away. He had never expected her not only to accept his ideas but to improve on them. He could no longer treat her as an ordinary girl.

That afternoon, Xie Jing meant to get into He Shun's lorry. She was still worried about his going to the oil depot, but he had no other assignment and, besides, had handed in his self-criticism. There was no reason to prevent him from going. If she went with him, she could keep an eye on him. But somehow this made Liu Sijia feel jealous. She often talked and laughed with other drivers, but always kept him at a distance. Though both of them realized this, neither mentioned it. Now he was jealous of He Shun. Did she think him worse than that bastard? He could not help shouting, "Xie Jing!"

"Yes!" Xie Jing made for him, thinking, "So he's unable to hold back any more."

With a set face, Liu demanded, "You help this one and that one, why don't you ever help me?"

"You're a reliable driver. Do you need anyone to give you a hand?"

"Do you trust me?"

Meeting his eyes, she said, "All right, I'll learn something from you today. You're a model driver who has driven a hundred thousand kilometres safely."

As she got into his cabin, Ye Fang ran up holding a piece of paper. "Xie Jing," she said, "the traffic police just phoned to ask you to take part in the test tomorrow."

Thinking she would soon be a real driver, Xie Jing was delighted. "Come with me tomorrow, will you?"

With a sneer, Liu said, "Fine. When you get your

licence, we'll be your tools for ever. You can do whatever you like with us. What shall we do?"

Xie Jing tossed her head and retorted, "Do you think I should be your tool for ever?"

Liu was lost for words. His expression was strangely depressed yet admiring as he started the engine and slowly followed He Shun.

"When are you going to get the award?" Xie Jing asked without looking at him.

"What award?"

"The award for your diagram." She smiled. "You know that, don't you?"

"It's not my work." He made up his mind not to admit it. If he admitted it, he thought, that meant she was one cut above him. He regretted not having made more investigations and thinking more carefully before drawing it. He could not accept an award for a diagram so greatly altered. Others might have wanted to take the credit for it, but he would be ashamed to do such a thing. He would rather give up that fifty yuan than make a fool of himself.

Xie Jing feigned surprise. "What's to be done then? But it's your handwriting, I can recognize it. So when I went to the head office on business this morning I got the money for it."

"Perhaps it was drawn by Big Head Sun."

"Everybody knows Sun doesn't draw. If he'd done it, he would have given it to me instead of throwing it on the floor. He's my instructor, you know. During the day Ye Fang teaches me how to drive. When Sun's on night duty, he teaches me about a lorry's structure and maintenance. I know him well. Besides he won't accept this kind of financial help from you. He didn't even take the money sent him this morning when He Shun let the cat out of the bag. Didn't He Shun tell you?"

Liu Sijia had no inkling of this, while she knew everything. His buddies had really let him down. Why should that bastard He Shun keep it from him? To make off with the money? His face darkened. He made an effort to keep cool, but his cheek muscles twitched.

"It seems you overestimate individual ability and brotherhood, while belittling the strength of an organization, a collective. No matter what difficulties our plant is facing at the moment, ours is a socialist state-owned enterprise with over ten thousand workers and staff members. There's a Party committee. There's the Party branch in the transportation team. You can help Sun, but would the Party ignore a worker when he's in difficulties? Of course I don't mean all cadres are perfect. The chairman of the trade union always tries to whittle down the subsidy regardless of a man's problems. But Tian's partly to blame for not making the matter clear. Tell you something, the medical expenses for Sun's wife will be covered by the plant, every cent of them. You don't have to tamper with the attendance record. He's asked for leave. But as a special case, he'll still get full pay."

Liu was silent. Her tone was mild, but he found this lecture hard to take. Normally he would have jumped to his feet and shouted her down. But today he was speechless. He could refute other people with his eloquence and wit, but not this girl. He would have to make a great effort to break even. He regretted having invited her into his cabin.

Once out of the entrance, the lorry raced towards

the general oil depot of the city. Lorries seemed to
have the same temperament as their drivers. He Shun's
lorry was fast and tough. One hand on the steering-
wheel, a cup of tea or cigarette in the other, he joked,
laughed and behaved so recklessly that his passenger
would have his heart in his mouth. Liu's lorry was fast
but steady. When driving, he kept quiet, his face
serious, his eyes fastened to the road. Keeping a firm
grip on the steering-wheel, he looked confident and
alert. One felt safe enough in his cabin to have a doze.
Xie Jing admired his skill and liked his motto: Driving
a lorry is like riding a tiger!

Neither of them spoke. It was awkward for both of
them. If only He Shun or Ye Fang were present. Xie
Jing looked out of the windscreen. Poplars flanking
the road were already tinged with green. Tower blocks
made of cement had been erected, and people were
moving in. On the street were wedding cars and
hearses. Spring was a busy season. Schools, shops,
stalls flashed past. Having left the road circling the city,
the lorry headed downtown. Here the streets were nar-
row and crowded, and Liu had to slow down. At last
he raised the question puzzling him, though without
looking at her, "Zhu Tongkang asked you to punish
me, didn't he? Why haven't you asked me about selling
the pancakes?"

She shot him a glance. There was nothing she could
keep secret from someone like him. "I saw no need to."

"Why?"

"What's the point of asking you? You didn't do it
for yourself, in the first place. Secondly, you weren't
just fooling about but trying to help a friend. It was a

fine deed deserving to be praised. Who would dare
punish you!"

Though her words were double-edged, his lips curved
for a second in a faint smile. So, after all, she did not
know everything.

"I'm thinking of writing an article about your good
deed, to be published in our plant's paper and then
broadcast. That would be to your credit. How about
it?"

"That's the last thing I want you to do, you know
that."

"Yes, of course. That's in character. And you know
what's best for you. There's no need for anybody else
to worry about you."

"Tell me what your character is."

"Fight against all trends which make people pessi-
mistic, vulgar, selfish and apathetic, and be someone
who's useful to others and to society."

"Oh, stop preaching! People are the cause of all evil
and the source of all goodness as well. They are dreadful yet pitiful creatures. But they're powerless in the
face of social disorder and the mysteries of fate."

"You sound very philosophical. It's too bad that
your theory's wrong. Still, what you said reflects your
mentality. We've been together for two years. In my
opinion, you're too proud, too stand-offish. I know
you often go to restaurants, and fool around with He
Shun, Ye Fang and the others. But at heart you're
lonely, bored. You're only looking for some stimulus.
This was your motive in selling pancakes. What you
said to your pals this morning was true, but it wasn't the
whole truth. You don't like certain things in the plant
and are angry about them, so you deliberately make

trouble to stir up the whole plant. You make things difficult for the management without breaking any laws, then delight in watching them flounder. But you're wrong. Actually the more trouble you make, the worse you feel. Just because you're alive and kicking, with feelings and a good brain, you don't want to destroy yourself. . . ."

"Stop it!" Liu braked all of a sudden and the lorry screeched to a halt. He put his head on the steering-wheel, his shoulders shaking.

Xie Jing was astonished. From what she had heard and from her own observation, she was certain that Liu was not as cold and apathetic as he appeared to be. She had meant to shake him up, not expecting her argument to go home so effectively.

"Sijia," for the first time she addressed him with feeling. But at once she blushed, her heart beat faster. Controlling herself with an effort, she asked softly, "Are you all right?"

Liu neither replied nor looked up. So she had seen through him. His self-respect, his show of calm and his cynicism — she found them laughable. His buddies flattered him, listened to him, but none of them under-stood him. And he despised them. Because he found it hard to get along with such muddle-headed people, Ye Fang included. Everyone thought her a beauty, but she was shallow, tasteless as a plastic flower. The deputy team leader now sitting beside him was not on good terms with him and they often clashed, but she was the one who really understood him. She was a person you could trust and confide in. However, his self-respect prevented him from doing this. He looked up, a strange expression on his face, both tractable and full of vitality. He dared not look at her, yet felt strongly attracted to her. He longed to be close to her, to understand her, but felt this attraction a threat. If he gave in to it, that would be the end of his proud aloofness and his prestige. So he tried with all his might to resist this attraction and even spoke sarcastically to cover up his confusion.

Xie Jing's remarks had touched a raw nerve. He felt as though he had been stripped bare, unable to hide anything. He had even lost his calmness and his mental defences had completely collapsed.

Xie Jing asked him to change places with her. Liu complied without a word.

The lorry drove on. Her attitude as she drove and the expression on her face were charming. A faint dreamy smile played on her lips. Though not as beautiful as Ye Fang, she was profound, tranquil and idealistic, like a poem or a painting. She was so fond of driving that whenever she held the wheel she felt elated. Liu eyed her ardently, trembling slightly. His feeling for her had overwhelmed him too suddenly, it was too strong to resist. He was almost out of his senses. For two years he had cultivated hostility towards her, but now he realized how much he loved her. He wanted to cry, to laugh with her and tell her what torment he was in. He had read that a man in love would pocket his pride. True. But did he really love her? Could there be such a strange, abrupt love as this? Ye Fang ran after him, loved him, and sometimes he did feel fond of her, but he had never experienced his present feeling for her. But he could not tell what Xie Jing thought of him. He dared not speak his mind for fear that she might despise him.

Xie Jing noticed his changing expressions in the mirror in front of her. She said, "Like you, I've been through disillusionment and painful mental struggles. But that helped me to realize certain truths. So I decided to take a new road and regained faith in life. Some people tried to destroy our generation, but we can't give up on ourselves as hopeless." She knew what was on his mind, what he wanted to say. But she could not let him love her or give him the chance to say this. A man with such strong self-respect might do something desperate if his offer of love were turned down. She must distract his attention.

"What's your faith then?" Liu asked. "Now you can drive, you're a team leader who has a skill. With your political record and technical knowledge you should go far. You may even end up with the post of manager. . . ." He broke off, shocked to have spoken as he had. He felt so drawn to her, yet had retorted so sarcastically. He was filled with remorse. Perhaps he could never say anything kind, no matter how hard he tried. He did not want to hurt her. But since he had started, he would have to go on.

"How can you talk about regaining faith in life without a definite aim? You're a star in this plant, with good prospects. You've nothing to worry about. But what about me? In primary and middle school, I always came first in my class, showing that I'm not inferior to anyone else. But after those years of nightmare, I had no way out. Climb up by hook or by crook? I can't. I despise such behaviour. Go to university? I've no time to review all the textbooks. Besides, I'm over age. Someone suggested that I study at night school and learn a foreign language. But what's the use? My parents taught me electrical engineering. I bet I could've been a very good electrician if I had been assigned to work in that line. But unfortunately my job is driving a lorry. I aim high but the odds are against me. So I'm just a mediocrity and that gets on my nerves. . . ."

Xie Jing swept her eyes over him. She knew what he was saying was true. But this was not the time to console him. She should goad him, not express her sympathy. So she said tongue in cheek, "Don't be so modest! There's no need to be ironic either. You're not a mediocrity at all! You're a somebody in the plant."

"Right. I like to make fools of the management. Don't they keep yelling: We're short of work, short of money, can't afford to give bonuses? To annoy them, I do something to rake in money. They're not short of money, they simply don't use their brains. There are loopholes everywhere and they don't do a thing about them. If I were the manager, I could overhaul the plant within three years. Unfortunately I don't want to be an official, just a real human being. This is also my advantage. Because I have more freedom than you officials."

"You are an official without a title, a man with real power. In our team, more people support you than me. This is something you can be proud of, something I admire. You've won your mates over because you look down upon cadres. I don't mean you're envious of them. You think you're smarter and that's probably true. Take me for example. You're far better in administration, management and expertise." She was very much in earnest.

But Liu felt as if sitting on pins and needles.

With her eyes on the road ahead, she continued,

"But don't let your indignation interfere with your judgement. Bitterness is bad for health, and prejudice stops you from thinking clearly. Quite a few of our generation are very bitter and always try to hurt other people. Not to give a damn for anything seems to be all the fashion. To show that they're different from the common herd, they even mock at things they know nothing about. Those who think themselves a cut above other people and are cynical are really to be pitied. They're lowering themselves. Using cynicism to cover up their ignorance and boredom."

Xie Jing had hit the nail on the head. Liu seemed to be someone who could be coaxed, not bullied. But in fact, you had to be hard on him and push him. So she had decided to touch him on the raw, to find out what was really in his mind.

Liu felt so hurt that a shiver shot down his spine. However, he was pleased not to have said a word about his love for her. So in her eyes he was no better than He Shun, an ignorant good-for-nothing! She had avenged herself for her past two years of hard treatment. Without using abusive language she had made a shrewd and wounding analysis. She was too clever for him, a girl without normal feelings. She had simply made fun of him. You would never get the better of such a person. He wanted to take over the steering-wheel and kick her off the lorry. As he reached out for the steering-wheel, he inadvertently touched her hand. His own hand jerked back as if he'd got an electric shock. He blushed and looked away.

Xie Jing did not look at him. She was keeping a firm grip on the steering-wheel. The oil depot was in sight, lorries coming and going busily to fetch petrol. All of a sudden, a few people ran out of the entrance in great consternation, waving their hands and shouting to her, "Stop! Stop!"

Xie Jing braked. Liu opened the door and inquired, "What's wrong?"

"There's a fire in the oil depot!"

"Ah!" Xie Jing and Liu jumped to the ground and ran towards the depot.

9

Dark clouds of smoke were rising in the depot, a lorry loaded with petrol cans had caught fire. The flames were crackling and roaring. Since the petrol pump operated automatically there were not many attendants in the depot. A few women, scared stiff, did not know how to work the fire extinguisher. Someone splashed water on to the lorry but the fire blazed even more fiercely, spreading fast. Some petrol cans were leaking. The whole lorry was a ball of fire! The whole depot was endangered. For just on the other side of a thin wall was the worksite where they were enlarging the depot. Stacked on the ground were timber, oxygen cylinders, acetylene cylinders. Worse still, there were scores of oil pipes and, not too far away, nine huge oil tanks. If the fire spread there, great explosions might wreck all the buildings near by, engulfing the whole place in a sea of fire. Even the housing estate in that neighbourhood was threatened. A disaster seemed imminent. Some people rushed out of the depot; others stamped the ground at the entrance, not knowing what to do.

Xie Jing, Liu Sijia and He Shun dashed towards the gate. Xie Jing shouted, "Don't stand and watch, put out the fire!"

"Too late," Liu yelled back. "That lorry must be driven away!"

But who dared to risk it? The lorry was aflame, the paint on the cabin burning noisily. It was impossible to stay near it. Besides, those oil cans might explode any minute. One blast would start a series of explosions and blow the lorry sky high. Anyone in the cabin would be burnt to ashes. Who dared to risk his neck like that?

"Whose lorry is this?" Liu bellowed.

"Mine," a middle-aged man beside him replied. His honest-looking face was distorted with terror, his body shaking all over.

With a grim smile, Liu boxed his ears, his eyes bloodshot. The man staggered and fell, but no one paid any attention. Just as Liu whirled round to run to the lorry he was caught by He Shun. "What do you think you're doing? We didn't start the fire. None of our business!"

Liu was stunned for a second. He Shun was right in a way. Why should he seek the limelight by risking his life? He hesitated. He wanted to see how Xie Jing would react. She was a deputy team leader, a Party member who had the gift of the gab. What would she do? But when he turned his head, he found Xie Jing gone. Somebody screamed. He looked back and caught sight of a small figure dashing towards the lorry. It was Xie Jing! Repulsed by the fire and smoke, she tore off her jacket and flailed out at the flames on the cabin.

Then she jumped on to the running-board and got into the driver's seat.

Liu could have kicked himself. A hefty young fellow letting a girl risk her life! What's more, she was only a novice. She might lose her life yet fail to avert the calamity.

Whether out of fear or tension, He Shun's grip on Liu's arm was still tight. Liu wrenched himself away.

"Sijia ... you! ..."

Liu spat out a curse, "You bastard!"

Then he made for the lorry.

Xie Jing had already started the engine. Liu shouted frantically, "Take it easy! Don't rush! One jerk will trigger off the blast!"

The lorry began moving. Liu leapt into the cabin and stretched to grip the steering-wheel while speaking at the top of his lungs, "Easy! The steadier the better! No jerking! Ah — Right! Easy! Easy! Turn a bit to the right, a fraction more. Once out of the gate, turn left. . . ."

Xie Jing eased the lorry out of the depot. People exclaimed in amazement. But she heard nothing. The back of Liu's jacket caught fire but he did not notice it. While looking ahead of him, he continued cautioning Xie Jing and helped her control the steering-wheel with his right hand. The lorry, like an erupting volcano, drove out of the gate.

The threat to the depot had lessened, but the lorry's danger had increased. Liu was fully aware of this. They would speed up once on the road and when they reached somewhere quiet they would jump off. Suddenly he felt a burning pain on the back. When he looked over his shoulder he saw flames. He peeled his jacket off and threw it away.

"Let me drive, you get off!" he ordered Xie Jing.

"Leave me alone! Jump off quick!"

Xie Jing's face, lit up by the fire, looked stern but proud. Liu shot a glance at her. He would never forget her expression. He did not want to take his eyes off her. He felt he was beginning to understand her. She was quick-witted, tough, intelligent and dauntless. He moved over roughly and grabbed the steering-wheel.

"Get off at once! I'm going to accelerate!"

"No! You get off!"

"This isn't your job! Why should two of us take the risk?"

Liu stood up and gave the door on the other side a vicious kick. Then he pushed Xie Jing over there shouting, "Jump off!" He gave her a shove. With a cry Xie Jing fell out.

Hearing her cry, his heart contracted, his eyes brimmed with tears. It had been a long, long time since he last shed tears. Luckily no one could see him. He wanted to have a good cry. She was such a wonderful girl! Too good for him. And she had such a low opinion of him. Liu gritted his teeth and accelerated.

Now the cabin was swallowed up by the flames. The iron partition behind him was red-hot, the glass panes had cracked. The sputtering sound of burning paint increased. Leaping tongues of fire assailed the cabin from both sides and almost touched Liu's face. The lorry might explode any moment now.

"Danger! Jump out! Hurry up!" someone shouted.

He wanted to turn round and see how far he was

from the depot. But he could not make this out through the fire and smoke.

Stop here? No! There was a school on the left where children were having their lessons. Stopping here would endanger them all. Damn! How could they build a school by an oil depot! Better go a bit further.

Stop here? No! There was a store on the right.

It was a hardware store.

Well, here again a building had just been completed, and there was a big character "Happiness" on the lintel. . . .

"Oh blast! I'm in for it today!" He was perspiring profusely. With his eyes wide open, he trod on the accelerator and pressed the horn which sounded like a fire-engine's siren. The fire ball raced on. He gave up the idea of pulling up by the road, for he saw a pond on the left not too far ahead. "Get the lorry over there and see," he said to himself.

"Get off! Jump!" people cried while making way for him.

Three hundred metres! Two hundred metres! One hundred! He veered sharply to the left and shot towards the pond. He tried to slow down but the brakes no longer worked. Oh hell! But he must not miss that pond! Further on there was another housing estate. He ripped open the door and leapt on to the running-board. Immediately he was engulfed by the flames. He gave the steering-wheel a hard pull to the left and jumped off. He fell on the ground and rolled over to put out the fire on his clothes.

The lorry lurched forward, then plunged into the pond.

Bang! A flaming oil can rocketed up almost thirty metres high and then dropped into the water.

The cans exploded one after another. Petrol floated on the surface of the water and in a minute the hundred square metre pond was enveloped in fire and smoke.

Lying on the roadside, Liu took a deep breath and said to himself, "Lucky there's a pond here!"

Suddenly he thought of Xie Jing. Was she badly hurt? He struggled to his feet. He felt a pain in his leg and almost fell; but he knew he was all right, no bones were broken. He limped back anxiously. If a young man prepared for the jump felt so badly bruised, then what about Xie Jing?

Very soon he was surrounded by a crowd: the heads of the oil depot, people from the school, the store, the chairman of the neighbourhood committee and some others. They admired him and were immensely grateful to him. If not for him, there would have been a disaster. He was snowed under with questions.

"Comrade, where do you work? What's your name?"

"We are so grateful to you. We'll go and tell the head of your unit what you've done."

"We'll request that you get rewarded."

"You're a hero! You must be a model worker!"

"What was in your mind just now?"

. . . . . .

Liu was flabbergasted. After a pause he burst out, "Clear off, all of you!"

He elbowed through the crowd and broke into a run. Then he stopped abruptly and shouted over his shoulder, "If you have time, better do something useful yourselves instead of praising others!"

Then, ignoring them, he limped on.

People were stunned by his rudeness. Had the shock crazed him?

On the road, other people kept greeting him in admiration. He ignored them and ran forward. They had no idea what was wrong and ran after him. Very soon there was a crowd trailing behind him.

Xie Jing was worrying about him too. She staggered along to meet him.

"Are you all right, Xie Jing?" Liu called out, walking towards her.

Xie Jing was very pale, beads of sweat standing out on her forehead. With a faint smile she said, "I'm all right. How about you?"

"Fine!" Shooting her an anxious, intense glance, Liu made for his own lorry.

10

Was there anyone in the world who could scare He Shun? Was he ever ashamed or embarrassed?

Maybe.

This had been a good chance to be in the limelight, with that horrifying accident which had nearly finished off the oil depot. Luckily it had nothing to do with him, a notorious trouble-maker. He witnessed the whole business, knew all the details. Presently a crowd gathered, making wild guesses, unable to find out the truth. He Shun could have given them an embroidered account so that all these wide-eyed people hung on his lips envying him this experience, while he enjoyed holding forth, the centre of all attention. Liu had jumped on to his truck and driven away. Now the heads of the oil depot and enthusiastic passers-by were anxious to track down the hero. So He Shun could have told them at great length about Liu, about his good relation with him and even about the girl driver whom Liu had pushed out of the cabin. He could have taken their breath away and gained some kudos himself too, not like in his team where he was a nobody.

Usually, He Shun would have grabbed at such a chance.

But today he was not in the mood and even hoped that no one would recognize him. The hero and the heroine who had saved the depot were his best friend and his deputy team leader. He should have been proud of this, but instead he felt ashamed of himself, felt under tremendous, invisible pressure. In these circumstances he would not admit that he knew either of them.

Presently Xie Jing limped over. Flustered, He Shun whirled round and leapt into his truck, then drove off to fetch petrol. All of a sudden, he realized that it was Xie Jing who had put him in such a strange mood — it was she who scared him. In the past she had criticized him, mocked him; only that very morning she had given him a piece of her mind. But he had never taken it to heart. In his eyes, she was nothing. He would often laugh or crack a joke to make light of her rebukes. But he was afraid of her now. Not her rank but her personality, her way of doing things. She was like a torch throwing light on him, showing him up as a petty hooligan. He was truly a bastard as Liu had said. Fearing Xie Jing, he instinctively made off.

He Shun helped a woman worker to fix the nozzle of the petrol pump to his truck. When the valve was opened, the petrol gurgled into the tank. He stole a glance at Xie Jing, who was surrounded by people. He had never dreamed that a girl, a priggish cadre who hadn't even got a driver's license, would dare to get into that flaming cabin and drive that damn truck away! Had she overheard what he had said to Liu and been so indignant that she dashed to the truck? No! Not a chance! She couldn't have heard him, for by then she was already sprinting towards that truck. Oh, He Shun! If you didn't want to go, fair enough; but why should you say such a thing? If you had gritted your teeth and charged ahead, what airs you could have given yourself now! You wouldn't have been killed or badly hurt, at most a few cuts or bruises. Just imagine! If you'd known, you wouldn't have run away from this good chance to shine. Hell, what's the use of thinking this way? Instead of shining I made a fool of myself! ... Well, not exactly that. I wasn't the only one to hang back. A lot of people rushed out of the depot, they were the only two who went to the rescue. I was just like most of the others. Even the driver of that truck fled. Why should I be ashamed to face her?

He Shun reproached and defended himself in turn. But he still had a guilty conscience. The more excuses he made, the more he despised himself.

Shit! Xie Jing was heading towards him! She had come here on Liu's truck. Now that Liu had gone, did she want a lift from He Shun? He grew nervous. Without checking to see if his tank was full or not, he closed the nozzle, rolled up the pipe, slipped into his truck and drove away like a thief.

Left in the lurch by He Shun, Xie Jing felt frustrated. She was aching all over. Exhausted, she sank down on the steps of the entrance, waiting for another driver to give her a lift. At once she was surrounded by the cadres of the depot, repeating their chorus of praise and gratitude. Some wanted to send her to hospital for a check-up. Others urged her to rest in their office. Hanging her head in silence, she sat motionless, neither accepting nor turning down their offers. The pain grew worse. She felt thoroughly disgusted. Who were those people? Where had they been when the truck was aflame? It was simple to get the flaming truck out of the depot, but difficult to deal with people like these. It was Liu who was smart. She admired his alertness, his swift decision to ditch his assistant and drive off without filling up with petrol. The people around her had introduced themselves as the director, Party secretary, head of the Political Section, head of the Public Relations Section and so on. Would she have done the same in a similar situation if she had still been the deputy head of the Public Relations Department? Yes, she would. It was part of the job.

In desperation she cried, "I've told you time and again, I didn't drive that truck. It was Liu Sijia, a driver of the No. 5 Iron and Steel Plant. I'm still only learning to drive, I couldn't have done it. But Liu hates flattery, he won't let you thank him. He may even sue you."

"Sue us? What for?" they exclaimed.

Xie Jing regretted her blunder. However exasperated she was she shouldn't have used the word "sue". That was a gaffe. But now it was too late to take it back. Anyway, today's accident had shown up the loopholes in the depot's safety precautions. "As heads of the depot," she said, "you're legally responsible for this fire. How can you run a large oil depot like this, with no strict precautions against accidents? When one happens you just can't cope. Those few rules you have on your gate about fire prevention aren't taken seriously. So instead of thanking us you'd better examine your work."

To her surprise the ominous word "sue" failed to rid her of those people, who only expressed their gratitude more profusely. She was at a loss when Ye Fang elbowed her way through the crowd and came to her rescue.

"Xie Jing!" she called, hugging her as if they were long-parted friends, "How are you? Badly hurt?"

"I'm all right. Help me into your truck. Let's go straight back."

The heads of the depot urged her obsequiously to stay or let them take her to hospital. Just then, Liu suddenly appeared. He jumped off his truck and set about filling the tank, then strolled over casually. He had changed out of the clothes in which he had driven the flaming truck away and was now wearing a brown western suit, a black tie with white dots on it, brown leather shoes and large sun-glasses. He looked like a smart foreigner or someone just back from a study trip abroad, not at all like a truck driver. Ye Fang was on the point of calling him when Xie Jing gave her a pinch on the arm to stop her.

But Liu asked Xie Jing in his usual mocking way, "Well, how does it feel to be a heroine?"

"Why...?" She meant to ask him why he had come back, but changed this to, "...Have you come for petrol too?"

"What a question! You fixed the quota so I have to

fulfil it, don't I? I've never missed a single day. Why make an exception today? I'm not like you, surrounded by crowds of admirers. Of course, you don't have to bother about your quota."

Xie Jing smiled at him a sweet, understanding smile. Ye Fang felt all at sea. Xie Jing, however, realized that Liu was not taking a dig at her but explaining why he had had to change his clothes. He was also, by way of a joke, testing other people to see if they could recognize him in this disguise.

Indeed, all turned to stare at this smartly dressed young man who looked perhaps a bit too foreign. However, disgust and contempt registered in their eyes. Only one of them murmured dubiously, "He looks like Liu Sijia who saved us from the fire."

But some cadres snorted, as if to say: How could such a fellow be Liu Sijia, the hero? Just look at him. A Chinese in a western suit! He even keeps his sunglasses on while talking to his deputy team leader. A loafer and a rascal like that could never be a hero! Impossible!

Again people turned their attention to Xie Jing. No one so much as glanced at Liu any more.

He laughed heartily and said loudly to Xie Jing, "I realize now that it's easy to be a hero but difficult to cope with such lavish praise. No wonder some model workers change once they become well-known. It's not entirely their fault. Those who keep praising them to the skies are to blame. Xie Jing, as a deputy, you must be careful. Ha, ha. . . !"

His words aroused indignation. Luckily the girl at the pump came to his rescue by calling, "Your tank's full!"

"Coming!" Liu made for his truck singing:

"All the colours of the rainbow,
Life's like a kaleidoscope.
How should we live our lives?
I know how to manage."

He jumped into the cabin, tooted his horn and drove off quickly in a cloud of dust. The onlookers backed away at once, inwardly cursing the inconsiderate driver. Taking this opportunity, Xie Jing asked Ye Fang to help her into her truck. Then Ye Fang started the engine and the two of them left the depot.

Ye Fang drove slowly, very preoccupied with her thoughts. She knew how Liu and Xie Jing had averted an accident, and sensed that he was drifting away from her and growing closer to Xie Jing. She had no proof of this, she simply felt it. Who in the team dared to offend or mock Liu? Only Xie Jing. Yet strange to say he took this lying down. It was like her own case. She would hit or swear at anyone but him. To him, she behaved like a lamb. Yet the more she gave way to him, the colder he grew. Why? He had a pair of cold eyes, but some times they shone with warmth when he stole a glance at Xie Jing. Ye Fang was very jealous. When had he ever looked at her like that?

The year before last, she remembered, they had gone for a meal at the Yellow Bridge Restaurant. For fun, He Shun had urged her to play a finger-game with Liu. If she won, Liu would have to get under the table and drink a cup of wine as punishment. If Liu won, she would let him kiss her and they would get engaged. She lost on purpose and paid the forfeit. Later she took this business seriously although Liu did not seem to think it binding. Once he even joked, "Can love be determined by a bet? Must I make amends by cutting off my lips?"

So he had never loved her after all. He had simply been amusing himself with her. That afternoon when about to drive to the depot, he had asked Xie Jing to go as his assistant, and she had agreed readily. Then that accident had happened and together they'd gone to the rescue. Now each wanted to give the credit to the other. Their love was cemented by that life-and-death struggle. Even the gods were on their side.

Ye Fang's heart ached. A girl, however tough, is sensitive and perceptive about such matters, able to feel the same happiness or distress as her more delicate sisters.

Presently Xie Jing leaned back, her eyes closed.

"Xie Jing," Ye Fang asked softly, "are you asleep?"

"No."

"Still in pain?"

"I feel a bit better."

"Where did you fall?"

"On my thigh and side."

"Any bones broken?"

"No."

Reluctant to speak, Xie Jing did not open her eyes.

But Ye Fang's mind was in a turmoil. She had been good to Xie Jing, but now Xie Jing had taken away her lover! Though she knew that she was no match for the other girl, she could not take this. She would make a scene. But first she must sound out Xie Jing's attitude towards Liu. She blurted out:

"Xie Jing, be frank with me. I've been good to you, haven't I?"

"Of course, and I'm grateful to you."

"Honestly, Xie Jing, do you love Liu?" There was a quiver in her voice though she spoke softly.

Xie Jing sat up and fixed her eyes on Ye Fang's. She took in the situation at once and realized what her answer would mean to this girl. Putting her hand on Ye Fang's hand, which was gripping the steering-wheel, she said sincerely, as if to her best friend, "Ye Fang, are you out of your mind? Have you lost your senses because you're head over heels in love? Nobody's going to take your Liu away from you. I already have a boy-friend."

"Have you?" Overjoyed, Ye Fang shot her a flustered glance.

With a smile Xie Jing tapped her head.

"Where does he work?"

"Let's not talk about him now. Let's talk about you." Xie Jing went on more seriously, "You're head over heels in love with him, aren't you?"

Ye Fang nodded.

"Does he love you too?"

It was hard to reply. It would be too embarrassing if she said "no". On the other hand, she really wasn't sure. But she could not lie to Xie Jing.

"Not sure, right?" Xie Jing could not help smiling. What a girl! She loved him but did not know if he loved her. "I think, he loved you before and will love you more in future."

"What about now?"

"Well ... he loves certain things about you, but not everything."

Not totally convinced, Ye Fang said, "You talk like a fortune-teller! What doesn't he like about me?"

Since Xie Jing had taken a great weight off her mind by telling her she had a boy-friend, she knew Ye Fang would listen to some home truths now. She said earnestly and bluntly:

"Remember how you criticized me? You said I was a girl of a single colour — red. You were right. One should have many colours, not just one. It's the same with clothes. We don't want to dress drably, but bright reds or greens would be gaudy. But how do you make life more colourful? Smoking, drinking, eating out, playing the fool, fighting, swearing, showing off and complaining all day long? No. Those are vulgar signs of boredom. In my view, it's morality, talent, study, knowledge, affection, good health, joy, anger, sorrow, happiness, as well as music, chess, calligraphy and painting which should bring colour to our lives. You must have noticed that Liu only fools about with He Shun when he's frustrated or bored. If you can sober him up and help him when he feels low, surely he will love you, won't he? Instead you get him to drink, and when you're drunk you may behave like lovers, but when he's sober again he finds it disgusting."

Ye Fang was convinced. No wonder Liu was drawn to Xie Jing though she often criticized him. Ye Fang did whatever he wanted, but he looked down on her for it. Was she able to control him?

"I'm not asking you to nag at him all the time," Xie Jing continued as if she could read her mind. "You can't be lovers if you fight all day long! Your life's too monotonous, eating, smoking, playing about and making trouble, that's all. How boring! What's the point of living like that? An animal just wants to keep alive, but we should really live. Our generation missed out on our schooling; we don't know much. That's our common weakness. We didn't have the right start. Now a new period's begun, and we mustn't lag behind again. The most complex, most difficult things in life, the most beautiful too, are still ahead of us."

Ye Fang understood only part of this. However, she began to think about it because it concerned her future happiness. Though already twenty-five years old, she was still uncertain how to live. In some ways she was amazingly mature, in others she was fearfully ignorant.

So without realizing it, Xie Jing was quietly influencing those around her. However, her own life was not all roses. She sincerely wanted Ye Fang to do better and win the happiness she deserved. But at heart she felt indescribably depressed, for today she had gained something then promptly lost it. However, she believed that this loss was all to the good.

II

Shortly before knocking-off time, Liu was notified by the plant's Party committee that two heads of the oil depot would be coming, accompanied by Zhu Tong-kang, to give him and Xie Jing a letter of thanks, award certificate and premium. This disgusted him. If they had taken proper safety measures, the accident would not have happened. Now even the Party secretary was condescending to come to their team to see him. Hadn't Zhu wanted to punish him as a bad example? Now all of a sudden he wanted to praise him as a good one. Those leaders were simply making fools of themselves, asking for trouble. In fact, he was not as bad as the Party secretary thought, nor as good as the heads of the depot believed. He was himself, neither wholly good nor bad. Living in this society he was limited by it. He was tempted to lie low and ignore them. But he thought better of it. Why should he upset himself? Didn't Xie Jing say "bitterness is bad for the health"? And some fashionable thinkers advocated: Make others lose their tempers but keep cool yourself. Right! They were not a bad lot, of course, but neither were they capable leaders. Since they wanted to come, why not play a little trick on them. He would set up his pancakes stall again and let those big shots look for him in the market. If they gave him a letter of thanks, award certificate and premium, he would accept them there. That would be fun!

In high spirits he went to find He Shun, who looked down in the dumps that afternoon. Since returning from the depot, he had kept to himself, hanging his head in silence. Liu thought he was embarrassed at having made off with all their takings that morning. But to him thirty-seven yuan was nothing, and he had no high opinion of He Shun anyway, so he pretended to know nothing about it.

"Get ready," he said merrily but as if issuing an order. "After knocking off we'll go selling for another hour."

"Selling what?"

"Pancakes."

"Again?" He Shun fished out that thirty-seven yuan and forty *fen* and gave it to Liu. "Big Head Sun won't take it. What do you say?"

"You keep it then."

"No, I won't. Let's go halves. We'd better quit selling them."

"What's wrong with you?" Liu was impatient. His eyes like slits bored angrily into He Shun.

Afraid of annoying him, He Shun hesitated, then muttered, "My belly aches."

Without a word, Liu whirled round and left. He had no time to deal with him at the moment, but he would certainly settle scores the next day. Who else could he find? He could not sell the pancakes alone. Besides, it looked more imposing to have an assistant. He thought of Ye Fang and knocked at the door of the women drivers' rest room. Ye Fang happened to open the door. There was no one else in the room. Very pleased to see him, she said:

"Just the man I'm looking for. I've something to tell you, Sijia. After we knock off and you've had your talk with those big shots, come here. I'll be waiting for you."

"Will you do me a favour, Ye Fang?"

She disliked his being so polite to her. "Did I ever refuse you when you needed my help?"

That was true. With a smile Liu asked, "Help me sell pancakes after work, will you?"

"What? Sell pancakes again?" She exclaimed, shaking her head. "No! I won't! I won't let you do it either."

Liu was puzzled to find her singing the same tune as He Shun. Had anyone said anything to them? Had Xie Jing talked to them? No, not likely. They were not people she could easily win over.

"Are you sure you won't give me a hand?"

"I'll do anything else for you. But selling pancakes won't do you any good. It's bad for you!"

Liu was surprised. He had never seen her so firm and confident.

"Sijia, don't look at me like that! I've never answered you back, and I'm not going to start to now, but it's high time I began thinking for myself. Haven't you let off enough steam? This is a lucky day, Sijia, for you and for me too. It gives us a way to make a fresh start in life."

Those were surely not her own words. Such an idea could never occur to her. Liu was staggered for a moment.

"Tell me why it's a lucky day for me," he said.

"Now everybody knows what kind of person you really are. I'm proud of you and so happy for your sake."

After a pause she added in a low voice, "Xie Jing told me that she's engaged and hopes sincerely that the two of us. . . ." She gazed at Liu, tears streaming down her cheeks.

Liu, usually so phlegmatic, was touched by the girl's sincerity. In the grip of a powerful emotion he toyed with his hair. "You're so good to me, Ye Fang, I must be honest with you," he said. "Xie Jing would never love me even if she hadn't a boy-friend. And I would never run after her. I'm just not up to her. I'm no good. You don't know me really. He Shun's rotten on the surface, I'm rotten to the heart. If I've seen through anyone I lose all interest in him. Someone like me is incapable of love and doesn't deserve to be loved. If you were to marry me, you wouldn't find happiness."

In frustration Ye Fang threw herself into his arms, crying as she pounded his shoulders with her fists.

Liu remained quite wooden, not moving.

Just then the door opened and in came Xie Jing. At sight of them she stopped short. Looking away, she said, "Liu, I've written an indictment against the heads of the oil depot. Have a look. If you agree, you can sign it. Then, as the two who helped prevent a fire, we'll take the case to court. If you don't agree, I'll do it on my own."

"An indictment?" Liu pushed away Ye Fang and took the sheet of paper from Xie Jing. Having read it quickly he looked up at her. She was tackling this much better than he would have by selling pancakes. They saw eye to eye, but she was dealing with this in a serious way which would really shake the heads of the oil depot. Then the law and public opinion would force them to mend their ways. Without any hesitation he signed.

"I'm all for it," he said. "I was planning to make fools of them."

"This isn't a laughing matter. Life's not a joke, so you can't treat it that way."

Xie Jing took the indictment back and showed it to Ye Fang, a sign that she would like to hear her opinion. Ye Fang was touched, though she had nothing to say.

"So that's that. They'll soon be here, and I'll show them this statement. We don't have to keep it from them. When things are settled, we'll accept their awards. No need to be polite. What do you think?"

"Fine. I'll do as you say," Liu replied. "Do you know why I sold pancakes? I was so fed up I wanted to make our bosses so mad that they'd come to lecture me. Then I'd have taken them to the free market and told them how to do business and make a profit. They're such old fossils! It's good to be honest, but they're too dumb to run this plant well. Last month, the price of steel ingots was three hundred and seventy-five yuan a ton, but they wouldn't sell. This month it dropped to three hundred and fifty a ton, and they have no choice but to sell. At the moment there are more than two thousand tons of steel in the warehouse, yet they've borrowed money to pay the workers. We're drivers, so they can't fool us. They simply don't know the market and how to make money from assets lying useless. Those things can fetch money, and money makes more money if you handle it the right way. They just have to start the ball rolling."

Xie Jing was amazed. She had only dropped a hint yet Liu understood it perfectly. This young man was really something. By transporting materials and goods, he had seen what was wrong with the plant's management and marketing. She herself had been too engrossed in the team's work to think about the whole plant.

"You're so full of ideas," she said. "Why don't you pass them on to the Party secretary and the manager?"

"I'm not a Party member, or activist like you, always reporting your thoughts to the leadership so they can voice your opinions, and showing your loyalty to the Party. People like us have our own way of making our opinions heard."

"Fair enough. I'll keep Zhu behind, and you can have a good talk with him."

"I don't mean that."

Someone outside called, "Xie Jing! Liu Sijia!"

"Let's go," she said, "they're coming."

Ye Fang caught hold of Liu and made him take off his western jacket and tie. "No time to change," she said. "Just wear your shirt. But not your sun-glasses."

Liu broke into a smile. Following Xie Jing, he walked out of the rest room, humming his little song:

> "All the colours of the rainbow,
> Life's like a kaleidoscope.
> How should we live our lives?
> I know how to manage."

May 1981

Manager Qiao Assumes Office

Comeback

THERE was an awkward and rather unusual silence at the enlarged Party committee meeting of the Electrical Equipment Bureau, especially since Huo Dadao, the head, was presiding over it. It was like the lull before a storm. Although the "gang of four" had been out of power for two and a half years, the Heavy Electrical Machinery Plant had never fulfilled its quota. The situation was intolerable. Unless the whole bureau was to be let down, a capable man had to be sent there to put things right. The problem was who to send. Quite a number of cadres in the bureau hadn't much to do but few were qualified and fewer still were willing to be appointed. People were anxious to be promoted, not vice versa; and who wanted to take over such a mess?

But Huo remained calm, his eyes closed as if in meditation or sweeping across all the faces in front of him.

Then his gaze fell on a dark tanned face, tough and fleshy, with bushy eyebrows, deep eyes, high cheek bones. An image of strength! He was Qiao Guang-pu, the director of the Electrical Appliance Company under the bureau. He was fidgeting with a cigarette he had taken out of Deputy Head Xu Jinting's packet. Though he had given up smoking ten years before during a period of illegal detention, he often fidgeted with other people's cigarettes or smelt them whenever he was agitated or concentrating on something. Staring at the cigarette, his lips firmly shut, he clenched his teeth in anger, while the muscle of his left cheek twitched. Huo smiled imperceptibly, certain who would break the ice and what would be the solution.

The expensive "Tulip" cigarette in Qiao's hand was crushed as he reached out for another. This time Xu stopped his hand and said, "Listen, Qiao, if you don't smoke, don't waste them like this. No wonder the smokers all steer clear of you at meetings."

Everyone roared with laughter.

Without raising his eyes, Qiao began to speak in a steady voice, "I'd like to work in the Heavy Electrical Machinery Plant. I hope the bureau Party committee will consider my request."

His words dropped like a bombshell. Aghast, Xu offered him a cigarette and queried, "You must be kidding, Qiao?"

It was indeed the surprise to end all surprises that Qiao should volunteer to work in a factory. He was already a company director, an important yet easy job. He had the help of the head of the bureau plus the factory managers to do all the donkey work. If things went well he'd be promoted. If the reverse, he could shift the blame on to the higher-ups or his subordinates. All he had to do was pass on instructions and issue orders. A director had a lot of freedom and power. An easy job for good pay, an ideal one in the eyes of many old cadres. Yet Qiao wanted to leave such a post to be a plant manager. What had got into his head?

Qiao's eyes scanned the meeting room and finally met Huo's. For an instant they exchanged significant glances.

"I'm fifty-six and pretty fit. My blood pressure's a bit high, but that doesn't matter. If I fail and the plant doesn't fulfil the quota set by the state, I'll pack up and go back to cadre school to raise chickens and ducks."

His determination left him no room for second thoughts. Huo raised his eyes and looked at him with deep appreciation. Here was a man of action, on whom one could depend.

"Is there anything else?"

"Yes. I'd like to have Shi Gan with me to be the Party secretary. I'll be the manager. We were old partners."

This caused another stir. Everybody knew that Shi Gan was no longer the man he used to be. A modest man, what he needed was a peaceful life. Would he be willing to take the job?

For a moment Qiao was silent; his cheek began to twitch again.

"That's what you think," someone said. "But how can you be sure Shi will want to be your partner this time?"

"I've sent a car to the cadre school to fetch him. He'll have to accept whether or not he wants to. Besides. . . ." Qiao turned to Huo and continued, "if the Party committee agrees, I'm certain he'll go with me. By the way, I'd like to say a few words about job transfer. A Party member must obey the Party's decision. Of course, one's opinion must be considered beforehand, but it is the Party which has the final say and which assigns posts to its members regardless of rank."

As he glanced at his watch, Shi happened to enter, looking like an old peasant. But the way he entered and his composure showed that he was an experienced cadre who had often frequented the room. He was small and slow-moving, while his shabby appearance concealed his shrewdness. Though he was just turning sixty, his lined face made him look older. He nodded like a stranger in response to their warm greetings, keeping his mouth shut as if afraid to utter a sound. Refusing the seat Huo offered him, he remained standing as if not knowing why he had been summoned and ready to leave at any minute.

Qiao rose to his feet and said, "Shall I first talk it over with Shi, Huo?"

Then he took Shi's arm and walked him out of the room. After they had settled themselves down in armchairs in Huo's office, Qiao looked at Shi, distressed to see that he seemed a different man.

In 1958, after completing his studies in the Soviet Union, Qiao had been appointed the manager of the Heavy Electrical Machinery Plant and Shi Gan was made the Party secretary. As a result of their efforts, the plant soon became a model. Shi was a witty, humorous fellow, and a good talker. During the "cultural revolution", much of what he had said was criticized. During his illegal detention, Shi often remarked to Qiao, "All my troubles were caused by my tongue. It spills out whatever's in my mind." He got particularly irritated when being interrogated by the so-called rebels at criticism meetings. If he kept silent, they accused him of being un-cooperative; if he answered them, it only added more fuel to the flames. Qiao, who was also often criticized at the same time, had a way of dealing with his interrogators. He called it switching off. At first, like Shi, he listened attentively to those criticisms, but the more he listened the angrier he became. Very often he perspired profusely and afterwards he was completely exhausted. Then gradually he got used to it. Qiao was fond of Beijing opera, so when a meeting was held he'd switch off and silently sing an aria to himself. Quite pleased with himself, he told Shi about his method. Alas, Beijing opera was not Shi's forte and it didn't work for him. Once, in the autumn of 1967, Shi was ordered to stand on a makeshift platform on two trucks. As he got down at the end of the meeting, he slipped and fell to the ground, unfortunately biting off the tip of his tongue. Saying nothing, he swallowed the blood in pain. Ever since then the two friends had been separated. Shi never spoke again in public. When his injury had healed, he was sent to do physical labour in the bureau's cadre school. Later, if he was offered work in the city he refused, saying he couldn't talk. When the news of the gang's arrest was announced, Shi went to the city and drank some wine in celebration. But he returned to the cadre school that same night, for he could not leave his "three armies". As he was responsible for hundreds of chickens, dozens of ducks and a flock of sheep, he was nicknamed the "commander of three armies". He had resolved to live in the countryside for the rest of his life. But early that morning, Qiao had sent a close friend to fetch him under the pretext that there would be an important meeting.

Having told Shi what was in his mind, Qiao waited hopefully for his support.

Under Shi's strange, inquiring gaze, Qiao became rather uneasy. It seemed to convey a disturbing remoteness and distrust between old friends. At last, Shi spoke in a low, indistinct voice, "Why on earth pick on me? I won't take the job!"

"Listen, Shi!" Qiao's voice was anxious. "Do you really want to hide away like a hermit in the country? Are you as scared of struggles as others say?"

Shi nodded. But Qiao jumped to his feet, denying it. "No! You're not like that! You can fool others but not me!"

"I've only got half a tongue.... I'd bite off the rest if I could!"

"Nonsense! You've got two tongues. One to help me and one to convince people. You often encouraged me in a crisis. No one can replace you. You're the best Party secretary I've ever met. You must come and work with me now."

Shi sighed, his eyes had an agonized expression for an instant. "I'm a disabled man," he said. "I can't give you any help. I may even disappoint you."

"Pull yourself together, Shi! You're more than a gifted speaker, you've got a good head on your shoulders. You've lots of experience and guts. On top of that, we've worked well together for years. All I'm asking is that you give me advice at crucial moments."

Still shaking his head, Shi replied, "I'm way out of date and I've no energy left."

"What crap!" Qiao was about to lose his temper.

"You're as fit as a fiddle. How can you talk like that? OK, you lost part of your tongue, but that doesn't mean you lost your whole head!"

"I mean I just don't give a damn any more!"

"What?" Qiao pulled Shi to his feet and looked straight into his eyes, then snapped, "Just say that again! Where's your confidence in the Party? Your courage? Your sense of responsibility?"

Shi tried to avoid Qiao's eyes which mirrored his thoughts and feelings. He felt shocked at himself for being so cowardly. But he would never admit it publicly.

In a mocking tone, Qiao said as if to himself, "It's ironical really. The Central Party Committee's determined to modernize our country and now the main obstacles have been removed. All we need is good leaders. Yet look at our cadres. No confidence, no guts! If you ask them to do something, they try to pass the buck or simply refuse with all kinds of excuses. Don't they have any sense of responsibility left as ordinary Party members? I'm like a soldier. Ask me to do something and I'll try my best. There's nothing strange in that, but some people these days take it as seeking the limelight. Perhaps others call me a fool behind my back!"

Shi was hurt again. Seeing his shoulders quivering, Qiao added earnestly, "Shi, you must come with me, even if I have to drag you there."

"Listen, giant...." Shi began after a sigh. The familiar nickname immediately warmed Qiao's heart. But Shi resumed his distant tone again, "So long as you won't regret it, I don't mind. If you think I'm no good, just tell me so. I can go back to the cadre school."

When the two returned to the meeting room, the members had already reached a decision.

"Qiao will take up his new post tomorrow," Huo told Shi, "and you can go there in a couple of days. Have a rest first. If you don't feel quite fit, go to hospital to have a general check-up."

Shi Gan nodded and then left.

Huo turned to Qiao and said, "Someone's anxious to take your place even before you leave!" He then eyed the others and asked, "Any other recommendations? Better put your cards on the table now and let us see them."

There was a deathly silence. They all knew Huo's rule: Speak up at a meeting or forget it.

Xu, Huo's deputy, broke the silence by saying, "Ji Shen of the Electrical Machinery Plant hopes to be transferred to work in the Electrical Appliance Company under the bureau, as he's not in good health." Following him, some other members made their recommendations.

His eyes gleaming, Huo said angrily, "Recommending oneself isn't something new. After all, Qiao recommended himself. But your recommendations are completely different. If we accepted them all we'd have fifteen deputies in the bureau. All the six companies under the bureau would have ten or fifteen directors each. I doubt if they'd accept that. If you aren't fit enough to work in the factories, how can you work well in the company? It isn't a rest-house. Or do you think the work here isn't important? All those who need to recuperate can take sick-leave. Go and register in the organization department. But we won't accept just anyone. We'd rather leave places vacant than appoint parasites at the expense of the country. I like Qiao's style of work. From now on, those who do well will be rewarded and promoted, while those who make serious errors will be penalized and demoted! Some cadres pester their friends to find them new posts when they fail at their own jobs. This only encourages officials to hold on to one job, while seeking a better one. No wonder the workers say that their managers aren't really interested in their work. How can a cadre run a factory well with such a mentality?"

Xu spoke up again. "Ji Shen is the manager of the Electrical Machinery Plant. Now we've decided to send Qiao and Shi there, what should he do then?"

"He can be the deputy manager," Huo said firmly. "If he does well, he'll be promoted. If he doesn't he'll be demoted until he can find a job he can do. Of course, this is my opinion. We can discuss it."

Xu whispered to Qiao, "Things will get worse when you go there."

Qiao shrugged as if saying, "I never expected it to be a picnic."

Assuming Office

It was late in the evening when Qiao got home. As the air in his room was rather stale, he opened the door and windows wide. He was dying for a cup of tea, but, as there was no hot water in the thermos flask, he had to make do with some cold water. Then, sitting at his desk, he selected a book entitled *Metallography* from beneath a stack of books. He drew out a photo, the background of which was Lenin's Mausoleum in Moscow's Red Square. In the foreground stood Qiao and a girl. In his light western suit, Qiao looked young and very handsome, but faintly ill at ease. The attractive girl beside him was smiling at him sweetly. Gazing at the photo, Qiao suddenly closed his eyes, and buried his head in his hands. The photo slipped from his fingers to the desk. . . .

In 1957 Qiao, already in his final year of study in the Soviet Union, had gone to gain some practical experience in the Leningrad Power Plant as an assistant manager. Tong Zhen, the girl in the photo, was a college student working in the plant on her graduation thesis. She was soon attracted to Qiao, who was handsome, intelligent and good at his work. He refused to tolerate fear, suspicion and flattery. Tong, who was similar, fell in love with him, despite the fact that he was ten years her senior and married. Qiao, too, was very happy to meet another Chinese in a foreign land and treated her as his younger sister, protecting her as if she were still a child. But that was not what she wanted. Sometimes she felt jealous seeing him brooding, perhaps missing his wife.

Qiao returned home first and was appointed the manager of the Electrical Machinery Plant, a new enterprise which badly needed technicians. Tong, after her graduation in 1958, returned home to work under Qiao. Tong had a nephew, Xi Wangbei, who happened to be an apprentice in the same plant. By chance he discovered that his aunt was in love with Qiao. Being headstrong and suspicious, Xi began to hate Qiao believing he was trifling with his aunt. Though ten years younger, he regarded himself as his aunt's guardian and kept an eye on her. He went out of his way to prevent her from meeting Qiao when he was alone. Quite a few young men wanted to court her, but Tong sent them away, saying she would never marry. This made Xi even more irritated and so he put all the blame on Qiao. In his eyes, Qiao was a playboy, who was ruining his aunt's life.

Seven years later, the "cultural revolution" started. Xi became the leader of a faction with Qiao as the main target of his attack. Apart from labelling Qiao as a "capitalist roader", Xi called him a "womanizer". To protect his aunt, he never went into details. Some of his men, however, were interested in the romantic angle and magnified the whole affair by making up stories about Tong and Qiao. Tong was greatly hurt. In her eyes, there were not many people like Qiao who were able to run a modern factory. He had enjoyed a high prestige before, but now his reputation was ruined. People did not really hate those who had not followed the Party line, but those who were immoral were always despised. How could she clarify the truth? She blamed herself for making Qiao suffer more than so-called other "capitalist roaders". She wrote to tell him that she had decided to commit suicide. But Xi, ever cautious, caught her in time. Since then, Qiao had felt indebted to the two women in his life.

Qiao's wife had been the head of the propaganda department in a university. In spite of the gossip about her husband, she had never doubted him. She died mysteriously when being illegally detained for investigation in early 1968. With bitter regrets, Qiao confessed before the portrait of his late wife that he had once wavered before Tong's passionate words and that he had sometimes felt drawn to her. He made a vow never to speak to Tong again. When his youngest son started university, Qiao was left alone, leading the life of a monk, as if deliberately torturing himself to show his faithfulness to his late wife and children.

Even he didn't know what prompted him to ring Tong up and ask her to come over. "What do you want?" he asked himself in surprise. If he had not volunteered to return to the plant, the affair would have been finished for ever. How could they work together again after all that trouble? Only ten years before, they had been cruelly slandered. Now Qiao realized that Tong was still important to him despite his efforts to forget her. His feelings were so subtle, so complicated, he could not work them out. "Better take a grip on yourself," he told himself. "There's a lot to do tomorrow." All of a sudden, he sensed someone at his shoulder. He looked up. His heart missed a beat when he saw Tong standing beside him gazing tearfully at the photo. He jumped to his feet and gripped her hands, whispering, "Tong Zhen! Tong!..."

Tong shuddered and withdrew her hands from his ardent hold. Then she turned round, wiped away her tears and made an effort to control herself. Her appearance had changed so much that Qiao was quite shocked. Though only a little over forty, Tong's hair was streaked with grey. Though her eyes were soft and feminine they conveyed a deep bitterness. There was no sign of their former warmth and courage. Qiao's heart ached. This promising and talented woman engineer could have done much. Now there was no sign of the idealistic, energetic girl. Was it only time which had made her age so quickly?

Both of them felt rather awkward. Though Qiao searched for warm yet suitable words to break the silence, in the end he blurted out, "Tong, why don't you get married?" He hadn't intended to ask this. Even the voice didn't sound like his.

"What do you mean?" she retorted.

He waved his hand as though brushing away all hypocrisy. Suddenly he came closer to her and said, "Why should I pretend? Tong, let's get married! Tomorrow or the day after tomorrow? Agreed?"

Though she had waited for this moment for twenty years, Tong was almost thrown off her balance by his proposal.

"Isn't it a bit sudden?" she said softly. "Why the rush?"

Now that the ice was broken, Qiao replied with his usual enthusiasm and strength, "Look, our hair is already grey. How can you talk about rushing it? We don't need to prepare anything for the wedding. We can just throw a party and announce our marriage, that's all."

Her face, glowing with happiness, looked younger. "You know how I feel," she murmured. "You decide."

"So it's settled," he said joyfully, holding her hand again. "When I go back to work at the plant tomorrow, I'll tell our friends and relatives that our wedding will take place on the day after tomorrow."

"Go back to the plant to work?" Tong was startled.

"Yes. The bureau Party commitee decided this morning that Shi Gan and I should go back to the plant. You know we're old partners."

"Oh no! No!" Tong protested automatically. She had imagined being transferred after their wedding to a new factory, where no one would know anything about their past and where they would live in peace. But how would people at the plant talk about Qiao's going back and their marriage? She shuddered at the thought of the gossip and slander. Moreover, Xi, who had been Qiao's most vicious persecutor, was now a deputy manager. How could they co-operate together?

"You're doing very well in the company," she said unhappily. "Why do you want to come back?"

"The work in the company doesn't suit me really," he replied. "I'm no man for office work."

"Our plant's a mess. Do you think you can sort things out?"

"Well, if we let all the big factories like ours remain in chaos, modernization will remain a dream. It'll be rather like commanding a battle during the war, getting the plant into shape! I don't like playing just a minor role. I'm not too old. I want to accomplish something before it's too late."

Tong's feelings were a mixture of surprise, joy and uneasiness. It had been his sense of responsibility to his work, his ability and his masculinity that had made her love him. Now many years later, though he was still the same, she was asking him to give up his career. She murmured, "I've never seen a man over fifty with such drive."

"Drive, like youthfulness, is independent of age. It doesn't only belong to the young, nor does it vanish with age." He saw how she had aged not only in her appearance but also in her thoughts and feelings. These days many people were fed up with politics. Their psychological wounds seemed the most difficult to heal. He suddenly felt that a big responsibility had been laid on him. Clasping her shoulders like a young man, Qiao said warmly, "I say, engineer, where are all the plans you kept whispering to me? Don't you remember you wanted to make 600,000, 1,000,000 or 1,500,000 kilowatt generating sets? We even hoped to build the first nuclear power station in our country with a capacity of a million kilowatts. Have you forgotten all that?"

Her engineer's heart began to thaw.

Qiao continued, "We must get the latest information from abroad. In the fifties and early sixties, we could keep up to date. But now I know nothing about new developments. By the way, will you teach me English for an hour a day after our marriage?"

Tong nodded, looking straight into his eyes with warmth. She felt secure beside him, more determined and confident. "Funny, you haven't changed in the least. You're still so idealistic after all you've been through," she said with a grin.

"How can one alter one's nature?" he chuckled. Not wishing to change the subject, he continued to encourage her, his eyes fixed on the slender woman. "I was put through the mill — so what? You know the old saying, 'Stone whets a sword, difficulties strengthen will-power'."

He asked her to show him round the plant. When she was reluctant he teased her, "What was the word you cursed me with? I remember, it was 'coarse', wasn't it? Funny, how this 'coarse' man can talk about love? Listen, love is a strong passion. You've longed for it. Now it's here, you don't have to fear it, let alone hide your feelings and suffer for it. I'm only worried that your passion is drying up like your interest in politics."

"Nonsense!" Tong denied, blushing. "A woman's

love never dries up." Overwhelmed by emotion, she kissed him passionately.

On their way to the plant, she persuaded him not to marry her right away on the pretext that, for her, her wedding-day was of vital importance and that she had paid a lot more for it than other women. She wanted to prepare herself well for it. Qiao agreed.

2

The two of them first entered Workshop No. 8, which was nearest the entrance. The familiar look of the shop floor made every bone in Qiao's body cry out for action. His hands were itching to touch the lathes. Then he thought of the twelve advanced workers whom he had trained, each in charge of a processing section.

"All your advanced workers are in other jobs now," Tong told him. "One has become a foreman, another a warehouse-keeper, a janitor, a checker and so on. Don't you remember how four of them condemned you at the criticism meeting, saying you had corrupted them with material incentives? Don't you have any grudges against them?"

"Oh no," Qiao brushed this aside. "At those meetings, everybody raised their fists and shouted slogans against me. If I begrudged that, I wouldn't be back here. If those twelve men are no longer pace-setters, then I'll have to train new ones. We must have the most skilful workers and best products."

While talking to Tong, Qiao walked from lathe to lathe. Nothing pleased him more than feasting his eyes on purring machines turning out top quality products.

Qiao halted before a young man who was casually throwing processed turbine blades on to a pile on the ground, while humming a foreign pop song. Qiao picked up some of the blades to examine them and found that most were defective. Staring at the young worker, he snapped, "Stop singing!"

Not knowing who Qiao was, the youngster winked at Tong and sang louder:

O mother!
Please keep your cool.
Young people are just loafers!

"Stop it!" Qiao bellowed, his authoritative voice and furious eyes startling the turner. "Are you a turner or a ragpicker?" he continued. "I bet you don't know anything about the operating rules!"

Obviously Qiao was an official, and his air of authority silenced the boy. Taking a white handkerchief from Tong, Qiao wiped the lathe. The handkerchief turned black.

"So is this the way you look after your lathe?" Qiao demanded, his eyes fixed on the young man. "Keep this handkerchief hanging on your lathe until you've cleaned it. Then you can have a white towel."

Many workers had gathered around them.

"Comrades," Qiao said to them, "I'll ask the equipment section to hang a white towel on each of your lathes tomorrow. Let the towel tell in future whether or not you look after your machines well."

Some of the old workers recognized Qiao and quietly withdrew. Red in the face, the young turner was too embarrassed to say anything. He nervously hung the black handkerchief on a lever which apparently he never touched. This brought him more trouble.

Qiao, having noticed the dirty, greasy lever, asked, "What's that handle for?"

"I don't know."

"But there's a notice explaining how to use it, isn't there?"

"It's in a foreign language. I don't understand it."

"How long have you been working at this lathe?"

"Six years."

"And for six years you've never touched that lever?"

The young man nodded. His face twitching in anger, Qiao asked the others around, "Who can tell him how this works?"

No one replied. Some certainly did not know, while others did not want to further embarrass their young comrade.

"Will you tell him then, engineer?" Qiao asked Tong.

Tong, to ease the tension, explained to him what it was for and how it worked.

"What's your name?" Qiao asked again.

"Du Bing."

"I'll never forget you, humming while you work and not greasing your lathe for six years." Then he changed from a sarcastic tone into a severe one, "Tell your foreman that this lathe needs overhauling at once. I'm the new manager."

When Qiao and Tong turned to leave, they heard someone whisper, "Just your luck, Du Bing. He's our former manager!"

Another said, "An expert like him, he knows at a glance what's wrong."

"With bums like him around," Qiao said angrily, "even the best equipment we import will be damaged."

"Do you think he's one of the worst?" Tong asked.

"Well, I find it shocking that not a single person bothered to look into such matters for six years. The cadres are so careless, so irresponsible. As a chief engineer, I must say, you're doing pretty well!" Qiao added, tongue in cheek.

"But if the manager is so negligent, how can you blame people like us?" Tong retorted indignantly.

They were talking like this as they entered Workshop No. 7, where they at once caught sight of a young German testing a boring machine. This visitor to China working night shift caught Qiao's attention. Tong told him that he had been sent by the German firm, Siemens, when snags with an electrical part occurred during assembling. His name was Therl and he was only twenty-three years old. This was his first visit to the East, and he had come via Japan, which was why he was seven days late. Afraid that this might be reported to his firm, he had worked extremely hard and solved the problem within three days instead of the scheduled seven or ten. Though he was an expert and a hard worker, he also liked fun and games.

"Though he's so young, he's able to do the job independently abroad," Qiao said in admiration. Then he sent Tong to get the foreman in charge of work that day. Before the man could greet him, Qiao said, "Ask all those under thirty to come here and watch how Therl works. And ask Therl to say something about himself and how he learned his skill. I'm thinking of inviting him to give a talk to all our young workers before he leaves."

The man did not query Qiao's identity but complied with a smile.

Qiao heard some people murmuring behind him and turned round. They were workers from Workshop No. 8, who had rushed to see him when they had learned that Qiao was the man who had roundly criticized Du Bing.

"You won't learn anything looking at me," Qiao told them. "Go and watch that young German over there." He sent a worker he knew to get all the young men in his workshop to come too, especially the young turner Du Bing.

Just as he finished speaking, an old worker pulled him over to a quiet corner and mumbled, "Do you want a foreigner to set us an example?"

Qiao was startled to see that the speaker was Shi Gan! In his overalls and old blue cap, he looked like a worker. Qiao was delighted to see Shi had started work. He had not changed. Though he had refused to come at first, now that he had agreed he would do his best. His appointment had not yet been announced, but he had come to work.

Shi was sullen, regretting his decision. Earlier that afternoon he had had a look round and talked to a few workers whom he did not know. Because of his injury, he spoke indistinctly, and people thought something must be wrong with him. In this way, he learned a lot that Qiao could not. The workers in this plant were rather confused ideologically. The idol many had worshipped had gone. They had even lost their national pride and faith in socialism. For many years they had been cheated, manipulated and criticized. They'd become demoralized. Moreover, in this plant there were three groups of cadres: those who had been cadres before the "cultural revolution"; or during it; or after the downfall of the gang when Ji Shen became the manager. The old people were still hurt, while the young felt resentful. Shi worried that one day they would flare up and clash head-on, causing renewed conflict within the Party. There was not only chaos awaiting him and Qiao, but also bitter political rivalries. They were up against a very difficult situation.

Shi was furious with himself for having got involved in such a mess. Political struggles had taught him a great deal. Now he seldom became excited or lost control of himself in public, and resented pretentiousness of any kind. With his feelings thus hidden, he believed he could resist any temptation. So how on earth had he been persuaded by Qiao that very morning? He was quite certain that his return would do both of them no good. Qiao would never be a politician. He had started working even before the announcement of his appointment. That was no way for a manager to behave. He did not want to talk to Qiao at this moment. But, surprised to see Tong beside Qiao, he could not help warning him, "You mustn't get married for at least six months."

"What do you mean?" Qiao was put out.

Shi told him briefly that the news of the management reshuffle had leaked out and that some were gossiping that Qiao had only come back to marry Tong Zhen.

"All right," Qiao said shortly, "I may as well be hanged for a sheep as for a lamb. We'll hold a wedding ceremony in the auditorium tomorrow evening. You'll be our witness."

Shi whirled to leave in a huff, but Qiao caught him.

Then Shi complained, "Didn't you ask me to give you advice? But when I do you just turn a deaf ear!"

Clenching his teeth, Qiao muttered after a while, "OK. I'll listen to you. After all, it's a personal thing. But tell me, the decision to reshuffle was made only this morning, how on earth did people learn about it this afternoon?"

"That's nothing unusual. These days, news travels faster on the grape-vine than through official channels. Rumours are proved by documents. Right now, the plant Party committee is having an urgent meeting. My instinct tells me it has something to do with our return." But instantly Shi regretted telling him what he only guessed. Emotion was something harmful. Shi found himself together with Qiao sinking faster into the swamp.

On an impulse, Qiao dragged Shi and Tong to the office block. The meeting room on the first floor was brightly lit, with cigarette smoke filtering out of its wide open windows. Someone was making a speech in a loud voice, talking about the next day's production campaign. This worried Qiao. He asked the other two to wait for him for a moment, while he went to make a phone call to Huo Dadao. Then the three of them entered the room.

3

People were surprised at the sudden appearance of the three gate-crashers. Ji Shen fixed his eyes on Tong, who immediately looked away, wishing to escape since she wasn't on the Party committee.

"What's brought you here?" Ji asked, as though he knew nothing about the reshuffle.

"Just having a look," Qiao said in a loud voice. "We heard that you were having a discussion on production. We'd like to know what you think."

"Fine! Fine!"

Ji looked haggard. He had mobile yet inscrutable features. "There are two items on today's agenda," he explained. "One, the suspension of Xi Wangbei at the request of the masses. Two, tomorrow's production campaign. I spent much time and energy on political movements in the past and not enough on production. But all the members of the committee are confident. Once the campaign gets going, things will improve. Comardes, we can be more specific. Qiao and Shi are the former leaders of our plant. Perhaps they can give us some good advice."

He was an experienced man, composed and steady. He was hoping to impress Qiao with how he conducted a meeting. That very afternoon he had learned of the bureau's decision by telephone, and he bitterly regretted ever having joined the bureau.

It was true that he had been persecuted by the "gang of four" for ten years. But he had not suffered much as he had been appointed the deputy principal of the Municipal Cadre School in the countryside. At that time, when the cadre school was regarded as a good socialist development, Ji realized that it was a safe place in which to lie low, with all its unfortunate prominent people. Being a deputy, he became acquainted with some former high-ranking officials. It would have been very difficult to get in contact with them if it had not been for the school. They had become his subordinates, and felt very grateful to him for making life a little easier for them in terms of accommodation, food, work and holidays. Besides, he found it easy to get on with people, and they, in turn, found him very agreeable. Now, since most of them had been restored to their former posts, Ji had friends in many high places and had become a man of influence himself.

Two years before, he had decided to work in the Electrical Equipment Bureau, fully aware of the importance of this industry for China's modernization. He only had experience in personnel work and knew nothing about production. In order to get some practical experience, he had asked to work in this Electrical Machinery Plant for a couple of years. Moreover, to be a manager of a big factory was very useful when construction and the economy were being stressed. It would pave the way for him to climb higher. He dreamed of becoming an important cadre in the bureau, where there might be chances to visit other countries. If you had been abroad, your future would be even brighter. Ji worked hard, but being only a bureaucrat and too cautious politically, he did things according to the way the wind blew. Naturally he was slow to act. When a knotty problem occurred, he tried to avoid it. Crafty and sophisticated, he put his individual interests above everything else. But with these values, how could he run a factory well where the problems were practical and specific? In another place he might have muddled along, but certainly not here under the eye of Huo Dadao. He knew that success was not merely a stroke of luck. It depended on ability and struggle. That was why he was banking everything on a new production campaign. If that raised production, he could leave the plant a hero. But that was not all. By dismissing Xi from his post, he would leave a thorny problem for Qiao to solve, which would certainly unseat him in time. Then no one would say Ji was incapable. Shi, however, smelled a rat, and Qiao too saw through Ji's trick.

Everybody at the meeting wondered what Qiao and Shi were up to, appearing so late at night. They were not really interested in the campaign business. Noticing the people's mood, Ji hurried to close the meeting, thinking he could thus achieve his ends. Just as he was clearing his throat to speak, Huo Dadao entered. His arrival caused another stir.

After asking what they were discussing, Huo, without any preambles, announced the bureau Party committee's decision to reshuffle. And finally he added, "Due to the chief engineer's long absence because of health reasons, the bureau has decided to promote Tong Zhen to be the assistant chief engineer."

Tong was taken by surprise and felt very nervous. She could not understand why Qiao had not hinted about it.

The announcement of these decisions came like a lightning blow to Ji Shen, who was almost speechless for once. Checking his anger with a great effort, he forced a smile and said, "Of course I accept the decisions. Both Qiao and Shi are old hands here, and I'm sure they'll do a better job than I." Then he continued, turning to Qiao and Shi, "Tomorrow I'll talk things over with you. Have you any opinions about the two decisions we've made at this meeting?"

Instead of speaking, Shi half closed his eyes lest they betray his thoughts.

"I hadn't the faintest idea about the suspension of Comrade Xi," Qiao said without formality. He could not help eyeing Xi, who was sitting in a corner. By chance he caught Xi's angry glare. Fearing to be distracted, he averted his gaze at once and continued, "I'm not for the campaign either. Well, Comrade Ji, you're suffering from coronary thrombosis, aren't you? Can you run at top speed five times from the ground floor to the seventh floor of this office block?"

Not knowing what Qiao was driving at, Ji gave a blank smile.

Qiao continued, "Well, our plant is like you, a man with coronary thrombosis. To make it leap forward will only mean suicide. To fulfil our quota by such campaigns from month to month is no way to run any plant."

His words struck the right chord, as the committee members had also been wondering why Ji wanted to launch a campaign to coincide with the reshuffle of the leadership. With a sneer Ji struck a match and lit a cigarette. It seemed there was something he wanted to say.

Noticing Ji's expression, Qiao, who had planned to say just a few words to show his attitude towards the decisions, shifted to another subject in a sharp tone, "I haven't seen any good plays for years," he said sharply, "so I can't tell if there are any good new directors around. But in industry, I know there are a number of political directors. Whenever there's a political movement or a problem in work, they call mass meetings, give pep talks and then organize a parade, shouting slogans, holding criticism meetings and launching campaigns. . . . Factories are their stages; the workers their actors and actresses. They direct them at random. They're no more than cheap propagandists. They can never make good managers for a modern socialist country. It's the easiest way to run a factory. No doubt there'll be endless after-effects. Modernization can never be achieved by a few so-called 'campaigns'."

Sensing something, he turned his head a little and found that Shi was winking to make him shut up. Qiao hurriedly finished, "I think I'd better stop here. Perhaps I've gone a bit too far. By the way, I want to tell you that Tong and I got married two hours ago. Shi was our witness. We didn't want to make a fuss since neither of us are young any more. We'll invite you for a drink later."

Surprised and delighted at this news, before the meeting was dismissed people began to tease Qiao and Tong.

Only Tong, Shi and Xi, for their own reasons, were greatly annoyed by Qiao's announcement. Tong was the first to walk out of the meeting room in a huff. Without a backward glance at Qiao, she went straight to the entrance of the plant.

Huo, noticing this, nudged Qiao and urged him to chase after Tong. After Qiao had gone, Huo stopped the others who wanted to tease the bride by saying, "He's a smart one, isn't he? I've never heard of marriage first and drinks later. What about going to his home tonight for a few drinks?"

Qiao had caught up with Tong. Her voice shaking

she said, "Have you gone mad? Don't you know how people will talk tomorrow?"

"That's just what I want," Qiao explained. "Now it's out in the open, you'll have no more worries and you can concentrate on your work. Otherwise you'd be nagging at me and tormenting yourself all the time. Even a mere glance at you walking with me would worry you to death. The more suspiciously you acted, the more trouble you'd land yourself in. Then we would be the victims of gossip and rumour again. I'm the manager. You're the assistant chief engineer. How could we co-operate under those circumstances? Now we've made it clear that we're husband and wife. Let those who wish to talk about us talk. They'll soon get bored with it. I made up my mind to announce it right on the spot. There wasn't time to consult you."

Under the lamp, her eyes glowed. Her anger lessened. This was a day of great significance for her.

Following Huo, Shi, no longer agitated, caught up with them. He gripped Tong's hand and nodded as though congratulating her on her happiness.

Some violent emotion seemed to be gripping Tong.

Huo told the two women committee members beside him, "Take my car and accompany the bride to her room. She may want to dress up. Then escort her to her new home. We'll wait for you there."

Tong said to Huo, "Don't bother. We'll go and register first."

"Will there be a big celebration?" one of them asked.

"Maybe. Anyway, at least there will be some wedding sweets." Everybody laughed.

Qiao and Tong, looking at Huo with gratitude, could not help smiling.

The Main Role

Just imagine, as the curtain rises, gongs and drums are beaten. The music starts and the hero swaggers in, but he neither speaks nor sings. How do you think the audience would react?

This was precisely the case with the Heavy Electrical Machinery Plant. It had been a fortnight since Qiao assumed office, but nothing had happened, no instructions, no meetings. He was not even in his office. What was the matter with him? He had never been like this before. It wasn't his style.

He was with the workers all day long. When you wanted him, he was nowhere to be found, yet he'd pop up right in front of you when you didn't need him. No one knew what he was up to. He seemed to have relinquished his authority and let the departments, offices and workshops go to pot. The workers without a leader did whatever they liked. The result was anarchy, and production dropped rapidly.

The bureau's operations centre felt the situation was intolerable. They asked Huo several times to go there and do something about it. Huo refused to raise a finger. When pressed too hard, he said tartly, "Don't you worry! Before the tiger springs, it crouches back a little. Don't you know this?"

Shi was anxious and puzzled too. He asked Qiao, "What are you waiting for? Have you a plan?"

"Oh yes!" Qiao replied readily. "Our plant is just like a sick man suffering from several diseases. We must find the right remedies to cure them. Before we start, we must make sure our diagnosis is correct."

Shi darted a glance at Qiao, who looked determined and self-confident.

"I've found out something important during the last two weeks," Qiao continued cheerfully. "Our workers and cadres aren't as apathetic as you imagined. Quite a number of them are really concerned about state affairs and our future. They make suggestions to me, argue with me and even criticize me, saying I've let them down. It's not a bad thing to have a short period of confusion. This helps us to separate the sheep from the goats. I've already picked out a few people in my mind, who will play an important role in my plan." He narrowed his eyes envisaging the plant's future.

"Isn't today your birthday?" Shi asked all of a sudden.

"Birthday? What birthday?" Qiao was puzzled. Leafing through the calendar, he suddenly realized it was. "Well, well! My birthday today. Fancy you remembering it!"

"Someone asked me if you were going to accept presents and throw a party."

"Hell, no! But if you'd like to come, I'll offer you a free drink."

Shi shook his head.

When Qiao got home, dinner was ready. On the table were food and wine. A woman has a good memory for such matters. Though just married, Tong remembered Qiao's birthday very well. Happily Qiao sat down to eat. But Tong stopped him and said with a smile, "I've invited Xi to come. Shall we wait for him?"

"Did you invite anybody else?"

"No."

Obviously she wanted the two to bury the hatchet. Qiao understood his wife's intention, but in fact he couldn't care less that Xi had once attacked him.

Instead of Xi, they were surprised by the arrival of a group of junior cadres from the plant, who had been on the management side before the "cultural revolution". While some were still the heads of certain departments, offices or workshops, others were no longer cadres.

"We've come to celebrate your birthday, Old Qiao," they all greeted him jubilantly.

"Forget it," Qiao said. "If you want some wine, there's plenty. But forget about the birthday business. Who told you that?"

One bald-headed man, a former head of administration, said meaningfully, "Old Qiao, you may have forgotten us, but we haven't forgotten you!"

"Come now! Who says I've forgotten you?"

"Well, haven't you? You've been back for half a month. All of us have been expecting something to happen. You've quite disappointed us. You know Liu, the manager of the Boiler Plant, don't you? The day he returned to his office, he threw a dinner party that evening and invited all his old cadres. What a feast! Of course, it wasn't the food or drink that mattered, but it gave them a chance to air their grievances. The following day, all of them went back to their former posts. Good for Liu! He didn't let his old comrades down!"

This got Qiao's back up, but he made an effort to control himself. After all, this was his new home, not the place for a showdown.

"In the two years since the gang fell, you still haven't let off steam?"

"The gang's followers are still around! Xi will soon be reinstated after only a month's suspension. . . ."

Talk of the devil! Xi suddenly entered and obviously caught the last sentence. Feigning indifference, he nodded to Qiao and sat down facing them. In fact he was ready for a fight. Sensing fireworks, Tong cleverly shifted the topic and led Xi to another room on some pretext.

The guests looked at each other and rose to leave. Their bald-headed leader said sarcastically, "Oh, I see. The feast isn't for us. No wonder that whizz-kid will be back in his job so soon. You've made it up. Fair enough, you're relatives after all."

Qiao did not insist on their staying but said coldly, "Wang, to put it bluntly, all you want is to go back to your old jobs or, better still, be promoted, right? Don't worry. Our trouble isn't that we have too many cadres in this plant. We need a lot more. Of course, I mean capable people who know how to do their jobs. There'll be an examination tomorrow. I don't think it matters if I tell you now. We've all been a long time in this plant and should know about such things as balanced production or what is standardization, systematization and universal specifications."

The men were flabbergasted. They'd never heard such terms. What shocked them most was that even the cadres had to take the exam.

Someone grumbled in a low voice, "This is very new, isn't it?"

"What's new about it?" Qiao retorted. "From now on, no one will be allowed to muddle along whether he is a worker or a cadre. To be frank, I'm most unhappy about the plant and have a lot more to complain about than you. It's time we got down to work."

After he'd seen them off, he returned to his drink. His expression was angry. When Tong brought him a bowl of rice after he had drunk a few cups of wine, he said to the young man opposite him, "You know pretty well, Xi, the decision to suspend you was not made by the new Party committee. Shi must have told you that your case has been cleared. Why do you still refuse to work?"

"I want the Party committee to make it clear to all the workers and staff members in the plant why I was suspended from my work. Now the investigation is over. It's been proved that, first, I never raided anybody's home or office; and second, I had no personal connection with the 'gang of four'. Why did you pick on me? Just because I was the head of a faction, or because I'm a so-called new cadre? How could you make such a decision based on rumour?"

Seeing him wave his chopsticks with indignation, Qiao thought, "So now you know what it's like! You slandered others, didn't you?"

As if guessing what was in his mind, Xi turned the conversation, "I request to work on the shop floor."

"What?" This was rather unusual. New cadres didn't easily quit their jobs lest people think they fell because they were involved with the gang. But Xi had the guts to ask for it. Was he bluffing? Anyway, Qiao called his bluff by saying, "Fine! I agree. In fact, respect doesn't come with an appointment. You have to earn it. Many people can be high-fliers. Some through their own efforts, while others are tossed up by the wind. I hope you're not looking for such a wind again."

Xi sneered. "I don't know what wind you're talking about! If I were an opportunist, I wouldn't have been suspended from my work. Twenty years ago I was an apprentice. I've been a worker, a group leader, a foreman, and when I was a little over thirty, I became a deputy manager, a 'whizz-kid', as some of them called me. I'm willing to go down to the shop floor instead of holding on to a post to the death like some others. Actually those who were once officials still crave more power and promotion."

The old cadres blamed Qiao for favouring the young, whereas the new ones insinuated that he was a bureaucrat.

Tong offered Qiao a lot of food, afraid he might lose his temper. But Qiao relaxed, chewing over what Xi had just said.

Xi knew that Qiao would never give him sympathy if he pleaded with him, but might soften if he was tough. A coward would never win his respect. Better to be tough with him.

"When will we Chinese rid ourselves of one-sidedness?" he went on. "During the 'cultural revolution', nearly all the cadres were attacked and removed from their offices. Now, though we talk about drawing a lesson from it, all new cadres have been dismissed. Of course, there are some followers of the gang among the new cadres, but they are only a handful. Most of them were fooled into believing they were following the Party line. If you're active in one political movement, you'll be a victim in the next. The safest way is to sit on the fence and do nothing. Once a movement starts everybody higher than a foreman is investigated. When a new man takes over the leading position, he puts in his own men and kicks out all the others. This is practised right down to the small units. People are divided into factions. The cadres spend all their time and energy on fixing people with whom they don't see eye to eye. In work they can't co-operate with each other. If things go on like this, despite all your high-sounding slogans, modernization will never be achieved."

Hearing this, Qiao grew quite alert though he said, "Come off it, Xi. You sound like a theoretician. Our country has suffered enough from too many critics, too much empty talk. What we need are hard-working and selfless people." He had imagined only the old cadres needed to vent their anger and had never expected such a complaint from a new cadre. It would be extremely damaging if the two forces clashed head-on.

2

Qiao went into action the following day.

First, he had all nine thousand workers and staff sit for the exam and have an appraisal made of their work. All those who were lazy, careless or unqualified were made to form a service team. Those who passed were capable and hard-working. After this, production began to pick up speed. The whole plant was stimulated by the new competitive spirit.

The workers felt that Qiao was a man of action. Once he had decided on something, he would go all out for it. As he had promised, a fine building for a kindergarten was soon completed. He had said that bonuses would be awarded if the production quota was reached, and so in August the workers got them for the first time. All skilled, hard-working people said that there could be no better manager than Qiao. At the same time he was hated by some of the service-team members, who were furious at having to work in it.

He dismissed the one thousand temporary workers who had been engaged in building and transportation. Their work was taken over by the service team. Qiao made a capable man, Li Gan, the head of the finance office, the team leader, and gave some of the temporary workers' wages to this team as a material incentive. Though they suffered no cut in wages, the young workers in it felt insulted and humiliated. Du Bing, for one, felt strongly about it, because his girl-friend had jilted him since he wasn't even a qualified turner. He was miserable and desperate.

But Qiao had other enemies. Worst were those angry cadres who had been sent to the service team. They in turn demanded that all the managers should take the exam too. Unperturbed Qiao went to the auditorium with a few deputy managers to sit for the exam.

The news soon got round, and the workers, having ended their day-shift, rushed to the hall which was soon packed to overflowing. They fired all sorts of questions at Qiao, who answered with ease. But Ji Shen did badly. When he got everything muddled up, the workers called him "a superfluous manager". Enraged he choked back his anger, inwardly cursing Qiao for laying such a nasty trap to make a fool of him in public.

Ji found being a deputy manager was rather demanding. Moreover, he resented being at the beck and call of others, especially so before the workers. Now that he had failed the exam, jealousy and resentment pushed him to join the opposition. He was Qiao's deputy only in name. His frowning face and his dark eyes seemed to be the source of all trouble in the plant. Wherever there was a problem in production, he had a hand in it. Yet he was too careful to be caught out. Qiao had to be both on guard against him and at the same time solve the problems he caused. He was really a damn nuisance.

So Qiao made up his mind to send Ji to the service team and ask him to take charge of construction, unaware that the service team was already a powder keg and that Ji's appearance would certainly spark off an explosion. It was thoughtful Shi who foresaw the impending trouble. Qiao, however, ignored his warning. Even more surprising, he promoted Xi to be the deputy manager instead of Ji, supervising production. Those who were capable were promoted. Qiao followed this rule, regardless of personal likes or dislikes. Xi, a personal enemy of Qiao, had become his assistant.

As Shi predicted, only a few days after Ji's transfer, grumbles in the service team became open protests, threatening to topple Qiao again.

Though Qiao was up to his neck in all sorts of contradictions and problems, he had no time to deal with the movement to topple him. What preoccupied him most was preparing for the next year's production. He hoped to get the output up to two million kilowatts. But the Power Company did not like the idea. They preferred to import some equipment from abroad. Besides, there were problems such as fuel and raw materials. Qiao decided to do some diplomatic work himself.

Unfortunately he met with an ignominious defeat. He had been ignorant of the gap between his wonderful plan and reality. Disorder and corruption made it impossible for him to reach his goal. He felt at the end of his tether. He needed large rotor forgings, the more the better; but the supplier would not listen to him. He wanted raw materials and fuel, but did not know how to get them. He was unaware of the unwritten rule that in return you had to give something the others needed. It was called mutual exchange. So it wasn't just a matter of clinching a deal. Anyway, Qiao learned something new: that it was not important whether or not a manager knew anything about metallography or mechanics. What was essential was to have a good "relationship" with others.

3

The first thing Qiao did when he returned was to see Shi Gan. Shi, flustered by his sudden appearance, stuffed some papers into his drawer. But Qiao, concentrating on other things, failed to notice this. They sat down and began talking when Li, the head of the service team, broke in. Seeing Qiao, he exclaimed joyfully, "Eh, Qiao, you're just the man I'm looking for!"

"What is it?" Qiao asked eagerly.

"The peasants are refusing to let us start building our apartment block. Xi is surrounded by them. There may be a scuffle."

"But the City Planning Bureau has given the go-ahead. We've paid the money."

"They want five tractors in addition."

"The same old story!" Qiao bellowed. "We're producing electrical machinery. Where in hell's name can we get tractors?"

"But Ji Shen promised them."

"Shit! Where's Ji? Go and get him."

"He's been transferred, leaving everything in a mess," Li complained.

"What?" Qiao turned to look at Shi.

"Three days ago," Shi explained, "he came to say good-bye to me in the morning. That same afternoon he went to the Foreign Trade Bureau. He knew a certain big shot there, who pulled some strings to get Ji the job. He didn't even say a word to the Party committee. But his file's with us. So he's still on our payroll."

"He can take his file with him. We won't pay him for doing nothing." Then he gestured to Li, "Let's go and have a look."

They got into a jeep and set off at once. On their way to the new building site, they met Xi racing along on his bike.

"Hey, Xi, what's happening?" Li called out.

"Nothing! It's all settled!" With that, he mounted and rode on as if on urgent business.

"Well done!" Li nodded admiringly. "He's got a good head on his shoulders." He asked the driver to turn around to catch up with him. When they were abreast of him, Li shouted, "What's the hurry? Anything wrong? You know, Qiao's back!"

Xi stopped to greet Qiao and then explained, "Workshop No. 1 has some problem with the coils."

Xi thrust the bike at Li and jumped into the jeep. As the jeep started for the plant, Li shouted after it, "Eh, Qiao, what about my problem?"

Problem after problem! There was no end to them. Since it was almost the end of the year and the workers were busier, problems were more likely to occur. Qiao feared that this new problem might mess up everything.

As they entered the workshop, they saw the foreman pleading with Tong Zhen. Calmly shaking her head, she was not budging. "What a stubborn mule!" the man thought to himself, his patience beginning to wear out. She did not raise her voice and she was still smiling. Though she spoke in an even tone, she refused to give an inch on technical questions. Even if you shouted at her, she remained the same, until finally you gave in and listened to her. Suddenly the exasperated man spotted Qiao. Immediately he dashed over to him, thinking he was the only person who could change Tong's mind.

"Qiao," he groused, "we were certain to fulfil this year's quota eight days ahead of schedule. We can do even better next year. But we've got a slight problem. You see, the puncture rate of the lower coil of a rotor is no more than one per cent. That's really nothing serious. But Tong insists we rewind the coil. Earlier this year, coils with a puncture rate around thirty or forty per cent were passed. So it's a lot better now."

"Have you found the cause of it?" Qiao broke in.

"Not yet."

"Yes, we have!" Tong butted in. "I've told you twice about it. All I'm asking you to do is to erect a plastic covering and take measures to protect the generators from dust. But you think it's too troublesome."

"Troublesome?" Qiao said in a mocking tone, "It's easy to turn out rejects, but aren't they troublesome to the country? What about quality? You did fairly well in the exam. Theory is one thing and practice is another, right? Do it again! No bonus for you and your workers this month."

The man was upset.

"You don't have to be so harsh, Qiao," Tong pleaded. "They're bound to finish the work in time even if they do it again. Why cut their bonus?"

"It has nothing to do with you," Qiao said coldly without even looking at her. "Just think of the time and materials wasted because of their carelessness!" Then he and Xi walked out of the workshop.

With a wry smile, the foreman said to Tong, "The service team wants to smash him, and we do everything possible to support him. I can't understand why he's so hard on us."

Tong said nothing. She was concerned with the technical side and had no say in such things. All she could do was try to console the depressed man.

4

Tong bought four tickets for a Beijing opera *The Forsaken Wife* to try and cheer up her husband. The other two were for Xi and his wife. As Xi did not turn up in time, the three of them set off first, leaving a ticket for Xi.

Just as they were about to enter the theatre, Li appeared out of the blue. Seeing him in such a flurry, Qiao sensed that something must have gone wrong. He asked the two women to go in first while he followed Li to a quiet place.

"What's up?" Qiao asked quietly. The look of authority in his eyes calmed Li down.

"Some people in the service team are out to make trouble."

"Who?"

"Du Bing. He's backed by Baldy Wang. They're making a noise about Ji Shen supporting them. Du's been absent for three days, so he's probably in touch with those having the sit-in. He appeared this afternoon and talked with a few of his cronies and then wrote some posters. He said they were going to put them up on the wall of the municipal government building, and even threatened to go on a hunger strike."

"Are you scared?" Qiao asked, sizing up this clever, capable man.

"Why should I be? It's you they're gunning for."

"Don't worry about me," Qiao said with a smile. "You just stick to the rules. Cut the wages of those who stay away from work without good reason. If they don't want to work here, fair enough. They can go somewhere else."

A leader must be firmer than his subordinates. Encouraged, Li grinned, "Watch out when you go home after the opera. They may mug you on the way. I must go now."

Qiao found his seat and sat down when the bell for silence rang. Some dignitaries entered and took their seats in the middle of the row in front of Qiao. Ji Shen was one of them. With his sharp eyes, he'd already spotted Qiao and Tong. Having sat down, he turned round and nodded to Tong. Then he proffered his hand to Qiao, saying, "So you're back, Qiao. How are things? A man like you always gets what he wants!"

Qiao just shook his head. He hated to talk loudly in public places.

Ji said condescendingly, "If you come to our bureau, look me up. I'm always at your disposal."

Qiao swallowed, feeling disgusted. Why was he so smug? Was it his promotion? Was he mocking?

Indeed, Ji now felt superior to Qiao, of whom he'd been so jealous only a few months previously. He'd never commit himself to boost production the way Qiao did, throw himself into a political movement. That was madness! To him, modernization was just another political movement, and Qiao was so stupid as to stake everything on it. He was on the brink of a precipice and could fall any minute. Now the Electrical Machinery Plant was already in a turmoil. Ji was proud of his prudent decision to leave the plant in time. Tonight meeting Qiao in such a situation made him feel on top of the world. He seemed to enjoy the opera, discussing it with the people sitting beside him.

But despite his efforts, Qiao could not concentrate on the performance. He racked his brains to find a good excuse to leave the theatre, so as not to disappoint the two women.

Xi groped his way to his seat with the help of an usher's torch. The two women inquired why he was so late and if he had eaten anything. He mumbled a few words, nodding his head. Then casting a sidelong glance at Qiao, he whispered, "Manager, how can you sit still? Let's get the hell out of here!"

Agreeing, Qiao followed Xi and took his leave. But Tong, running after them, caught them in the lobby.

Xi hastily explained to her, "I have to talk to him. He has the full support of the Ministry of Machine-building and has got some orders for generators from the Ministry of Electric Power. Our problems now are

materials, fuel and the co-operation between the factories concerned. Contracts, documents, and Qiao's
firmness aren't enough. This is where the deputy manager should come in."

Qiao had not expected Xi to be willing to do such a
job himself. Since he had failed, he couldn't bring
himself to ask a deputy to try. Besides, he doubted
whether Xi could succeed. Guessing Qiao's thoughts, Xi
was upset.

"Are you leaving tomorrow?" Tong asked. "Why the
hurry?"

"I've just discussed it with the Party secretary. He
agrees too. We've sent someone to buy the train tickets.
We'll probably leave tonight." Though Xi talked to
Tong, he intended Qiao to hear. "As a manager of a
big factory, Qiao has a fatal weakness. He knows nothing about human relationships. It's different from the
war years, or even a few years ago. Unlike robots, men
have feelings and thoughts. And it's most difficult to
influence men's thinking." Abruptly turning to Qiao he
went on, "You know how to run a big modern factory.
When there is important business in the bureau or ministry, you should go yourself, because you've a reputation and your words carry greater weight. As for public
relations, leave that to us deputy managers or chiefs of
departments. If things get out of hand, you can smooth
them out. But if you do everything yourself and get
into a fix, what can we do?"

"OK," Qiao said, "but stop giving me all your fine
theories! With you it's always theory before practice.
I'm sick of it all." He asked Xi to accompany the two
women, while he went to see Shi.

Tong gazed at her husband's receding figure. She

knew that he often covered up his anxiety and weaknesses and that he secretly tried to overcome them. He
never showed a trace of depression or hesitation at
home. He had to be tough for he shouldered a heavy
load. Now the plant was improving. If he backed
out at this moment, the plant would collapse. He must
not show softness or fear.

Xi was looking at Qiao's back smiling.

"When you two get together," Tong complained, "I'm
always afraid you'll come to blows!"

"Never!" Xi put his hand on her arm and said cheerfully, "Frankly, Tong, there aren't many people as good
as Manager Qiao around. Haven't you noticed how
many of our cadres are following his example? They'll
do well under Qiao's leadership. I confess I don't exactly like him, but I do admire his guts. Though he has a
great power of attraction, I'm resisting him with all my
might. I won't give in. He despises cowards."

He looked at his watch and exclaimed, "Hell! I'm
afraid I have to go too. Really to be his deputy isn't
easy!" So saying, he dashed off.

5

Under a lamp, Shi was carefully reading letters of accusation against Manager Qiao, which had been for-
warded from the plant's Party committee, the municipal
Party committee and even from the Central Party Committee. He felt a mixture of indignation, fear and
shame. All the letters attacked Qiao. Not a single one
criticized him, the Party secretary. On the contrary,
he was described as a victim of Qiao's despotism, as

only a figure-head, a living mummy. It was true that Shi had become very quiet and that quite often he pretended to be deaf, not answering certain questions. He had rather prided himself on his sophistication, but now he regretted it deeply and was angry with himself. He had never meant this behaviour of his to blacken Qiao and whitewash himself. Sometimes he had been fired by Qiao's enthusiasm, and very often his feelings overcame his common sense. On certain important issues, he sided with Qiao by saying nothing or simply acquiescing. He sometimes thought that if all cadres worked like Qiao, China would soon have a new look and that the Party would recover its vitality. But the letters were like a deluge threatening to swamp Qiao for good. Shi's heart ached. He had no idea what to do with the letters. He feared that Du Bing and his mob would gang up with some hooligans to turn the plant upside down.

While he was thinking, he heard someone call him. Opening the door, he saw Huo Dadao.

Huo looked round and asked, "So Qiao isn't here?"

"No."

"Well?" Huo sipped the tea Shi had poured him. "When I heard he was back, I went to see him right after supper. Unfortunately his door was locked. I guessed he would come here."

"He and Tong have gone to an opera."

"Then I'll wait for him. I'm pretty sure he won't sit through it all no matter how good! It's a pity that he has to disappoint Tong again." Huo chuckled softly.

"But he's a Beijing opera fan."

"I know. You don't believe me? You want a bet?"

Huo, in high spirits, seemed unaware of Shi's bad

mood. "What he's really keen on is his plant, his work," he added as if talking to himself. Glancing at the letters on the table, Huo asked indifferently, "Does he know about these?"

Shi shook his head.

"How was his trip? How is he?"

Shi shook his head again. He was about to say something, when Qiao pushed the door open.

Huo chortled and slapped Shi on the shoulder.

Qiao was puzzled by the laughter.

Shi immediately tried to hide the letters, but Qiao noticed his uneasiness. Walking to the table, he snatched up a letter.

Huo urged Shi to show him them all.

Having read some of the letters, Qiao was enraged and swore, "The dirty bastards!"

He paced up and down the room, his left cheek twitching, then went over to Huo, who appeared engrossed in reading a paper. So he turned to Shi and asked, "So what will you do?"

Shi shot him a glance and answered, "It's time you left this plant for the bureau. This year's quota will be fulfilled. I'll stay and stick it out. I won't leave while there's trouble."

"What are you talking about?" Qiao roared. "You want me to run away? What about the plant?"

"But what about you? If you're disgraced, a lot of people will be hurt. Who else will take up this job?" Shi meant this also for Huo's ear.

Huo looked at them calmly, not uttering a word.

Qiao, pacing up and down, snapped, "I'm not afraid of dirty slanders. As long as I'm the manager, I'll run the plant my way!"

Shi appealed to Huo, "What do you think, Huo?"

"A few letters and you're scared out of your wits?" Huo asked quietly. "Still you're his loyal friend. You tell him to get out first and then you'll follow later, eh? A good idea! I must say you've made great progress."

Shi's face became very red.

Smiling, Huo turned to Qiao and said, "Qiao, you've only been back for half a year, and one of your achievements is that you've turned this deaf and dumb fellow into a high-ranking official. We had to drag Shi here to be the Party secretary. Now he wants to be the manager as well! Come, Comrade Shi, there's no need to blush! I'm only speaking the truth. Now you're like a real Party secretary. But one thing I must criticize you for is Ji Shen's transfer. Why did you let him go without first consulting the bureau?"

Shi was very embarrassed. Old as he was, he had never got such a dressing-down from his leaders.

Huo rose to his feet and went over to Qiao. "You know I like the saying, 'Better to die fighting than in your bed!' Please tell me, how do you spend your time?"

"Forty per cent on production, fifty per cent on wrangles and ten per cent on slanders," was Qiao's prompt reply.

"What a waste of time! You should spend eighty per cent of your time on production and the rest on research."

He suddenly became very serious, "Modernization doesn't mean technique alone. You'll have to offend some people. Of course, it's safest to do nothing, but that's criminal. As for misunderstandings, being wronged, slanders, accusations, sneers, never mind them. Ignore them! If you want to achieve something, demand a free rein. We're racing against time. The curtain has just risen on our modernization drive. The real drama is yet to follow."

Seeing their faces brighten up, Huo continued, "The minister rang me up yesterday and told me that he was very interested in the way you are running the plant. He asked me to tell you to be even bolder. Experiment with some new methods. Gain experience. Know what our problems are. Next spring he wants us to go abroad to have a look. China's modernization will be realized by Chinese, but we must study the experience of other countries."

The three men sat down, sipping their tea and chatting. Huo suddenly suggested to Qiao, "You're good at singing Beijing opera. Sing us an aria."

"OK." Qiao drank some tea, lifted his head and began to sing. . . .

More About Manager Qiao

Competiton

EARLY morning. The sleety northwest wind stung people's faces like a wet lash. Qiao Guangpu arrived early at the plant as usual. As his car passed the gate, he caught sight of a familiar figure sweeping snow in front of the reception room. He frowned. Alighting from the car, he went back to the gate. In a joking tone he said, "Old Ma, why don't you leave your den? I hope to see you on the shop floor next time."

"I'm pretty well paid," Ma Changyou answered frankly. "And I'm getting on in years now. So I'm staying put."

"Then you're not entitled to a seventh-grade fitter's wage," Qiao countered. "You should be paid as a janitor instead. Wages change according to one's work like grain rations."

Ma chuckled. "Manager," he said, "it's not for you to decide. This is one of the advantages of socialism. Wages can be raised, never lowered."

"But that surely applies equally to the sense of responsibility of an old worker like you. This system of once in a job you can never get fired isn't necessarily an advantage of socialism, as you think. In my view, it goes against the Party's programme!"

Ma's face fell. "Manager," he asked, "be frank, how long do you intend to stay in this Electrical Machinery Plant?"

Qiao was taken aback. He realized that what was worrying Ma was Qiao's opposition lobby, the big-character posters and letters of accusation against him. Naturally there were people like Ma waiting to see which way the wind would blow. Things were unpredictable.

"This plant isn't mine and you're not working for me," Qiao answered gravely. "If I die, the plant will still be here, the machines will still run."

Ma had nothing to say. He watched Qiao leave with mixed feelings — compassion or compunction?

2

As the bell for work rang, three people came into Qiao's office. They were Gu Chang, the head of the manager's office, Li Gan, the former service-team leader newly promoted to be the general accountant, and Qiao's wife, the assistant chief engineer, Tong Zhen. Qiao, on Bureau Director Huo Dadao's advice, arranged his work in a scientific way to raise his efficiency. He had a strict timetable for each day, each week. The first half hour of the day, he and the deputy manager Xi Wangbei always had a talk with Li Gan and Tong Zhen. They were like his two hands, co-operating excellently with him.

"Why hasn't Xi turned up yet?" Qiao asked Gu.

"Gone to a meeting in the Foreign Trade Bureau."

"Oh?" Qiao grew alert.

"Ji Shen notified us. This meeting is about the sales rights of exported goods."

"Ah!" Qiao's heart missed a beat. Waving the question aside, he turned to Li, who handed him a short report. It listed production figures and the main problems. Drawn up by Li himself, it was simple and clear, with not one superfluous word. Qiao quickly looked it over. Seven quotas out of eight had been fulfilled. He looked searchingly at Li and asked, "Why's the production cost up?"

"Because of the moulding sand," Li answered. "Xikou sand costs forty-seven yuan a ton, Nandao sand ninety-one yuan. The quality is more or less the same, but we bought a big consignment of Nandao sand."

"Why?"

"I hear that a purchasing agent in our supply department accepted some presents from the Nandao people."

Qiao's jaws twitched and the muscles stood out. However, he did not explode. He nodded, signing to Li to go on.

"Ever since the 'cultural revolution', the supply department has stopped measuring its purchases of sand. They leave it to the sellers. When a consignment is brought here and unloaded, they pay whatever it says on the receipt. Yesterday, I measured all the loads of sand myself. Several were twenty tons short. One was thirteen short. I told the finance department to refuse to pay."

"Wasters! If they were buying food for themselves, they wouldn't be half a catty short." Qiao told Gu, "Make a note of this. Ask the head of the supply department to come to see me at two this afternoon."

Li continued, "According to the telegram from our men in Hongkong, a foreign firm has reduced the price of its dynamos by one tenth in order to undersell us. This puts us at a big disadvantage."

"Those foreign bosses!" Qiao stood up, a cold glint in his eyes. Soon after assuming office the previous year, he estimated that there probably wouldn't be enough material to feed the plant in the period of economic readjustment. So he had approached several suppliers himself, and finally he went to Vice-minister Che of the Ministry of Machine Building. The Vice-minister knew the market at home as well as abroad. He suggested that Qiao should launch two products. One was a hundred-ton diesel electric truck, which was mostly imported, and he encouraged Qiao to compete with foreigners first in this field at home. His other proposal was a light dynamo which could be exported to Hongkong and Southeast Asia. After a year and a half, Qiao's dynamos were stealing the market in Hongkong from a foreign company which had previously monopolized it. Now this company had slashed its price, hoping to force the Chinese dynamo out of the Hongkong market.

Qiao gradually calmed down. He said to Li, "According to the rate of production increase, we can pay the state four million yuan per year from the dynamo alone. If we cut the price by one tenth, how much will we lose?"

"Four hundred thousand," Li replied.

"If we don't, we'll be squeezed out of the world market. That would mean losing all the three million six hundred thousand yuan as well. Which do you prefer?"

Gu butted in, "But how can we reduce the price? That's up to the state."

"What a stickler!" Qiao remarked. "Certainly we've

the right to adjust the price of our own products. That's the way to do business."

"Ji Shen told me that the Foreign Trade Bureau is in charge of the sales of all exported goods. It seems that the municipal Party committee and Tie Jian, chief of the Economic Commission, have okayed it. We'll know for sure when Xi's back from the meeting."

"So that's the way it is!"

"Wherever Ji goes, he tries to block us!" Li complained.

"All he wants is to take over the sales right abroad so as to squeeze something from the profits. What does he know about management? If we leave our dynamos to him, we'll be out of the world market within half a year. Production and sales can't be separated!" With a toss of his head, Qiao added, "Forget him! Cut the price and notify Hongkong right away."

Li heaved a sigh of relief.

"Apart from cutting the price," Tong said, "we must improve the quality and appearance of our dynamos. For instance, our dynamos are grey, blue, red or green. Too gaudy. We must also study foreign dynamos and avoid their weak points. Many foreign customers would like to install a light dynamo in their homes and they naturally want one that looks attractive and has a fine finish. But labour abroad is expensive. Foreign companies may not be able to afford it. This is where we have the advantage."

Qiao broke in cheerfully, "A good idea! Specify what you want, and I'll ask the service team to see to it." He scribbled a few words on his desk calendar.

Tong was still calm, not affected by Qiao's enthusiasm. She continued, "Our new hundred-ton electric truck is promising too. Chuanxi Mine cabled to me yesterday that they find it excellent and want to order another fourteen next year. They used to import electric trucks, but they couldn't get spare parts, so most of their foreign trucks are now out of action. We must take this chance to launch our product. I've decided to send two capable technicians plus two maintenance men, whom I hope the manager will recommend, to Chuanxi Mine tomorrow as a technical team. We must not only sell products but also repair them and guarantee the prompt supply of spare parts. Foreign firms can't compete with us in this respect. If we can first replace foreign goods with our own in the home market, then launch into the world market, we'll have more orders than we can handle instead of not enough customers."

Qiao rubbed his hands in elation. Strange, she hadn't even hinted at such wonderful news the previous evening. "Think of all the mines there are in our country alone!" he exclaimed. "If our electric trucks sell well, we'll have a great future. Gu, make a note of that, will you? Tell the Party secretary what Tong just said. If he's for the idea of the technical team, ask him to persuade Ma Changyou to take a young fitter to join the team going to Chuanxi Mine and see Tong before setting off. Remind him, too, that this afternoon's our regular meeting. We must decide several things. First, to set up a sales department, because good salesmanship's of vital importance. We must pick as salesmen people who are strong politically, shrewd and capable like the Monkey King. Sales managers abroad are experienced professionals, who know the market well. Secondly, we must advertise our products more widely.

We'd better print some attractive brochures for distribution at home and abroad, or even send some free samples. We'll explain that our products have been strictly tested and give reliable data. All orders are welcome, and we'll guarantee to attend to them without delay. Thirdly, we must find places to start our own stores. Fourthly, we must set up a world market research centre to keep track of the situation both in China and abroad, and collect and study technical information and samples from other manufacturers. We must also learn how to deal with foreign capitalists."

When Li had jotted all this down, Qiao added, "I have to alter today's agenda a little. I'm going to the service team at nine."

The other three were nonplussed, and Gu, being a smart man, reminded him, "You should be in Workshop No. 5 from nine to ten this morning."

"Put it off till noon. I'll have lunch there."

"Skip your nap again?" Tong asked, throwing a glance at him.

Ignoring her, Qiao said, "You can go now if there's nothing else."

But Tong stayed behind to demand, "Why go to the service team all of a sudden?"

"A manager can go to any unit under him if he wants to. For more than a year now this team has been trying to topple me. I don't want to leave the problem till 1980."

Tong took a deep breath. Knowing her husband's hot temper, she said anxiously, "Don't fly off the handle. Keep cool. If you get excited. . . ."

Qiao shook his head with a laugh. "What is life if we can't get excited? Fact is, I'm going to give them

a good talking-to. Our plant has been forging ahead
for a year and a half. This shows that the changes
we've introduced are correct. Facts speak louder than
words."

His confidence made Tong more worried. She knew
that he was a never-satisfied, bold and capable factory
manager, who would push aside all obstacles in his way.
But he did not realize that the main obstacle was neither
Ji Shen, nor the service team, but the rigid economic
system which had evolved over a long period of time.
Any day, a storm might spring up and shatter his dream.
Now he was going to stir up a hornet's nest. This was
asking for trouble. She decided to ask Shi Gan, the
Party secretary, to try to stop him.

With a deep sigh, she turned and left. Qiao frowned,
saying to himself, "Damn! What's she fretting about?
It's hard to know what's in someone else's mind, no
matter how close you are. . . ."

A knock at the door interrupted these reflections.
The heads of the organization department and labour
and pay department had arrived as agreed. Qiao rubbed
his cheeks and shook his head a few times as if to shake
off the unpleasant impression Tong had made on him.
"Come in!" he boomed.

3

The woman head of the organization department looked
a typical office cadre, cordial but opinionated. Long
years of political work and personnel management had
made her highly principled and put a bridle on her
tongue. However, there was an aura of arrogance and

shrewdness about her.   The man looked capable and handsome, fair-complexioned, with a black stubble on his chin.   After sizing them up, Qiao suddenly asked the woman, "Hu, do you think the Monkey King can join the Party?"

She gaped in astonishment.

"Of course, this is only a metaphor. . . ."

Hu cut him short politely yet seriously, "Manager, did you send for us to listen to such a joke?"

Qiao's brows twitched.   "If you take it for a joke," he said, "you're greatly mistaken.   Both of you are in charge of people, and you judge them on the basis of the materials in their files.   You must see them as they are in real life and find out how they work in this plant. There'll be a wage rise soon.   Priority should be given to those who are capable and work well, and those who have made important contributions to the management."

Then he made his second point.   "The main duty of those in charge of personnel is to see that no talents are wasted, to find and train promising workers and give them key jobs.   Right now, special attention must be paid to raising the political status of experts and giving them better material conditions too.   Our people are very able.   Some, once they go overseas, discover proton and gluon and even win Nobel Prizes.   But they can't do that here in China.   Why?   What's stopping them? People like you ought to think about it and feel guilty. In a way, we've let down the country, the people."

Hu could not accept such a view.

Qiao went on to ask the head of the labour and pay department to find out how many skilled workers there were in the plant.   How many of them had left their workshops, and on what grounds?   They were the plant's greatest assets and must play more active roles. Qiao also asked him to form a "technical advisory group" of skilled workers.

Thirdly, Qiao gave them some reference material to read. He told them that "manpower-tapping" was an important factor in industrial development. In certain enterprises in Japan, the workers' intelligence and skill were considered as a kind of resource. The crux of economic competition was technological. And victory in this competition would depend, to a very great extent, on skilled workers and technical personnel.

Qiao had given them a work assignment and, at the same time, a lecture. The man found these questions fresh and interesting. But Hu instinctively felt repelled and bored. She forced herself to listen, dissenting at heart. To her mind, Qiao was peddling the handful of foreign wares he had picked up during his trip abroad earlier that year. Qiao realized this, of course, which made him more determined to convince her. If cadres at her level failed to improve their skill in management, how could ordinary cadres be expected to do it?

"I've given you three questions in your line of work," Qiao said finally. "When you get the answers, come and tell me."

To avoid a dispute, Hu grudgingly agreed. But as soon as she left the manager's office, she went to see Shi Gan. She wanted to have a serious talk with the Party secretary.

4

On his way to the service team, Qiao was overtaken by Shi Gan.

"Are you coming to protect me or stop me?" Qiao asked.

Shaking his head, Shi replied, "Neither. I've come to back you up. Besides, I've something to discuss with you."

"What?"

"Tie Jian, the chief of the Municipal Economic Commission, just told me that Tong Zhen is to be transferred."

"What?" Qiao was electrified. "What does this mean?"

"She's needed by a delegation which is going to negotiate with some foreigners. But I smell a rat. Another thing, Director Huo had a talk with me. He wants us to take Ji Shen back."

"Nonsense!" Qiao raised his voice. "Our plant's just been put into shape again. Now they want to take away the assistant chief engineer and send back that bum. Are they trying to destroy this plant? Nothing doing!"

Smiling calmly, Shi said, "People say you're like Director Huo. I think, you fall far short of him. Now I understand why Huo criticized me for letting Ji Shen leave this plant. What he meant, I think, was that a fellow like Ji would only block our way if he worked in a bureau. We should have kept him here and made him work, while keeping an eye on him. Have you the guts to take him back?"

"I'm dead against it!" Having said this, Qiao stalked away. Then he turned to add, "I'll go and see Director Huo myself. If necessary I'll see Tie Jian."

The winter wind in the north cuts like a knife. Qiao pulled down his safety helmet and quickened his steps

while Shi followed close behind him. Suddenly Qiao
noticed cement scattered on the ground. He looked up
and saw a man in a big fur hat pulling a barrow loaded
with three sacks of cement. The fellow seemed in a bad
temper for, instead of keeping to the road, he was jolting
his load at top speed along a rugged shortcut. From
one of the sacks, which had burst, cement was spilling.
As Qiao was about to call him, the barrow got bogged
down in a frozen puddle. The puller threw down the
shafts, as if on strike. Qiao and Shi hurried over and,
to their surprise, came face to face with none other
than Du Bing! Their paths were bound to cross!

"Ah, it's you!" Qiao said, tongue in cheek. "Isn't
your barrow like an ox running and urinating at the
same time?"

Instead of speaking, Du Bing glared at him, his eyes
full of resentment and rage.

While pushing the wheel, Qiao shouted to Du Bing,
"What are you waiting for? Take up the shafts!"

Reluctantly, the young man complied. Shi Gan
pushed the other wheel.

"Ready — go!" At Qiao's shout, the three men got
the barrow out of the puddle. Du Bing was about to
move on, when Qiao stepped forward, pressing down
the barrow shafts, and said, "Wait a minute!"

"What for?"

"Move that sack a little so that the hole will be on
top." Qiao met the young man's eyes. "Sulking
again?"

"A clay figure can't stand too much pressure, not to
say a live man like me!"

"A live man? Just how do you live? You're a
shiftless trouble-maker. Want to muddle along all your

life like this?" While speaking, Qiao moved the sack himself. Noticing that it was cement No. 600, he demanded, "What do you want this cement for?"

"To build a locker room."

"But you don't have to use such good cement. Do you know what grade it is?"

"No. Our section leader said any cement would do."

"Show me the requisition slip."

"Haven't one."

"Stealing it, eh?"

"I'm not taking it home, anyway."

"Take it back!" Qiao flared up.

The young man thumped down the barrow, then turned to leave in a huff. Before Qiao could explode, bald-headed Wang Guanxiong hurried out from the service team's shed to intervene. Smiling at Qiao and Shi, he shouted at Du Bing, "Young Du, what do you think you're doing?"

"But you...." Du whirled round to retort, staring at Wang, his section leader.

Wang tipped him a wink, urging him to clear off. Instead, Du Bing just stood there.

"Why didn't you issue a requisition slip?" Qiao asked Wang.

"We don't need much," Wang carefully weighed his words. "Besides, that red tape is troublesome, so we decided to scrounge a little near by."

"Section leader," Du Bing sneered, "why not tell the truth? We botched the job, wasted cement, but hushed it up. If we ask for more cement, we'll be in the red. Then we'll have no bonus at the end of the month. That was why our section leader told us to scrounge some."

"What do you mean by 'scrounge'?" Qiao asked. "It's theft, you know. Robbery! Where can you get sacks of cement like this except from our warehouse? You're upsetting the supply department's plan. Take this back. Write a report about the accident. You can ask for some inferior cement for the locker room."

"Right," said Wang and pulled the barrow away.

"Swine!" spat out Du Bing, then strode into the shed.

This big, roughly built shed was where the service team rested, where they held their meetings. The appearance of the manager and the Party secretary caused quite a stir, because the workers thought the management had forgotten them. The team leader called back all the workers outside. They politely invited Qiao and Shi to take seats. But Qiao remained standing. He noticed that a few workers were standing against the wall as if to hide something. He stepped over, pulled aside a young woman and saw a drawing on the whitewashed wall: a Taoist priest was about to go to Heaven, on his left was a boy sitting astride a dog, on his right a girl riding a chicken. The drawing had no title, no names identifying the three characters, but the implication was clear to anyone in the plant. The priest was the manager, the boy Xi Wangbei, and the girl Tong Zhen. Qiao's blood boiled, his eyes riveted on the drawing. But he had the sense to remember that there were many eyes fixed on his back. If he were to flare up, things might get out of hand. He checked his indignation, his cheeks twitching. There were other paintings. He looked at them one by one.

One showed a "gang of four" presiding over an examination. The examiners here were obviously Qiao, Xi, Tong and Li Gan while those being cross-examined were the workers. All were by the same skilful caricaturist, and the colour was very well applied. Who was the artist?

It was very still, everybody was preparing tensely for a storm. But the most worried was Shi Gan who knew Qiao's temperament. However, he could say nothing before so many people. All he could do was fix warning eyes on the manager, hoping Qiao would take the hint.

But Qiao did not even glance in his direction. In a calm, unfathomable voice, he asked, "Who painted these? I'd like to see him."

"It's me, manager. I'd like to have your instructions," Du Bing said provocatively, stepping forward.

"You?" Qiao asked doubtfully. "Never thought you had it in you. I'm not going to comment on your works. We all know what they mean. But some day you may be sorry you painted them. Still, you have a real aptitude. You must surely know how to mix colours?"

"Mix colours?" The young man was puzzled.

"Yes. You're with it. You can sing foreign songs, admire western ways, and know a bit about art. Can you tell us what colours foreigners like?" Du Bing was all at sea. Qiao had to explain, "You're a pitiful artist because all your talents are used for venting your spite and for slander. Take colours now.... Foreigners are not very keen on scarlet or bright green. They think them gaudy. Can you think of softer, more attractive colours?"

"Well. . . . Why not try rose-red? Or leaf-green?" Du Bing stuttered.

"What about blue?"

"Peacock blue is best."

"All nice names, aren't they?" Qiao grew jubilant. "Can you mix these colours for us to have a look?"

Du took out his pigments and brush from his locker, painted these three colours on a sheet of white paper, then handed it over to Qiao. Qiao examined the colours, muttering, "Good, we can try these." But all of a sudden he shifted his grave eyes to the young man who, no longer bellicose, awkwardly lowered his head.

"You're not a good turner," Qiao said cordially. "Nor a good mason. You don't even know the cement grades. But you may make a good painter. Try designing trade marks, painting advertisements. You ought to use your talents for a good cause. After a while, take those three colours you just mixed to the assistant chief engineer. If she's no objection, you can paint some dynamos with these colours. From today on, you'll work in Workshop No. 10. Okay?"

Du Bing nodded gratefully, too overwhelmed to speak.

Everybody in the shed sighed with relief.

Shi Gan seized this chance to say loudly, "Comrades, the manager and I have come to hear what grievances and requests you have. Setting up this service team wasn't just the manager's idea. It was carefully discussed and decided by the plant Party committee. We're going to have exams every year, and those who fail or can't man their posts on the production line will have to do service work. The young workers in this team will be sent in groups to technical schools or training centres to train. Those who do well and become skilled will be sent back to the workshops as technicians."

Qiao enlarged on this, saying, "Remember the mess our plant was in last summer? After seven every evening, some of the second shift knocked off to watch TV in the casual labourers' common room. Standing behind the casual labourers to watch, they worried about being spotted by the foreman. A casual labourer got from four to six yuan a day — much more than any of our regular workers. They were far better off and could afford to buy a large TV set for each common room. But the money they earned was the state's money. Our plant was over-staffed, with more than nine thousand workers. Just to watch the four gates we had several dozen men. Still, we hired over a thousand casual labourers. A Japanese told me that if he were running the plant, he would fire half the workers and double the production. I believe him. However, we can't do it his way. Our country has a thousand million people. Instead of firing workers, we have to find them jobs. But we mustn't let them muddle along in the old way, or our whole country including our plant will be ruined. That was why we laid off the casual labourers and formed this service team. Since you took over last year, you've saved one million two hundred thousand yuan. The bonus for the whole team is less than a hundred thousand. We've spent no more than six hundred thousand in building the kindergarten and the living blocks with the bonus thrown in. But still, we've saved six hundred thousand yuan for the state. Now tell me, wouldn't you have done the same if you were a manager?"

This startled Wang Guanxiong, sitting in one corner.

He took off his cap, exposing his shining bald head, and with a frown reflected, "A fixed sum is for a fixed purpose. When you sacked the casual labourers, that money should've been frozen. You've broken the financial rules. . . ."

Qiao continued, "To tell the truth, a plant can't be run the way ours was in the past. For years, the word 'competition' was taboo in our country as if it was something capitalist. We used to wait for the state to assign us work and then made over our products to the state. Any loss or gain was the state's. Workers could slack but they didn't lose their jobs — there was always the state to depend on. Most factories were in bad shape, losing money year in and year out. When there's competition, factories are forced to modernize or they're done for. Now we're competing with foreigners not only at home but also abroad. We're also competing with factories in our own line at home. Of course, this competition is totally different from the cut-throat struggle in capitalist countries. We have to carry out the state's economic plan, and we can't scrap socialist co-operation. It won't do in future for workers to get equal pay regardless of their skill and efficiency. Their wages will vary according to their contribution to the plant. Though we've a lot of people, we haven't many experts or specialists. All workshops and departments need capable people, so those who have special knowledge or skills can recommend themselves."

A telephone rang. It was Xi, who wanted to see the manager on urgent business. Xi also said that he would take the Steel Rolling Plant's special train to fetch two rotor forgings the following day. Qiao promised to go straight over, then turned and looked up. The workers were exchanging eager comments. He glanced at Shi and said finally, "I've been very frank with you. Don't get taken in by rumours. Now I'm going to tell you a fable. Truth and Rumour went together to bathe one day. Rumour, behind Truth's back, stole his clothes. When Truth finished bathing and stepped ashore, he saw no sign of his own clothes but Rumour's dirty ones lay on the ground. Of course he would not touch them. Ever since then, Rumour has worn Truth's beautiful clothes while Truth is naked."

The workers chuckled and, for the first time, the service team applauded their manager.

Whirlpool

Huo Dadao searched everywhere for Tie Jian the whole day, but in vain. If the director of the Electrical Equipment Bureau could not find his immediate superior, the chief of the Municipal Economic Commission, it must be even more difficult for ordinary people to approach him. Huo was a little annoyed because he was a busy man. But what could he do? He phoned Qiao and the two of them decided to catch Tie at home that evening.

After a quick supper, the director and the plant manager hurried to Tie Jian's home. It was a three-room house. As soon as they entered, they were flabbergasted. There in the centre of the room stood a big stove, on which Tie's wife was cooking noodles in a large cauldron. Some men dressed like peasants were helping her, one holding a wire strainer, another a large porcelain bowl. They called her either aunt or sister-in-law. The west room was like a room in a country inn. On the platform bed was a low table with a plate of fried bean-paste on it. Round this, half a dozen young peasants, each holding a bowl, were wolfing down noodles. As Tie's relatives, though rather distant ones, they wanted him to help them to get some material or equipment for their commune-run factories, or some tractors or chemical fertilizer for their production brigades. They were proud that their district had produced such a big shot as Tie Jian. The chief of the Municipal Economic Commission was in charge of the whole town's economy and factories. At a nod from him, there was nothing that could not be done. However, the only peasants who could find him were a few very close relatives whom Tie had to meet and help. But everyone who came to his home would at least get a bowl of hot noodles and, if he could not get a hotel room, could stay there for a couple of days. The country folk stood on no ceremony. Tie Jian earned more than two hundred yuan a month, which to them was a great deal of money — he could easily afford them a few bowls of noodles. But for Tie, this meant quite a big outlay, and he could only offer them noodles and bean-paste because he had too many relatives and fellow villagers.

In the east room there were several city people who had been Tie's subordinates in the Economic Commission or the units directly under it. Some had come to ask for fair treatment both politically and financially after their hard time in the "cultural revolution". Others wanted better jobs or to have their housing problems solved. But they could not find him either and had to wait in vain.

Mrs Tie felt dizzy from overwork. She was too busy

to give Huo and Qiao more than a greeting, though they were here for a different purpose. She was a kind-hearted woman, brought up in the country. In her eyes, all those who came to her husband wanted some favour from him. She sympathized with them, knowing that they had no one else to turn to. Nowadays it was common knowledge that you could only get things done through connections. But at the same time, she disliked those people who obliged her husband to stay away from home. And she, wife of a leading cadre, had to serve as an inn-keeper. As soon as she opened her eyes in the morning, she had to receive callers, who kept her busy serving them all day long.

Noticing that she had not recognized him, Huo stepped forward and said, "Madam Tie, don't you remember me?"

Used to all sorts of flattering words, she replied without even raising her eyes, "No, I don't. My eyesight's so bad these days."

"I'm Huo, Huo Dadao," he had to announce himself.

She sized him up through the steam and, wiping her hands on her apron, came to greet him warmly, "Oh, it's you! I'm too old to see clearly."

Having introduced Qiao to her, Huo said, "We've got to see Tie Jian on urgent business. We've been looking for him the whole day. When will he be back?"

"He won't come home today. He's back once or twice a month. This home's like a railway station and he's a train. He pulls up for a moment, then off he goes again. There's no stopping him." She had raised her voice as if for those in other rooms to hear too.

Huo had to leave. But Tie's wife followed them out. She beckoned them to turn left and entered a quiet, pleasant-looking room furnished in a modern style. Several smartly dressed girls were cracking melon seeds and listening to a foreign song played on a cassette recorder. They looked annoyed by this intrusion, and Tie's daughter, Tie Hua, glowered at her mother. But seeing Huo behind her, she had to stand up to greet him. Before her daughter, Tie's wife, usually a commanding character, was like an old wet-nurse. In a low voice she said, "They've got to see your father. Will you please take them to him?"

"Oh, Uncle Huo, is it so difficult even for you to see him?" Her lips curved in a smile. "There's a foreign film being shown to a limited audience tonight in the municipality's small hall. My father must be there. I'll take you to find him."

Huo and Qiao looked at each other, but said nothing.

The daughter's friends said good-bye and left. Tie Hua's mother put a pot of fried chilli paste and some stewed chops into a basket and asked her daughter to take it to her husband. The canteen where Tie had his meals was not very good, and she sent him better food from time to time.

2

Having shown Huo and Qiao into the small hall of the municipal building, Tie Hua pointed to a lounge. "Would you like to see him right now or a while later?" she asked. "All the big shots are in there, and Ji Shen too."

"Ji Shen?" Qiao said, surprised. "Does he rate such treatment?"

"You're as honest as you look." The girl chuckled. "He has remarkable ability, just like the Monkey King."

"Oh no, he hasn't," Qiao corrected her.

"He's Secretary Wang's favourite anyway."

"Come off it," Huo said sharply. "You're still too young to know about such things."

"Don't think only you officials know what's behind the scenes," the girl retorted shrewdly. "I probably know more than you. If you ask me, I'd advise you to go to the lounge when the film has just started. By then everybody will be gone except him."

"Isn't your father going to watch it?" Qiao was puzzled.

"Only after the light is off and the film has started."

"Why?"

"For fear people might spot him and pester him with some difficult problems."

"Who would come here to catch him?"

"What're you doing here then?" Tie Hua winked. "As soon as the light's off, go in there and intercept him." This said, she handed the basket to Huo and left.

Sure enough, by doing as they were told the two of them caught Tie Jian. The chief of the Economic Commission smiled wryly, disappointed that once again he would miss the film. But he was a man of great patience. No matter how put out, he would never reveal it.

Qiao riveted his eyes on this man.

A little over sixty, he was tall and grey-haired. His polite smile showed his dignity and self-control. The deep lines on his forehead and round his eyes seemed to be the evidence of experience and wisdom acquired through arduous struggles and hardships in the old days.

Under his grey, bushy eyebrows, his piercing eyes made people feel like keeping at a distance. He appeared to be questioning everything, as if warning himself to be on his guard. He knew immediately what they were there for, but he waited, silently.

"Comrade Tie Jian," Qiao blurted out, "why let the Foreign Trade Bureau take over the sales right of the products exported from our plant?"

"It's not finalized," said Tie, shaking his head.

"Why has Tong Zhen been transferred?"

"It's the municipal Party committee's decision. But she'll only be away temporarily."

"So Secretary Wang has really accepted Ji Shen's suggestion," Qiao persisted. "But does he know this is like sabotaging our plant?"

There was suddenly a trace of worry and distress in Tie's eyes. "Don't get carried away by your feelings, comrade," he said. "We must have the whole situation in mind. Ask someone to take over Tong's work and let her report to her new office as quickly as possible."

"What if the plant Party committee objects?"

"Are you talking about the committee of the Communist Party? How can a plant committee disobey the municipal committee?"

"What if she refuses to leave?"

"That's exactly what some people are waiting for. They would accuse you of running 'a family shop'. To be frank, there're people who hope you'll raise a hullabaloo and Tong will refuse to be transferred, because then they will make use of it to crush you."

Qiao drew a deep breath, rose to his feet and said to Huo, "I'm off now." He opened the door and left.

Tie gazed blankly after him while Huo's eyes remained fixed, challengingly, on his chief. "When they move one step forward," Huo complained, "you withdraw a step. When they have a request, you try to whittle it down but do what they want in the end. You're retreating bit by bit, making things impossible for us under you."

Huo had been Tie's subordinate for a long time, but still what he said hurt. Tie lost his temper. "What can I do? I'm like an eldest son's wife in a big feudal family. I'm in the middle, catching crap from all sides, from parents-in-law down to brothers and sisters-in-law. I try to iron out disagreements, but everyone complains to me. My own men are dissatisfied with me, and so are my opponents. I live as an ascetic, yet they're calling me all sorts of names. People pester me with their problems. What power do I have? If I spent all my energy on the Economic Commission, I might get something done. But what is my time taken up with?" He began to count his titles sardonically, "I'm in charge of sports, the environment, family planning and flood control. But my job is industry. What have I got to do with ball games or the birth rate? You may think it's a sign of trust. I don't! Do you suppose I don't know that behind my back people call me 'the arbiter'?"

Huo felt a sudden compassion for this veteran. Tie looked calm and aloof, but in fact he was under a terrible strain, as if walking on a tight-rope. However, Huo remembered what he had come for. He must not be soft-hearted or he would have to return empty-handed. So he said, "Do you know what Ji Shen has done since joining the Foreign Trade Bureau?"

Tie was silent.

"He's like a country moneybags shopping in Shanghai

in the old days. He wants everything he sees, the more expensive the better. As a result, he's taken in and imports a lot of junk. He simply squanders foreign currency. Why doesn't the Economic Commission look into the matter?"

Tie said coldly, "Why is Ji Shen so unscrupulous? Because he holds two trump cards. One, he protected Secretary Wang of the municipal Party committee in the 'cultural revolution'; so Wang out of gratitude always supports him. Two, quite a number of cadres are hankering after foreign consumer goods. Ji Shen's an experienced hand in taking advantage of the situation. He even says publicly, 'Opposition to imports means opposition to China's modernization. It shows that ultra-Leftist ideas are still making trouble.'"

"Are you scared?" Huo asked. "The higher a man's position, the more cowardly he becomes. I've written a detailed report about the problems concerning foreign trade in our town. You know me pretty well. If I don't see things set right, I'll fight it out. If the municipality can't solve these problems, I'll take the case to the central government."

"Take it easy, Huo." Tie preferred procrastination to making a hasty decision. He would not burn his boats, nor would he allow others to do this.

But Huo would not let things slide. He insisted, "Ji Shen's transfer to the Foreign Trade Bureau last year was not in conformity to the usual procedure. Since he belongs to the Electrical Machinery Plant, he must go back there."

Tie began to waver. He did not approve of that transfer himself. What was more, Ji would not be satisfied with just being in charge of foreign trade. He might al-

ready have an envious eye on Tie's post. Why not take
this chance to send him back to the plant? Tie was fond
of men like Qiao Guangpu, but Qiao's way of doing
things sometimes worried him. Ji Shen might hold him
in check. He weighed up the pros and cons from both
the public and his private angle. And finally he consented. Smiling, he said cheerfully, "Huo, don't press
me. I need time. Some foreigners laugh at us for our
slow tempo. Well, that's how it is. There're a lot of
things out of our reach. There's nothing perfect in the
world anyway."

They exchanged views on certain other issues, and
Huo got what he wanted. Yet he left with a heavy
heart. He had known Tie Jian for some twenty years,
yet quite often the man struck him as a total stranger.
One minute he seemed so close, and the next so distant.
He was hard to fathom. Thinking of Tie's nickname
"the arbiter", Huo could not help feeling worried.

3

It is said that true love comes only once in a lifetime.
There may be some truth in this. Though over forty,
Tong Zhen loved Qiao as tenderly yet ardently as a girl.
Qiao's feeling for her was less passionate.

In the evenings at home, Tong liked to chat. But
Qiao, who went to the plant early in the morning and
never had a siesta, used to come home exhausted. He
might talk a bit about work. When his wife began to
chat, he would nod off.

They saw eye to eye in work but their interests in life
were different. Tong realized that but not Qiao. He

was very happy with her. When he was late home and missed the English lesson on the radio, his wife would coach him, and he appreciated this immensely.

It was already eleven that night when Qiao got home. Tong saw at a glance that something was wrong. "What's up?" she asked.

"It's been decided that you're to transfer to the Economic Commission tomorrow." Qiao tried to speak calmly, to cover his frustration.

"Are you sure?" She had never dreamed that she of all people would be transferred at a time when the plant badly needed technical know-how. "Who'll take over my job then?"

"Who?" Qiao repeated sulkily. "No one for the time being. You keep the title of assistant chief engineer. Later maybe you can come back."

Tong forced a smile and said, "You're really too honest, too naive."

Qiao sighed and answered with a note of regret, "I shouldn't have rushed things by announcing our marriage. I meant to bind you, me and the plant together, to get you to take a fresh interest in your work. I'd no idea that we'd be accused of 'running a family shop'. Now we're paying for my rashness, and so is the plant."

Surprised and angry, Tong said, her lips quivering, "All right then. It's not too late now for us to split up. I'll go to the Economic Commission tomorrow."

Qiao looked up in astonishment and saw that her face was deathly pale. Aware, for the first time, of how blind he was to a woman's sensibilities, with a wave of his big hand he sighed.

Tong fought back her tears. What could she do? That was what her husband was like. She had forgiven him umpteen times. Today, again, she forgave him, knowing how hurt he felt.

4

On the following day, Tie Jian called Ji Shen to his office.

Meetings, talks seemed to make up Tie's life. Drained of enthusiasm he had assumed a mask of cold reserve.

He was very reluctant to see Ji Shen, yet he had to talk affably to him. "The production in the Electrical Machinery Plant is rocketing. There's too much work for Qiao and Shi to cope with, and they need your help. After all, you're the assistant manager."

"Oh?" Ji was taken aback. This was the last thing he had expected Tie to say. His lean, lined face flushed scarlet. After a moment's hesitation, he asked, "What about the work in the Foreign Trade Bureau?"

"You can keep the post there if you want," he continued. "But if you're too busy, let your director and the other deputy directors see to things there." What Tie meant was: he must work full-time in the plant.

Ji understood this. He could also see that Tie was not dismissing him entirely from the Foreign Trade Bureau. It was not that he hadn't the power; he hadn't the guts. He stood up and said, "Fine. There are still one or two problems in the bureau which I can't hand over to others. I'll go to the plant tomorrow. For the time being, I'll work at both places."

How could he let go the post in the Foreign Trade

Bureau? He had no special interest in foreign trade, it was power that tempted him. Banqueting with foreigners, in front of cameras ... this had gone to his head like strong liquor.

As soon as he got home, Ji phoned Wang Guanxiong to ask how things were in the plant. Initially, Tie Jian's talk with him had been a disappointment. But on second thoughts, it pleased him. Nothing else exported through the Foreign Trade Bureau sold so well as the Electrical Machinery Plant's dynamos. If he could take over the sales right, apart from the fringe benefits to the bureau, he could make use of the demand for them to lay his hands on plenty of foreign goods. But Qiao had refused to let the sales right go, in spite of Ji's manoeuvres in the bureau. Now that he was to go back as assistant plant manager, he would be in a better position to realize his goal. But Qiao was a tough customer. If he failed to get the upper hand of him, he would not be able to control the plant.

Wang Guanxiong went straight to Ji's home after his shift. Ji, cordial in the extreme, treated him to dinner and soon steered the conversation to what he wanted to know. Overwhelmed by this favour, after a few cups of wine Wang began to list his complaints against Manager Qiao. When he described how Qiao had laid off the casual labourers and set up a service team and how Li Gan had misappropriated funds, Ji's eyes sparkled. "Is this true?" he asked with a show of indifference.

"Every word."

"Good. You'd better write a report." Ji handed him a pen and some paper.

"What for?" Wang was puzzled.

"I must report this to the municipal Party committee. I can't trust my memory."

Wang's suspicion was dispelled. When Ji had this report, he cheerfully saw Wang off.

5

A few days passed. Xi Wangbei was due back with two large forgings. Qiao went to the loading dock to meet him. There a crowd had already gathered, eager to have a look at this special train.

Before long, a train chugged slowly into the plant. Qiao smiled wryly at sight of this unique train with dining-car, pantry and hard-sleeper coaches in front, and the parts of a heavy rolling mill on the middle and rear sections.

The Steel Rolling Plant in this town had ordered a heavy rolling mill from a machinery works elsewhere. The rolling mill weighed several thousand tons. When assembled, it would look like an iron hill. All the parts of the machine had been completed a year before and the Steel Rolling Plant had been keen to set it up and get it into production. The problem had been the transportation. Small bridges on the long way had needed reinforcing, the stations it had passed had been consulted. It had been almost as difficult as the Long March!

That spring, Xi had happened to order two large forgings of generator rotors from the same machinery works. Again there had been the problem of transportation. Hearing that the Steel Rolling Plant had the same problem, Xi went to its manager, a Comrade Lin. He offered to make the arrangements and rent a freight train plus a few coaches, provided the plant covered all the expenses. Since the cost was high the manager was reluctant. Xi argued that if the rolling mill started production a month earlier, the plant would get all the money back. Otherwise, he might not get it for another two years. If the parts were not well packed, they would rust in the rain. And the plant would have to lump it!

Manager Lin was convinced. He entrusted the whole thing to Xi, who agreed on two conditions: "First, give our two forgings a lift and we'll pay for their transportation. Secondly, wherever the train stops, I'll see to the liaison work, but not accept any hospitality because I've cooked up the idea. If I start living it up there's bound to be talk."

When Xi talked it over with Qiao and Shi, Qiao kept shaking his head. But since it was an agreement between the Steel Rolling Plant and the machinery works, and all Xi had asked for was a lift, he let it pass. Sure enough, the plan was carried out without a hitch. The parts of the mill and the two forgings were now arriving.

Xi jumped off a coach, looking haggard and travel-stained.

The workers unloaded the rotor forgings, which Qiao sent right away to the Experimental Workshop.

Just then, Gu Chang, the head of the manager's office, cycled over at top speed and handed Qiao a newspaper. Qiao looked at him in surprise, then opened the paper. On the first page he saw a letter from Wang Guanxiong accusing Li Gan, their general accountant, of malpractices. It was based on the material Wang had written for Ji Shen. Ji had added some finishing touches and sent it to Secretary Wang, who had given the go-ahead for publication. Qiao skimmed through it. Sneering, he suppressed his anger and threw the paper to Xi. As Xi read it he frowned.

"Ji Shen's back," Gu said. "He wants to hold a plant Party committee meeting right away. And Old Shi wants to see you."

Xi was shocked to hear this.

On his way back to the office block, Qiao noticed that many workers had hold of newspapers and were discussing the letter. On seeing him, they broke off to eye him in a speculative way. He slowed down deliberately, hs face glowing, looking resolute. He went from shop to shop till he came to the service team's shed, inside which he could hear a great commotion.

"Baldy Wang, what a bloody hypocrite you are! You fight for each cent of your bonus, yet you write to the paper attacking the plant."

"Hit the jackpot, eh? Fame and money, you've got them both. How much did the paper pay you?"

Wang was blustering. If he couldn't clear himself, he had to brazen it out.

Qiao opened the door and spotted Du Bing among the crowd bawling at Wang. On his blue overalls were blotches of red and green paint. All the drawings on the wall had gone.

The workers thronged round the manager, all talking at the same time. Some voiced their support for Li Gan, others criticized the newspaper.

Deeply moved, Qiao gripped the shoulder of a

youngster next to him. Never before had he felt so close to the workers. What a fine lot they were! He had come down on them hard, had criticized them. But now that he was in trouble they sided with him. He felt somewhat ashamed of himself.

6

When Qiao reached Party committee's office, most of the seats around the long table were already occupied. He threw a glance at Ji Shen who was chatting away with a smug look on his face.

When all members of this committee had arrived, Shi Gan announced coldly, "We're holding this emergency meeting at the request of Comrade Ji Shen. Ji, will you speak first?"

Ji opened an elegant imported notebook and drawled, "Last night, Secretary Wang sent for me. He told me to look into Li Gan's case. The whole town is talking about it. Li Gan, will you tell us all about it?"

Li, quite unruffled, opened a folder and said, "From the start of the "cultural revolution", our plant employed a thousand casual labourers every year, and their wages came to one million two hundred thousand yuan. When Manager Qiao took over, we laid them off. In the last year and a half, we've saved one million eight hundred thousand yuan. According to regulations, the money allocated for their wages shouldn't be put to any other use. But I spent a hundred thousand on bonuses for the service team, and five hundred thousand on the kindergarten and housing. I did this on the fourth of August last year, and on the same day I wrote a self-criticism. Here it is." He handed it to Shi Gan.

Xi and some others could not help chuckling.

Hu, the woman head of the organization department, asked sharply, "Since you knew the regulations why did you still do that?"

"Why not? I put the money to better use."

"But didn't you consider the consequences?"

"Dismissal from my post?"

Ji Shen broke in, "You didn't have the nerve to do that on your own, did you?"

Li grinned. "Want me to say that it was the manager who put me up to it? Sorry to disappoint you. I guessed this would happen, so I acted on my own, from the very beginning. You can check the accounts and records. All bear my signature. Qiao's neither my relative, nor my old friend. Why should I protect him? I say, this plant can do without Li Gan, but not without Qiao. The head of the financial department is not so important. If Qiao's ousted, the plant will suffer. It's up to the committee to decide. I've sorted out all my records and I'm ready to hand them over at any time."

"A hero, eh?" Ji said, tongue in cheek. "There's nothing more to discuss. We'll have to take disciplinary action."

The committee members contested this. Most of them were against punishing the accountant.

"Comrade Ji Shen," Xi asked, "are you here as a committee member or the envoy of Secretary Wang? You talk as if you were sent by the municipal Party committee. Does this mean that the municipal Party committee has no faith in this plant Party committee? Otherwise, why didn't Secretary Wang ask Comrade Shi Gan, as he should've done, instead of telling you to look into the case? So what's the point of our discussing it? You make the decision."

This put Ji Shen on the spot.

But Hu of the organization department, who welcomed Ji's return, snapped indignantly, "Special cases should be treated in a special way. When there's a scandal like this, of course the municipal Party secretary should send someone to look into it. Li Gan's isn't an isolated case. The plant committee is partly responsible. Our committee's too weak. In our plant, what the management says counts, not what the Party committee says."

"Well said!" Ji elaborated this point. "Shi Gan's a very good comrade. But we all know he's only a figure-head. All our Party branches' secretaries are here. I doubt if the superintendents of workshops listen to you. What is our policy in running a factory? Do we want one-man leadership or leadership by the Party committee? Who is the head of this plant, the Party secretary or the manager? Is the Party the soul of the enterprise or is profit? Li Gan's mistake was no accident. We must change the policy in running the plant."

As soon as he finished, Qiao said, "Since it's me you're gunning for, why pick Li Gan as a scapegoat? If you want to discipline someone, discipline me."

Now Shi Gan, hitherto silent, stood up, his eyes sweeping the room. His stern look induced absolute quiet.

Though he could not speak clearly, his words carried weight. "Li Gan should not be penalized," he began slowly. "Let's first look at the way we're running the plant, the policy that Ji Shen was talking about. Is it right or wrong? If wrong, it's Qiao and I who should be penalized. Li just carries out our directives. If basically right, the work of the Party committee over the past year shouldn't be repudiated. If it was wrong to re-allocate those funds, that can be criticized. As for the leadership of the plant, I hold that we have adhered to the system according to which the manager assumes responsibility under the Party committee's leadership. This can't be regarded as 'one-man leadership'. By the way, Comrade Ji Shen, are you officially back?"

"So it seems. But I'm still a deputy-director of the Foreign Trade Bureau."

This answer infuriated Qiao. But he controlled himself and said cuttingly, "An assistant plant manager under the Electrical Equipment Bureau is at the same time a deputy-director of the Foreign Trade Bureau. Incredible! But, Ji, a plant is a plant, you can't come or go as you choose. Either go back to your bureau and leave this plant for good, or come here to work full-time. If you prefer the latter, you're still in charge of construction. Before you make major decisions, please consult me. If you want to ask for leave, go to the Party committee's office."

But Ji Shen would not knuckle under. "I have to do the work assigned me by the municipal Party committee," he said.

They were still at loggerheads when the meeting broke up.

Stalemate

It was after ten o'clock when Qiao got home. Since his wife had left, he found the evenings so boring that he stayed in the plant till late. He was very hungry tonight and had a few bites of bread. He found it tasteless and put it aside, but couldn't be bothered to open a tin or cut himself some sausage. He paced the room irritably, as though something was missing.

With Tong Zhen away, he felt lost. He picked up his *Scientific English Reader*, but couldn't concentrate on it. He threw himself on to the bed, his head aching from lack of sleep, but he could not fall asleep. His drowsy mind was preoccupied with Ji Shen's sinister smile, Hu's recriminations, the threat to dismiss Li Gan, Baldy Wang's letter, the strange "arbiter", Secretary Wang who was such an unknown factor, the fight over sales rights. . . . These fantastic people and events seemed to be intertwined as if to hem him in and crush him. Letting out a bellow, he threw off the quilt and sat up, his hands clamped round his head. He felt fearfully lonely. He jumped to his feet, rushed to the telephone and picked up the last telegram Tong had sent him. Having found her address, he lifted the receiver and asked the operator to put him through to Tong Zhen. He had a strong desire to see her. If he could talk to her, no matter how briefly, he could vent his frustration. It was not difficult to put through a long distance call at night. Presently Tong's voice sounded at the other end. Hearing it, Qiao burst out, "This is Guangpu! I must see you, right now! Come back, will you?"

Tong was taken aback by his vehemence. "What's the matter, Guangpu?" she asked.

"Well...." Qiao realized how stupid he was. "Nothing important really. Just missing you very much."

Tong laughed, her tears brimming over. "Are you all right? Don't sit and doze off when you get home or you'll catch cold. Don't just eat bread for supper. Make yourself a soup. I forgot to tell you all this."

"You don't have to worry. I've no appetite and I can't sleep."

Alarmed by this, Tong said, "Tomorrow's Sunday, isn't it? I've got something to report to Director Huo, so I'll fly back first thing tomorrow. Have a good rest."

"Fine. As I can't sleep, I'll go to the airport now to wait for you."

"Don't be silly! I'm not sure if I can catch the plane. Promise to have a good rest. Do you hear me?"

"All right." Qiao rang off. After a little thought, he phoned the night duty office in the plant. "Is that Liu?" he asked. "Will you tell Assistant Manager Xi, Li Gan and the heads of the design office that the assistant chief engineer will be back tomorrow. If they have any problems, they should get their blueprints and materials ready. Pick important problems. Don't bother her with trifles. She can only stay one night."

2

Early the next morning Qiao cleaned up his flat — the first time he had done this since Tong left. Then he took a string bag and went shopping. He had never been to a food market and had no idea what it was like on Sunday. He was stunned by the long queues. He queued up a couple of times, but then lost patience and left. He wasted half an hour like this without buying anything. Several times he wanted to give up. But there was nothing at home. What could he give his wife to eat when she came back? Would she have to queue up herself? He decided to stick it out. But that made it too late to go to the airport. When he got home with his shopping, Tong was already there.

Qiao eyed her intently.

"What's wrong with you?" she asked.

He gripped her hand and led her to the sofa. "I'm hopping mad. There's so much I want to tell you."

Tong smiled affectionately. "Get on with it then."

"Problems! What you said was right: just a few of us can't remove the obstacles. If I fail to push the rocks away, they're going to crush me to death!"

"But surely the Party will see that they're moved away."

Qiao took his wife in his arms, his cheek against her hair. Tears welled up in his eyes and fell silently on her head. She lifted his face and wiped his eyes, then asked compassionately, "Why are you crying like a little boy?"

"Yes, crazy, isn't it?" He was not embarrassed. "What's dreadful is that our economy is suffering from anemia. Not having enough blood, we can only shed tears."

"You've overworked yourself since I left. So you're run down and depressed."

Qiao said earnestly, "I've realized during your

absence that we two depend on each other not only in work but in spirit. When you were here, I wasn't aware of this. When you were away, I came to know how important you were to me...."

They were interrupted by a shout outside, "Is Tong Zhen in?"

Several section heads of the Electrical Machinery Plant had arrived. Tong's desk would soon be piled with designs and papers requiring her attention.

Qiao rolled up his sleeves and went into the kitchen. He had to cook for his wife today. But what kind of meal could he make? Normally so self-confident, for once he was unsure of himself.

3

Tie Jian, the chief of the Economic Commission, paid a surprise visit to the Electrical Machinery Plant and asked Shi and Qiao to show him round the main workshops. A former director of the Municipal Industrial Department, he was experienced in running industry. Before very long, he noticed that the atmosphere here was quite different from most other plants. The well-swept roads, flanked with trees and flower-beds, were a refreshing sight. And hardly any loafers could be seen — something unusual in Chinese factories.

The first workshop he entered was warm. The men there seemed to be racing against time. The cement floor was spotless, white and green lines indicating the production process. The layout of the shop floor was excellent. Tie was very pleased and, as an old hand, offered one or two tips to Qiao. The way the plant was run was typical of Qiao, he thought. He said to Shi, "Qiao's certainly benefited from his tour abroad. To run a modern plant like this, we need people with vision and knowledge."

Tie Jian's visit caused a stir among the workers, who wondered what lay behind it. When he got to the office and took a seat, his enthusiasm vanished. Though he still had a smile on his face, it conveyed a vague disappointment. It seemed he was going to raise some serious issue.

Tie started off sternly, "Li Gan's made a mess of it! And by not keeping cool yourselves you've given other people a handle against you. Wang Guanxiong's accusation isn't the only one; some of your committee members are grumbling too. Secretary Wang's very angry. Right or wrong, rules are rules, and since Li Gan has broken them he can't get off scot-free. Comrade Shi, you have only two choices: Punish Li Gan, or punish both Li and Qiao — in which case you'll be involved too. It's up to you."

"Well. . . ." Shi did not know what to say.

"Go on. Take action against Li Gan and report it right away to the higher-ups."

"Nothing doing!" Qiao protested vehemently. "How serious is Li Gan's mistake after all? Tong Zhen's already been transferred. If Li's dismissed, you'll have taken my two best people. Then how can I run this plant?"

Tie's lips trembled, his hackles were up. In the municipal committee, he had spoken up for them, defended them, but instead of appreciating this they were turning a deaf ear to his advice. He retorted, "It seems

I have to wash my hands of the Electrical Machinery Plant." With that he strode out of the office.

Shi Gan hurried after him and caught up with him on the landing. He wanted to persuade him to change his mind. But Tie brushed him aside. "Comrade Shi," he said, "the injury to your tongue seems to have healed, but a damaged reputation doesn't heal so easily. Now you've once more aroused public opinion against you. As a Party secretary, you've failed in your duty. You haven't held Qiao in check."

Shi Gan watched his receding back, speechless. Tie eased himself into his car which turned and sped out of the gate. Shi wondered, "How could a good Party worker become such an 'arbiter'? He poses as impartial, but in fact he supports wrong trends and opens fire on revolutionary forces. That's no way for our Party's leading comrades to behave!"

4

Qiao returned to his office thoroughly depressed. He had recently been very busy and grumpy. The Foreign Trade Bureau had held up the export of his dynamos on the pretext that they had too much work to handle. As the plant was still paying taxes and fines, this meant its capital turnover was affected. Telegrams kept pouring in from foreign customers demanding delivery of the goods they had ordered. Qiao was pretty sure that this was another of Ji Shen's dirty tricks, to force him to give up the sales right. But Ji, when questioned, fobbed him off by saying that he could do nothing about it since he had left the bureau. Qiao discussed it with Xi, but they could find no solution. Driven to desperation, he made up his mind to see Secretary Wang.

The door opened to admit Shi Gan, Li Gan and several others of the production department. Li handed him a few telegrams. Qiao looked them over and flew into a rage. Some big foreign firms were cancelling their contracts because the goods were not delivered on time. Others claimed indemnity for the long delay. The sum totalled three million yuan!

"Damn it!" Qiao flared up. "Attack from both inside and outside." He threw the telegrams on the desk and started out. But Shi barred his way to ask, "Where are you going?"

"The municipal Party committee. If I can't win this case, I'll resign. Make Ji Shen the manager. They can do whatever they like."

"How shall we answer these?" Li Gan asked, pointing to the telegrams.

"If they want to back out, let them. If our goods are delayed, they have the right to fine us. We're the ones who've broken the contracts and lost credit! Where's Xi?"

"He's directing the test of rotors in the Experimental Workshop," Li replied. "After that, he'll have to go to the warehouse which is packed with dynamos — can't hold any more. With the end of the year coming, a lot more will be turned out. Where are we to put them? He's got to tackle the problem."

Qiao turned to Shi and said, "Tell him to take charge of the production of the whole plant. If our problems can't be solved in the municipality, I'll go to Beijing."

Li reminded him, "Our sales group in Hongkong wants to know whether or not to accept new orders."

"No! The Foreign Trade Bureau is on our necks now. If we accept more orders, we'll break our contracts again and be fined more money." Having said that, Qiao turned to leave.

"Just a minute!" Shi stopped him, and after a moment's thought said, "No matter who's responsible for the delay, we Chinese are to blame. We mustn't let feeling interfere with our judgement, or lose our temper with our customers."

"Yes! Right!" Li supported him.

Shi told Li Gan, "Reply to our customers in good faith. We'll pay for their losses according to our contracts. Explain to those who want to cancel their contracts that, first, we admit our fault, secondly, we hope they'll wait and we'll dispatch the products as soon as we can. Accept new orders in Hongkong and sign contracts immediately. We can't turn away prospective customers. Qiao, what do you think?"

Qiao looked at the Party secretary for a moment, then signalled abruptly to Li Gan. "Do as Shi says."

Li and the others left in high spirits.

Shi fixed his sharp eyes on Qiao, looking very serious. "Qiao," he said, "what's the matter with you these days? You lose your temper far too easily. What do you mean by resigning? Forgotten your resolution? Forgotten what you said when you hauled me back here? The truth is, I'm raring to go now. The boat is in mid-stream, but you want to throw away the pole! You're not yourself! You ought to have been prepared for all this. The climax is yet to come."

Lowering his eyes, Qiao muttered his agreement.

"You stick to your work here," Shi went on more mildly. "Leave the other business to me. First I'll go to the municipal Party committee. If nothing comes of that, I'll round up Director Huo and go to Vice-minister Che of the Ministry of Machine Building. If necessary, we may ask him to take the case to the State Council. If all this should fail, we can give up the sales right, but our dynamos mustn't be delayed any more. Anyway, all money earned goes to the state."

Before Qiao could speak, there was a sudden hub-bub of voices outside the window. The noise came nearer and nearer, approaching the door.

As soon as Shi and Qiao stepped outside, they were surrounded by a crowd of people all talking at once. Some even gripped Qiao's sleeve. It was impossible to hear what they were saying.

Ma Changyou, the old fitter just returned from the technical team's tour, waved vigorously to quieten the others down. "Stop making such a row! Now listen to me! Manager Qiao belongs to the Electrical Machinery Plant, to its nine thousand workers and staff members. We workers support him. No one can dismiss him at random. We need him! We trust him!"

"Hear! Hear!" the others exclaimed. "We need him! We trust him!"

The old man continued, "Let's send two representatives to the municipal Party committee. Tell them what the workers think of Qiao."

"Fine! Ma counts for one...." There was another roar of approval.

Shi called for silence. In a calm voice, he said, "Who says Qiao's been dismissed? Don't you believe it! I give you my word as Party secretary. If Qiao were to be dismissed, I'd have to be punished first. I've done less work than he has but made more mistakes."

The workers looked at their leader and were silent.

A sudden sting in his eyes, Shi shook his head and cried, "If you trust me, I'll be your representative. I'll convey your support for Manager Qiao to the municipal Party committee."

"Hear! Hear!"

Qiao did not speak. Fighting back tears, he gripped Shi's hands, then headed for a workshop.

Pages from a Factory
Secretary's Diary

March 4, 1979

I went to the factory an hour earlier than usual today because I wanted to say goodbye to Manager Wang, who was leaving for good. I reckoned that a man like him wouldn't kick up a fuss about it but would go quietly before the workers arrived.

Wang himself had asked for the transfer, but in fact, I'm pretty sure he felt unable to continue working in this factory. He was simply squeezed out by Assistant Manager Luo Ming. It was an open secret, yet people kept mum, especially in front of Wang. No one would rub it in. It was really awful.

As a factory secretary for four years, I've seen off two managers. Now Wang is the third.

When something is wrong with the management in a factory, a transfer is the most convenient remedy. That's probably true everywhere. Each time I say goodbye to a manager, I examine myself. It takes me a week to get over it.

I decided to use my power for the first time to order our only jeep to take Wang to his new place.

But a janitor told me that he had left half an hour before!

"All on his own?" I asked.

"Party Secretary Liu carried his luggage for him."

"But where's our jeep?"

"Luo had it out on business last night."

I was very upset. I'd hoped to get to the factory to give Wang a hand. But obviously the man behind all this dirty business had pipped me at the post.

I had a sudden feeling of resentment against Liu, the number one in our factory. What a weakling! Shandong, his home province, has been famous for its heroes since ancient days. Where were his guts? Numbers one and two squeezing into a bus with all that luggage!

As I was musing, the jeep sped in in a cloud of dust. Luo got out, beaming.

"Hello, Wei!" he said in a mocking tone. "Why so early? Seeing Wang off? Has he left?"

"Yes."

I'm laconic, especially when I'm in a bad mood. The least said, the soonest mended! A secretary must watch his tongue. A blunder can bring a lot of trouble.

Luo fumbled in his pocket and fished out a few fire-crackers. Passing them to me, he said, "Have some fun!"

Refusing to take them, I replied, "I don't dare light them."

He snorted, "You're no man!"

"You often carry them in your pockets?"

"Left-overs from the Spring Festival. I'll set them all off and clear the air!"

Crack! He lit one and guffawed.

A cold shiver went down my spine. Wang was lucky

to have left already. How would he have felt about this?

Manager — a post which is so enticing to certain people! In an attempt to remove the word "assistant" in his title, Luo had pushed out three men. But twice new managers had been appointed. Will another come or will Luo be promoted? If the latter, I'll have to consider leaving too, quitting the manager's office and going back to the production department to work on statistics again.

March 11

"Wei, have you heard that Luo's been promoted to manager?" Quite a number of workers tried to sound me out.

"No, I haven't." My answer was the same.

Then someone would probe, "Oh, come off it! Surely you've heard it."

Poor fellows! Having no say whatever in the factory, yet wanting to know everything. Pointless curiosity! No matter who's the manager, you'll have to work all the same. It's none of your business!

"Manager Luo, you're wanted on the phone!" People have begun to address him like this these days. Even some workshop reports start with "Manager Luo". "Assistant" has been omitted. Those cunning cadres, who have already trimmed their sails to suit the wind, are more pitiful than the workers.

"Wei, don't you smell a rat? Luo works hard these days. He's got a finger in every pie. He's all over the place. Always with a smile on his face. Even his voice is louder."

"No, I don't." You're here to work, I thought, not to watch others' expressions. Perhaps it's my professional weakness, my nerves have gone dull or numb. I've got used to all kinds of speeches and facial expressions. I take nothing to heart.

Since I know there are some who watch my expressions and weigh my words carefully, when I have to address Luo, I always take the trouble to say his full title — "Assistant Manager Luo".

When certain documents require a manager's perusal, I give them to Liu, the Party branch secretary, according to the rules. I then pass them on to whomever he tells me. I don't intend to flatter Luo. He's probably sensed it. However, since I haven't been officially informed about his promotion, he can't do anything about it.

I don't care whether or not he's going to be the manager. That's none of my business. If the higher-ups ask my opinion, I'll object. He's been in this factory for ages, knows everything about it and he has quite a following, yet he'll never be a good manager. What he cares about is power, not responsibility. He lacks the necessary qualities and abilities of a good manager.

March 12

It's strange. Luo's daughter, Luo Jingyu, came to my office and chatted for some time.

She's been job-hunting since she came back from the

countryside two years ago. The trouble is, she's too choosy. She won't work in a collective-owned factory, nor in a job she doesn't like and she refuses to go somewhere a bit far from home. As she rarely comes to our factory, I couldn't work out at first what she was up to, yacking away in the office. Then she mentioned the question of her job at last and said, "I want to work here."

"You must be kidding!" I said doubtfully. "Though we're state-owned, we're small, only two hundred people. Nothing to write home about. Besides, there's no job you'd fancy here."

"It's difficult to get a good job, and I've been waiting for two years." She told the truth. "I'm already twenty-six. I can't afford to wait any more. A chemical factory has its advantages. The production costs are low, but the profit's great. So your bonuses are high."

"That's quite true. Have a word with your father then."

"He would find it embarrassing to help me. Wei, will you do me a favour?"

Here was an opportunity for a man who wanted to butter up his superior and climb up the social ladder. If it was inconvenient for a manager to do something, then it was up to his secretary to help him out. He should run errands and do the job in all kinds of names if necessary to achieve his superior's aims.

When I had failed to resist the Party branch committee's decision to appoint me as the factory secretary, I made a rule for myself that there would be nothing personal between my superiors and me. No matter who he was, our relationship was strictly business! Public affairs should be conducted in an orthodox way. Personal considerations shouldn't intrude.

"Wait till I ask the Party branch committee," I replied.

She was totally unprepared for such an answer. She thought that, as she was the daughter of the manager and I was her father's secretary, I should naturally serve her too. She was very cross and, after a snigger which was just like her father's, left with a slam of the door.

March 15

"Our new manager will come soon," Secretary Liu told me jovially in a low voice.

This down-to-earth man was as innocent as a lamb. He had received three managers in the same jovial mood and sulkily seen them off, carrying their bags. Today he was again in high spirits.

I was neither very happy nor disappointed. I was simply bored.

March 18

The telephone in the office kept ringing. I heard it from quite far away. People mock those who enter the factory gate just as the bell is ringing. But I enter the office five days out of six just as the phone is ringing.

Calls at this time are usually for managers. It is the right time to catch them. Half an hour later and they're nowhere to be found. Even I have no idea of their whereabouts, let alone what they are busy with.

Brr. . . .

As a secretary, I was used to it. No matter how urgent it sounds, I am never in a hurry. I opened the door, hung up my bag, had a bite of my bun and finally picked up the receiver.

"Hello! Is that Secretary Wei? Would you do me a favour, Wei? My father died yesterday and he's to be cremated today. Could you have a word with the manager and say that I want to borrow a car? Do help me out, please!"

Startled, I inquired, "Who is it?"

"This is Pang. Pang Wancheng. Sorry to trouble you."

"Why didn't you let me know earlier?" I complained.

"How could I know he would die so soon?"

I was hard put to it. "You know that we've only one jeep and one lorry. But they went to fetch raw materials from the countryside yesterday. They won't be back for a day or two. What can I do?"

Pang was a very simple, honest crane-operator and he would never ask the factory for help if he wasn't desperate. Despite what I told him, he stubbornly continued pleading, "Wei, I'm in no position to ask Manager Luo for such a favour. But you've been a secretary for years. You know much better than me how to solve the problem. I've no one to turn to. The time for the cremation has been fixed. All our relatives will come soon. What shall I do if I can't get a car?"

In the eyes of the workers, I seem to be a man of power too. They don't realize I'm just the manager's errand-boy and mouthpiece. However, I couldn't explain that to him at that moment. It seemed that I was the only "important person" he knew, his last hope.

While I was still talking, a stout, short fellow suddenly appeared behind me and said smilingly, "Let me speak to him."

Astonished, I asked, "What — what are you doing here?"

This bloke had a charming round face with a pair of big sparkling eyes.

He looked like a salesman from a factory who had come on business. Pointing, I said, "The production department's the third room on the left."

He shook his head and introduced himself, "My name's Jin Fengchi. I'm sent by the Bureau of Chemical Industry to work here."

The new manager! My heart missed a beat.

I cursed myself. A secretary shouldn't be so snobbish. Why did I judge a man by his appearance?

I handed him the phone. When he spoke, his voice became serious and concerned, "Don't worry, Comrade Pang. Tell me, when do you need a car?"

He took a biro from his breast pocket and I gave him a piece of paper. While repeating Pang's words, he scribbled on the paper. "Ten o'clock, fine. Your address? No. 8, Fifth Lane, Jinzhou Street. Good. What's your name again? Pang Wancheng. OK, Wancheng, wait at home and I'll send you a van. Don't be so polite. Anything else I can do for you? My name isn't important. Anyway you can stop worrying now. But don't be too upset. Better take care of yourself. Have a few days off and rest."

He rang off. Taking the receiver in his left hand, he

dialled a number. "Is that the Chemical Machinery Repair Plant? Who's speaking? Du! Guess who's speaking to you? Ha! Ha!... Yes, I'm in my new job. No choice. Very sad to leave you and our factory too. Look, I've a slight problem here. Can I borrow your van? Excellent! Ten o'clock. Tell Young Sun to go to No. 8, Fifth Lane, Jinzhou Street and look for a man named Pang Wancheng. Sorry to trouble you. Phone me whenever you want me."

Having put down the receiver, he turned to ask me, "How many telephones do we have?"

"Ours is a small factory, so there are only three. There's one here, one in the production department and another in the reception office."

Pulling over a stool and sitting down, he produced a cigarette case and handed me a cigarette. Having lit his, he said slowly, "Surely you must be Secretary Wei, a very capable man I hear."

"My name's Wei Jixiang. I'm a square peg in a round hole, not really qualified."

I wanted to impress on him that I had no interest in my present job.

"I'm new here," he said politely. "I need your help."

I quickly waved my hands to show I could do very little.

His face fell. "I'm not being polite," he said seriously. "Cadres learn from the people and a manager from his secretary. It's the secretary who drafts the manager's speech for mass meetings. All a manager does is to read it aloud from the platform. A manager's competence largely depends on his secretary's level. If the secretary's lousy, the manager probably won't be any good either. You read all the documents first and then pass them on to the managers concerned. Besides, you have to attend to the managers' odd jobs. Managers may be the leaders of the factory, but you're their boss."

I was fidgeting, feeling, in turn, comfortable and uneasy. My face was burning. I couldn't figure out whether he was flattering me or being sarcastic. I am considered a man with some education in the factory. But today I was all at sea, unable to tell whether or not he was serious.

It is too early to jump to conclusions, but one thing is certain, he's no fool!

At noon, Pang came straight from the crematorium and asked me to take him to the new manager.

Secretary Liu was showing Jin round the workshops as Pang, a black band round his arm, and I searched everywhere for him. Not knowing what had happened, many people followed us.

On seeing Jin, Pang went over and kowtowed in the traditional way. I was shocked!

Jin was surprised too. He hurriedly helped him up and said, "Comrade Pang, what on earth are you doing?"

Pang was very grateful to him. Too emotional, he stuttered when he spoke, "A th-th-thousand thanks, M-M-Manager Jin. If you hadn't sent the van, goodness knows how long my father's body would have remained at home. He'll be grateful to you too in the netherworld. Thank you very much."

Jin wanted to pat him on the shoulder to comfort him but he was too short. So he gripped Pang's arm instead and said earnestly, "Don't talk like that, Pang. Nowadays those who have influential connections use them. Those who have power use it. But what about the workers who have neither? We can't blame the workers for their resentment, nor can we complain that they are less enthusiastic than before 1958. We can't say that they're selfish and only thinking of themselves. If nobody seems to care about them, they have to look after themselves." I was flabbergasted. He was really bold to talk like that! Though new, he seemed very frank with the workers. He talked in a way as if he were defending them.

What he said touched their hearts. The admiration in their eyes and their whispered comments showed that his words were more effective than an "inaugural address" at a mass meeting.

Liu was delighted to see the workers responding positively to the new manager and said earnestly to Jin, "The workers of this factory are a fine lot, aren't they? They like you."

Jin turned to Pang and continued, "Wancheng, your father's dead now, but don't let it get you down too much. Take a few days off. You must look after yourself too."

He had said that over the phone and now he was repeating himself in public.

Deeply moved, Pang didn't know what to say. Flushing, he replied, "No. I won't have a rest. I'll come back to work today."

Having said that, he began to put on his overalls. He had only taken half of his three days' leave for the funeral.

Liu led the manager to another workshop. As I turned to go to my office, I spotted Luo standing at the back of the crowd. Gazing after the two receding figures of

Liu and Jin, he puffed vigorously on his cigarette. The pale pock-marks on his face became more distinct, an indicator of his feelings. When he was in high spirits, they disappeared. When he was furious, his red face seemed to make the marks whiter.

He went to Pang and said smilingly, "Pang Wancheng, I never thought that a big man like you could be so yellow-bellied! So a van can make you grovel on your knees!"

Unprepared for this, Pang stammered, "Manager Luo, you're. . . ."

Luo is a ruthless man, liable to get nasty any minute. Very often, he would suddenly scold for no obvious reason. I pretended not to have seen them and went to the office.

But he caught me up and walked abreast with me.

"Wei," he spoke up, "our new chief certainly knows how to win friends and influence people!"

I said nothing. I've always avoided rivalry between managers. I'm impartial to all.

But no doubt our little factory will soon have troubles again.

March 23

"The first thing Manager Jin did was to borrow a van from outside for the most honest worker of our factory."

The news soon got round. After much exaggeration, it assumed an air of romance.

How easily people are satisfied and moved!

April 2

Manager Jin and I got into the jeep and went to the company to report on our work. However, neither of us spoke for some time.

But suddenly he asked me a very peculiar question, " 'I may be a dragon here, but I'll be no match for you, a snake in its old haunts.' Do you know which opera that line is from?"

"*Shajiabang*," I said, throwing him a glance.

Another silence. But I understood perfectly what he meant.

It was not until we got out and entered the office block of the company, he ventured again, "We must speak first. At the beginning, people tend to be formal and the big shots would like to listen to others first. So it's an opportunity for a small factory like ours. Besides, at the start of the meeting, leading comrades are attentive and listen carefully. But later their concentration wanes. They'll begin smoking, drinking tea or going to the lavatory. No one will really be listening."

He was sharp. But I was still worried. What had he got to say? He'd been in the factory less than a month!

The company had notified us that there would be a managers' meeting. Liu, thinking Jin was far too new, suggested that Luo attend the meeting. I knew Luo liked to appear on such occasions. But Jin smiled and said, "Better I go." It was very subtle. Was he against letting Luo attend the meeting as a manager or was he eager to seek the limelight himself?

Sure enough, as the meeting was declared open, he spoke first. He was eloquent and his example of Pang only taking half of his three days' leave was vivid and moving. While he commended the worker, he impressed the listeners with his art of leadership.

We were praised at the meeting, unusual for a tiny factory like ours.

I felt more and more that Jin was not as simple as he seemed.

When the second man began his report, Jin whispered to me, "Jot down the good points, Wei, particularly others' experiences and the company directors' instructions. I'm going out for a moment."

He was away for several hours, only reappearing shortly before the meeting ended. Very strange!

April 25

It gets more and more peculiar. The marks on Luo's face are less visible. Has the power struggle come to an end? Luo is not a man to easily knuckle under. Has he thrown in the sponge? Not likely!

When I entered the office at noon after lunch, I saw Jin talking over the phone, Luo beside him, wearing an obsequious look, which was very rare.

". . . Her name's Luo Jingyu, a relative of mine. You must help her however difficult. I'll expect your answer within a week. OK. So it's settled?"

The penny dropped. I have no admiration for Jin's way of doing things, but I have to admit that he certainly has a good head on his shoulders. Luo is a difficult man to co-operate with, but he knows thoroughly our production and has quite a following. If he is under

Jin's thumb, Jin can consider himself really settled in the factory.

But I had never expected that Jin would do such a thing. He certainly knows how to win over a philistine. No wonder people remark behind his back that he is as slick as a snake.

May 10

Jin and I went to a meeting at the bureau. Not long after it had started, he again whispered to me, "Keep notes, Wei. I'll be out for a moment."

Whenever we had meetings either in the company or the bureau, he always played the same trick. What on earth did he go out for? What could keep him that busy?

After a short while I left the meeting too. It was quite warm and many offices had their doors open. As I went up to the second floor, I happened to see Jin wandering from room to room. He seemed to have dropped in to have a chat or a laugh with practically everybody from the department heads to staff members. He had brought with him plenty of good cigarettes and offered them generously to everyone who smoked. But it was not just one-sided, he was given cigarettes too. He was very familiar with the people working there. Drinking and smoking, he was utterly at ease. Sometimes he had business to do, sometimes he came just to chat. A couple of hours were easily killed this way.

Our factory is a tiny unit in the Bureau of Chemical Industry. That a manager of such a factory is on good terms with many people including some cadres higher than himself in the bureau is really something remarkable!

On the way back to our factory after the meeting, I told him, "I hear you've got a lot of friends in the bureau."

"Didn't you realize that this afternoon?" He grinned at me.

I couldn't cover up my embarrassment.

"Wei," he said buoyantly, "we've been together for some time now, and I've come to know that you're a very good comrade. Your handwriting's absolutely beautiful and you write quickly. Day after day, you run your legs off, working harder than any manager. However, I must say, you're a bit of a stick-in-the-mud. Tell you what — in capitalist countries, money counts, but in our country, it's your connections. That's something I've learned through experience. This certainly won't change in the next three to five years. Ours is a small factory and we've no big cadres. That means we've neither power nor position. If you don't have good connections and don't butter people up, you can do nothing."

An amazing theory! I could not decide if he was admirable or despicable.

May 12

Luo was all smiles when he spoke to me in a cheerful voice, "Wei, I've got a job for you. Will you bring Manager Jin to my home for dinner tonight? He probably won't come alone, so I'm roping you in too. Do everything you can to persuade him."

"Toadying to the boss!" I thought. "So humble, just because he's found your daughter a job."

But what else could I expect of someone who had been a pump-keeper, then joined the Party and become an assistant manager by chance? I'd never have dinner in his home! In the past, I always made some excuse. "Just my luck!" I said. "My son's got pneumonia! I'll have to take him to hospital after work today."

His face darkened at once. "I suppose I'm not important enough! Well, don't trouble then. Just send Jin to my home, OK?"

What could I do? I was a factory secretary after all. Gazing after his back, I cursed, "I'll be damned if I'll let my son be a secretary!"

I went to Jin when it was time to knock off. He accepted the invitation bluntly and urged me to accept. I told the same lie again. Narrowing his eyes, he grinned and said, "Don't make it up, Wei. You're no good at lying. Your face gives you away!"

"But it's true, every word!" I defended myself hastily.

"Oh, come off it!" he guffawed. "You don't even bother to change your lies! Always the same story. Your little fib is known all over the factory. People say, 'When Wei doesn't want to go somewhere, he excuses himself by making his wife or children ill.' You're an educated man. Can't you invent some other story?"

I shook my head, smiling wrily.

Patting me on the shoulder, he continued, "You poor innocent! The assistant manager is throwing a dinner for us. That's our good luck, you know. I won't take a sip of any liquor under two yuan a bottle! Come with me. You don't have to say a word, just eat your fill! Isn't it great?"

I didn't go anyway. But I learned that Luo's daughter had started work in a state-owned radio factory today. So that was why Luo threw the dinner. Jin is really quite a character to have tamed a fellow like Luo.

When the Party spirit, discipline and laws don't work for someone, personal feelings and favouritism may have their place.

But I'm unimpressed by Jin's way of doing things. In fact, his simplicity and kindness, which made such an impression on me the first day he arrived, have changed. (*I have omitted my diary entries from June to September.*)

October 9

The complications among the leading comrades reflect those in society and people's thinking.

Now Luo and Jin have ganged up, while there's a growing tension between Jin and Liu. This morning, there was the inevitable show-down over bonuses at the Party branch committee meeting.

A government document circulated in September said that a factory was entitled to bonuses proportionate to its profits. The raw material our factory needs is others' waste material. The capital is small, but the profit remarkable. As a rule, the smaller the number of workers in a factory, the easier the bonus is given. It was calculated at the end of September that each worker could get a fifty-yuan bonus and an office worker more than forty. That meant most of the workers would get double their rate of pay.

Being an honest and straightforward man, Liu was astonished to hear this. Forty yuan a month extra was, of course, something he needed, for his living standard was the lowest among the top leaders of the factory. But he was against it. Shaking his head, he protested, "That won't do! Such a big bonus? Out of the question!"

"What's there to be afraid of?" many workers countered, disappointment showing on their faces. Everybody welcomed having some extra cash. But the members of the Party branch committee sat on the fence, staring at the manager and the Party secretary, waiting for a decision. They wanted the money but were hesitant about bearing the responsibility.

"Speak your mind, Luo," Jin urged the assistant manager.

Luo was very blunt, "Give the bonus to the workers. Act according to the document."

Liu retorted, "The document applies to enterprises in general. But ours is an exception. We can't take advantage of this. We must thoroughly understand the spirit of the document. Besides, the leaders might not approve of it if they knew."

"What would you do with the money?" Luo asked. "Hand it over to the state for nothing?"

"Put it in the bank for the time being. It'll come in handy for the community welfare fund."

Silently Jin smoked. No one knew what he was thinking. He is expert in handling people, always weighing the pros and cons carefully. He would never risk his position for a few dozen yuan for the workers. What if he should offend the company or the bureau? Surely he knew which side to back. He would never lose a lot to save a little. Besides, the Party secretary had already made his attitude clear. He wouldn't oppose Liu.

I thought too that Jin would surely be against the large bonus.

As I'd expected, Jin said, "Liu's right. The sum's a bit on the large side. . . ."

"You —" Luo uttered, his face suddenly red.

Jin wagged his finger at him, as if there had been an agreement between them. I realized all of a sudden that Jin was making use of Luo, a headstrong fellow, to sound out Liu first.

Jin continued, "We're the leaders of the Oriental Chemical Factory. We needn't worry about the state. Our chief concern is the welfare of the workers of this factory. If we offend them, we'll certainly get into trouble. We've read the document to the workers. If we don't issue the bonus according to the document, we'll be breaking our promise and damaging the image of the state. It'll put us in a bad light for sure. Even worse, the workers will be disheartened, and production will drop. So I vote for giving the bonus, every cent of it. If the company inquires into it, we can say we were carrying out the instructions in the document. If other factories raise questions and poke their noses into our affairs, we'll tell them we acted according to the principle of 'more pay for more work'. Our factory's doing well. We've made a good profit for the state. Of course we're entitled to a big bonus. Now what do you think?"

As most of the members agreed with what he'd said, it was decided thus. Liu felt it wrong to give such a big bonus, but he had no convincing argument. Though it was a majority vote, he was still uneasy. He asked Jin to stay behind after the meeting.

Work had already ended, but I didn't go home since I still had some urgent business to attend to. The window above the door leading to Liu's office was open. While writing, I could hear clearly the conversation in Liu's room. I am worried about him. He is too old-fashioned, too inflexible. In the past, he'd been fretting a great deal about the friction between the manager and the assistant manager. Wang had suited him very well, a decent and upright man, honest and frank to both his inferiors and superiors. But he was narrow-minded, and often sulked. He couldn't brazen it out and finally left after less than a year in the job. Jin is shrewd and able and hits it off well with everybody. Even Luo has succumbed and co-operates with him. Liu should be having an easy life. Yet he goes looking for trouble. In the past, he and Wang had failed to contain Luo. How can he now deal with Jin and Luo single-handed?

Liu's voice in the next room became louder and louder. "... To be a leader, one must play fair. It's wrong to pander to one faction or try to please everybody. What's worse is to curry favour by giving away the state's money. Jin, some people have complained to me about you. You ought to watch your step."

It was terrible. How could a Party secretary speak to a manager like that? To ease the tension, I hurriedly sent them the material I'd just written.

Jin was really smart. He listened with patience, no sign of anger on his face. Seeing me, he smiled and remarked, "You've come at the right time, Wei. Let's talk it over together. This Party secretary of ours is really impossible! No wonder the leading body of this factory was so ineffective and always at odds with each other. Instead of helping his subordinates out of difficulties, he needs them to help him out. Now tell me, Liu, how am I not playing fair? You accuse me of currying favour by giving away the state's money, but didn't I do it according to the spirit of the document?"

Liu sighed, waving his hand and replied, "As for money, the more the better. I know the workers won't be very happy if we lessen the bonus. But as leaders, we must think about their long-term interests. We must guide them, educate them. Doesn't the document also say that part of the bonus can be used for the community welfare fund?"

"If you hold back the fifty yuan, you'll enrage the workers. What exactly do you want that money for?"

"For some future use. For instance, we must ensure that we can give a bonus every month, no matter how small. Even if we fail in fulfilling the production quota, we can still give a bonus, just in case. Besides, if we've put aside enough money, we can build a few more houses for the workers."

"Forget it, Liu! Haven't you had enough?" Jin then turned to me, "As a secretary, Wei, you must have learned this lesson. Act promptly while you've power in your hands. The document says you can give the bonus, so give it! If you hesitate now, you can do nothing about the money later if the directive is changed. As for the housing problem, I tell you frankly, it won't be easy to build a dozen houses for a small factory like ours. The construction departments will want a couple of them when the houses are put up. Then there are those in charge of electricity, water, coal and even food stores.... How many rooms will be left for us? You'll spend the money, sweat over it, and then what will you get in return? Troubles, abuse! What benefit will the workers of this factory really get? Better put a lump sum in their hands!"

Though Liu didn't quite agree, he said nothing more, however.

Jin offered us cigarettes, but Liu refused. Instead, he took out his own. Jin wasn't offended, lighting his cigarette calmly. Drawing on it deeply, he continued, "Liu, the way you handle things was OK before 1958, but it won't work now. Take the document. Abide by it, but don't be too strict. There's a lot to learn. For example, how many times have you got yourself in a fix? Those who had been sent to the countryside during the "cultural revolution" were allowed to come back to town and were allocated jobs. But you didn't act quickly enough, and it was soon stopped. You lost the opportunity and everyone was mad at you. Then all those whose wages had been frozen were to be refunded. Those who got in first were lucky. Those who were slow got nothing. There are lots of examples. If you're inflexible, you'll lose every chance."

Jin hoped sincerely that Liu would change a bit. But I think, Liu was disgusted by his theory.

October 10

The bonus was issued, and everybody talked about it. What upset me was that they seemed to know all the gory details about the disagreement the previous day,

even better than my minutes! Liu became the target
of all their gripes, while Jin was worshipped as a hero.

It is unfair to put Liu in such a bad light.

Jin decided to hold a mass meeting to mobilize the
workers at this favourable time. At the meeting, he
made a short yet moving speech. There was no draft,
but he knew what he was talking about.

"All the bonus is given to you, every bit of it. Some
people were shocked at such a big sum. Frankly, if we
work harder, our profit will rise even more, and next
month you'll probably get an even bigger bonus. So
long as I'm in charge of the money, I assure you that
all that you're entitled to will be given to you without
delay, without a cent deducted!"

November 2

It was just my day! From early dawn till mid-after-
noon, I only caught a couple of small carp. On my
way home, I ran into Jin. He'd got a crateful, so I
asked where he had been fishing. Instead of replying,
he smiled. I reckoned that he must have known the
keeper and had fished in his pond. Despite my refusal,
he gave me half his fish. When I passed his home, he
invited me in. It was difficult to refuse. Besides, I
wanted to have a look at his home. A capable man
like him, I guessed, must have a nice flat with fashionable furniture. But to my surprise, it was so simple
that I could hardly believe it was his.

He asked his daughter, who was doing her home-
work, to cook, while he offered me a drink. Glowering

at him, the girl took up her satchel and went into her granny's room.

So he had to turn to his mother. Reluctantly, the old woman went to the kitchen grumbling. I soon learned why from her complaints.

Jin earned seventy yuan a month, but he only contributed a little for the house-keeping. He smoked good cigarettes and drank good alcohol. Every evening after work, he boozed. When he got home, he made do with a snack. So his wife had to keep his mother and the two children on her salary.

He was no boss at home, not like in the factory.

I never realized Jin was such a bloke.

December 31

The bell had long since rung but the cadres still stayed in the factory at the request of Jin, who had phoned from the bank. The bonus for each worker at the end of the year was a hundred yuan. However, the bank refused to pay the money. Jin had gone to the bank taking the document with him. Trying to persuade them to agree, he had stayed there for a whole day, not even returning for lunch, but no one knew why he asked the cadres to wait for him.

He returned at last. Elated, he told the cadres, "Make it snappy, everybody! We must divide the money and give it to the workers today."

Overjoyed, everyone was raring to go. Under the direction of the head of the financial department, they put into each red envelope a hundred yuan.

Liu called Jin to my office and said emotionally, "Jin, we can't do this. It's all wrong to give bonuses at random! It's not stated in the document that the workers should be given a big sum at the end of the year, is it?"

"But it doesn't say we shouldn't either, does it?" Jin was edgy after a hard day.

"Jin, it's a mistake. We're not going to close down after the New Year, are we?"

"Oh you! You're impossible!" he snapped, barely concealing his irritation. "How many times have I told you that we must give all the bonus to the workers? And we must do it today. Or why did I waste my time at the bank? The higher-ups keep changing their minds. Who can predict the new rule next year? If a new document comes freezing bonuses, then we'll be in trouble! The workers will be furious with us."

"Don't worry! I'll answer for it!"

"But it's been decided at the Party branch committee meeting. You can't change it now." Jin pushed open the door and left. This was the first time I had seen him in a rage.

January 3, 1980

As soon as I began work today I received several documents, one of which stated that all the 1979 bonuses were frozen.

I showed it to Jin. He chuckled and said, "I knew it would happen."

When it was read among the workers, they felt all

the more grateful to the manager. Even the cadres couldn't help talking about it. It was really lucky! One day's delay and the bonuses would have been lost. Our manager was a man of vision and action!

This afternoon, we elected a delegate to the People's Congress. The candidate was chosen by the workers themselves this time. It was really democratic. The whole factory was divided into five groups: four workshops and one group of cadres. Jin won the election by an overwhelming majority in the three workshops. He almost got full votes in the cadres' group except three. It had been expected. But one person from the fourth workshop wrote on his voting slip, "Jin Fengchi is an old fox!"

The workers, who were chosen to count the ballot, told someone about this, and it was a blow to Jin's pride.

After work, Jin came to me, a bottle of alcohol in his hand. "Don't go, Wei," he said. "Have pity on a homeless man! Have a drink with me."

He produced some peanuts from his pocket.

"Why don't you go home?" I asked.

"My wife and I had a quarrel last night. I can't go home today, or we'll fight again." He poured himself a drink and gulped it down.

"Jin, you ought to look after your family," I chaffed. "From next month, I'll take most of your salary to them."

He smiled. "Chin-chin! Even an upright official finds it hard to settle a family quarrel. We've been at odds for twenty years, and she can never get the better of me. You want to try? Cheers!"

He drank like a fish. There was nothing to eat except the peanuts, which he nibbled. Before long, his eyes became bloodshot.

He stared at me and remarked all of a sudden, "It's very difficult to please people nowadays. They're a mixture of any and every sort. No matter how hard you try, somebody's always grousing."

I knew what he meant. But it was hard for me to say anything. He had another sip and continued, "I've offended the Party secretary in the interest of the workers. If I'd pleased the Party secretary, I'd have offended the workers. Do you know who cast the three votes against me?"

I was startled. How could he know who voted against him? He must have suspected Liu. But Liu was open and obviously wouldn't vote for him.

"I don't know," was all I could say.

"Luo's one of them. No question!"

I was so shocked, I could hardly believe it. "But he admires you a lot, doesn't he?"

He grinned. "I did him a favour. Anyway, his little tricks can never fool me. He's a ruthless character and very ambitious. But he was right not to vote for me."

"What about the third one?"

Pointing at himself, he said, "That was mine."

He was either drunk or making fun of me.

"It's true," he said, tossing down his drink. Now the liquor had really gone to his head. "I know you must think that I'm as slick as a snake. But I wasn't born like that. The longer you muddle along in this society, the smarter you become. After a few slips and falls even you'd wise up. The more complex the society, the sharper the people. Liu's a good man, but he didn't get as many votes as I. How can good men like him cope in future? If I'd listened to Liu and run the factory in a rigid way, production would have dropped. I'd have offended the workers and there'd be no profit. The state and our leaders wouldn't have been happy about it. Don't think I'm glad because I've got most votes. On the contrary, I feel very bad. I knew Liu wouldn't vote for me, but I voted for him. . . ."

"You're a bit tipsy, Jin," I said, helping him to a bed which was for those on night duty. "Have a rest. I'll go home and fetch you some food."

I deeply regretted that I'd voted in his favour. Though he got most votes, he is not of the calibre of a people's delegate, even in these times.

I'm certain that he'll lose the next election.

How I Became a Writer

GENERALLY speaking, the writer's road is a long and tortuous one. This is true all the more if one's own fate has been closely linked with the development of a literature. So how did I first set foot on this particular road? Was it due to luck or misfortune? Was it inevitable or just sheer coincidence? Was it the result of something innate or of something acquired? There are so many unanswerable questions. For me one of them has always been quite why I have such an indissoluble bond with literature.

Did I perhaps start along this road very early in life? If so, I was totally unaware of it.

The distance between Beanshop Village (my native place) and Cangxian County (a small city in Hebei Province) is only 25 *li*. To my child's mind though, it seemed like 25,000 *li* and that it required superhuman strength to get there. On Sundays or festival days, I would follow the grown-ups going to the country fair ten *li* or so away and was as happy as if I had gone to Cangxian. It was said that people in the town went to fairs every day. For me, my earliest and most frequent entertainment was in listening to stories about gods and spirits told by the "supermen" in our village. These stories, fascinating and terrifying at the same time, were always recounted with gusto, as though monsters and ghosts might appear at any time and at any place. Every time a story was finished, I would be so frightened that I dared not even go outside to pee. In our village, these "supermen" were particularly looked up to and whenever they dropped by anyone's house, the host or hostess would always entertain them with cigarettes and tea.

One day, in order to see what a passenger train looked like, I walked 12 *li* to the railway tracks. Having glimpsed the iron python passing through with its great grumbling engine, my eyes at once opened wide. It seemed far more wonderful even than the giant python which, as described in legends, could walk up and down mountains. I lingered a good while, enjoying myself so much that I forgot to go back home until nightfall. Shortly after that, somebody told me that trains were an even more magnificent sight by night, and that the headlights blazed even more brightly than the huge eyes of any monster. So, one moonless night, I ran over there once again. Long after my curiosity was satisfied and my eyes had feasted on this rare sight, it occurred to me that I ought to return home. But just at this moment, I was suddenly seized with fright. On my way back, I heard noises which sounded like "Sa, sa, sa. . ." coming from the fields on either side of the road and I didn't know whether it was a ghost or an immortal. In absolutely no doubt that there was some monster in hot pursuit, I raced along as fast as I could and dared not look around even once. At the western end of our village was a pine forest filled with scattered graves. Whenever I went into that wood, I used to shake with fear since it was there that all the terrible things happened in the legends that circulated among the villagers. I was in such a state of panic I felt as if every hair on my head was standing on end and as though my scalp was going to split into little pieces. Covering my face with both hands, I would dash through and out of the forest like a frightened rat. When I got home, I would be absolutely soaked with sweat. After getting back to normal though, I was rather pleased at having had such a miraculous, exciting adventure. The next day, in order to win a "tiger-skinned bird", I made a bet with some of my little friends. To prove I'd been there, I stuck one of their chopsticks on top of the largest tomb in that forest at midnight.

When I was about ten, I began to develop a liking for theatre (both Beijing opera and Hebei *bangzi**). During New Year's Eve and the March Temple Fair, I would follow along behind the theatrical troupes, wandering with them all around the neighbouring district. I never got tired of watching their productions and was soon so familiar with their programmes that I could easily recite quite a few of the famous speeches and imitate the actions and gestures of some of the leading actors.

This, then, was the sort of literary education I had in my early childhood.

It was beyond my wildest imaginings that when I was only a fourth-grade pupil in primary school, I would become a story-teller myself, one of the "supermen" of our village. Almost every single night, a great number of villagers, old and young, male and female, would crowd into the three northern rooms of Second Aunty's courtyard, some of them sitting on the

---

* A local opera popular mainly in Hebei Province.

kang, others on the ground. Unaccustomed to sitting properly for so long, I would lie down on the *kang,* reading a story out loud to them under an oil-lamp placed on the windowsill. Being the only literate person in the whole village, I had the honour of playing the starring role on these grand occasions and no matter how bad-tempered I was, my fellow villagers would excuse it completely. Instead of having a fixed repertoire, I read at random whatever works they offered, things like *The Three Kingdoms, Outlaws of the Marsh* and so on and so forth. Consequently bizarre things often used to happen. Once, when I got to the end of the 17th chapter of a historical epic, the succeeding chapter was still nowhere to be found and I was forced to continue with the 23rd chapter, leaving out the missing chapters 19 to 22. And whenever I paused to ponder over an unfamiliar word in a passage, the audience would quickly become impatient and urge me on, saying they could guess the word from the context.

Usually, my readings only came to an end when I grew so tired that both my eyes and tongue failed to respond to my command and Second Aunty had already prepared a red-date tea as a reward for me. As a result of my special function as story-teller, I had a chance to read all of the things that my enthusiastic audiences had collected from their friends or relatives. So I always had a lot of novels put by and read them voraciously. It was, therefore, no surprise that the sheep would be herded out to pasture in the morning without my being in the slightest aware and that I would put off cutting grass until it was nearing high noon. I was often forced to gather some haphazardly, hurrying home to account for myself with a small pile loosely heaped in my basket.

I don't know whether this sort of experience could be seen as my first real contact with literature. To tell the truth, I was absolutely fascinated by those stories and characters, yet it didn't seem to bring about any particular improvement in my language ability. I was also fond of solving arithmetical problems, of the "How many chickens and hares are there in the cage?" kind and consequently it was easy for me to get top marks in the maths exams. In language, however, and in composition in particular, my results were as mediocre as ever.

When it was time for me to attend middle school, I went to Tianjin, a big city which was quite alien to me and which I didn't like at all. Despite the fact that I was always one of the top three in the class, I was still looked down on by my schoolmates who had all been born and raised in the city. They made fun of my clothing and my rural accent, and behaved as if the fact that I was a monitor of our class was an insult to them. Whenever I gave instructions from the front row, they would boo and hoot in the rear and I was subjected to all sorts of indignities. Finally unable to stand it any longer, I got into a fierce fight with them, at long last venting all of my pent-up anger. Precisely as a result of this act of revenge, however, I was immediately dismissed from the class committee. Only then did I begin to grapple with the complexities of life and to learn that if one wanted to have a secure position in society and live without being humiliated by others, you must fight against evil.

In early 1958, I was framed by two classmates, neither

of whom had previously borne a grudge against me, and I suddenly became the main target of criticism in the school. I was accused not only of disobeying orders (I had refused to study at the pedagogical school arranged by our educational authorities), but also of reading novels all day long. I was also accused of not being discerning enough in my reading, indiscriminately swallowing whatever came into my hands, such as Ba Jin's *Family*, *Spring* and *Autumn*, Stendhal's *Le Rouge et le Noir*, Tolstoy's *Resurrection* and so on and so forth. Before all this happened, these two classmates had investigated my reading record in the school library and had even asked me my opinion of these works. However, not being particularly vigilant, I probably just blurted out a lot of off-the-cuff remarks. They wrote down everything I said in their notebooks, though I myself had long since forgotten. The conclusion, roughly, that they drew from these materials was as follows: "So influenced by bourgeois ideas is he, that he wants to be a writer in order to pursue private fame and gain." Besides this, I was also accused of having a passion for reading historical romances full of feudal ethics. In meetings they would attack me by saying: "Before you fancy your chances as a writer, why don't you pick up a mirror and look at your reflection? If the forty people in our class were all writers, then you would be one too. But if there were only thirty-nine then you wouldn't be included!"

Although I withstood all of this criticism, I couldn't put up with their insults and mockery. As a matter of fact, my ambition then anyway was to get into a training institute specializing in tractors. I got top marks in all of my 14 subjects except for composition. The reason was clear: Although I still hadn't broken my old habit of reading novels all day long I still took no interest in composition. It had never occurred to me that they would not only unjustly accuse me of trying to become a writer, but that they would hold me up to such mockery and sarcasm. Unfortunately, I had no time to avenge these false accusations since we all went our separate ways immediately after graduation. In reality, however, what chance did I have of defending myself against a mass movement? After suffering all this contempt and injustice, I suddenly started coughing up blood. Afraid that the illness might have an unfavourable effect on my job assignment after graduation, I didn't have the nerve either to go to hospital to have a checkup or to tell my family, nor did I wish to allow my persecutors to congratulate one another on hearing this news. So I hid myself in the depths of a forest reserve beyond the railway, stealthily writing stories and essays. After finishing a piece, which took on average a day or two, I would offer it to a newspaper or magazine, in the hope that at least one would be carried so that I could win credit for myself and irritate my enemies: Hadn't they said that I wanted to become a writer? As a result I was determined to do my utmost to get back at them. Nevertheless, these painstaking plans and attempts were all in vain, since none of my pieces was ever published. I felt that I just didn't have the makings of a writer, and what's more it taught me a home truth: Don't recklessly criticize literary works. Certainly, things are sometimes poorly written but if you tried to produce something yourself of even that standard, you'd probably fail.

After this first setback, I dropped for ever my ambitions of becoming a writer and went to work at the Tianjin Heavy Machinery Plant. The factory was quite wide-ranging and had very sophisticated equipment. With a veteran revolutionary as its director, it was one of the key enterprises in the country and turned out to be far more than the tractor construction workshop I had admired on an earlier visit. Feeling quite at home, I threw myself immediately into studying mechanics. To my great astonishment I found that I, the son of a peasant, had a talent for mechanical things. Two years later, I became the head of a production team and in addition my boss assured me that, since I was so clever and quick, I would soon be further promoted to senior crafts-man level (i.e., a grade 8 worker), if I could only over-come my old defect — my fondness for reading novels and going to the theatre. In his eyes, it was ridiculous for a young apprentice to go to watch Mei Lanfang per-forming at a cost of two yuan a ticket. From then on, I devoted myself to my speciality and was willing to spend the rest of my life at it, no longer thinking about writing. As a result, the wound in my heart gradually healed and the blood-spitting ceased too. When I went to hospital for an examination, all my medical certificate said was that I had some calcification in the left lung. However, my "chronic disease" continued — I just couldn't live without books; no matter how late it was nor how tired I felt when I got back to my dormitory, I would still pick up something to read.

While I was working at the factory, conscription sud-denly began and, being the right age, I was drafted at once. It seemed a shame to give up my newly acquired skill, yet I thought of the advantages of joining the forces, of how it would broaden my horizons and enable me to travel and so I resolutely put on a uniform. I served in the navy for several years, although I remained shorebound, mostly engaged in surveying and drafting. The new work really did open my eyes and cause me to see the whole world. Whatever happened abroad would instantly be reflected on our maps. Eventually I became familiar with the world's geography, and with the major ports of every country. I was also up on the latest military information, on things like the current situation of our own navy and the degree to which the Soviet Union and the United States had developed their navies. I learned that the building up of armed forces depended mainly on the development of heavy industry and that a modern war could only be won by producing an adequate quantity and quality of iron and steel, in other words on the level of both science and technology. So ultimately I gained experience of the agricultural, industrial and military fronts.

When I was in the navy, the literary and artistic propaganda team was popular with the troops, and once a month we would hold an evening meeting. As the head of a squad, I had to compile programmes that would make a good showing of our unit. The old saying, "Pick a general from among the dwarfs", was brought to mind when the chief of our troop, thinking I seemed to have a talent for writing, put me in charge of compiling programmes for the propaganda team itself. From then on, I wrote whatever was needed, one-act plays, comic skits, ballads, or lyrics. Looking back on all of this I realize that preparing programmes for the propaganda team was really a good chance to learn writing skills. I also learned some basic principles. One must always take the mood of an audience into account before starting work and make things easy to understand and full of genuine feeling. I found that that was the only way an audience could be moved.

The success of our performances taught me a lot. I was naturally highly pleased, even a little intoxicated, by conversations with marshals and generals, with the praise of troupe leaders and the hearty applause and repeated curtain calls from the audience, but none of this upset nor radically changed my earlier views on literature. I still regarded propaganda work as a temporary job and draftsmanship as my real work, my lifelong undertaking, and saw the task of writing programmes as something of a lark. When I was transferred to the propaganda team, the leaders of our troop had quite a divergence of opinion: the man in charge of political work insisted on nominating me for transfer while the director of our detachment in charge of management flatly refused to carry out this order. The unit I worked in was a very professional one, and talented staff were highly thought of. Having been recently promoted to deputy head of the brigade (similar to a platoon in the infantry), I took charge of all the occupational business and was able to handle the workload. Had I ignored my proper duties, it would surely have offended my direct superior, who could have prevented me from further promotion.

Once when we were performing in a village, some of the peasants started weeping bitterly when we started reciting poetry and the sound of sobbing then spread throughout the hall. Obviously each of the peasants in this poor, backward village had suffered greatly, and poignant memories had been aroused by their empathy with the characters in the poem. As a result, they spontaneously poured out all their pent-up grievances.

The bitter weeping of these peasants sent a shiver of recognition through me. It reminded me immediately of the people who listened, absorbed, to the stories from ancient legends which I stuttered out by the oil-lamp's dim light ten years earlier. With this scene before me, my approach to literature change. In the begining, art was created by people in order to express anger, to laugh, to sing and to record their lives and so poetry, music and literature came into being. Though literature has developed into a very sophisticated medium, it should still belong to ordinary people. Literature is the voice of the people and thus they are its very soul. Literature must voice their heartfelt wishes and aspirations. Only after integration with people's real experience can the indignation aroused in a writer's heart have a significant effect.

Literature is by no means a frivolous matter, neither is it the property of those who only seek fame and personal gain. It is ignorance and prejudice to regard creative writing as a way of achieving these things or to think that people who write do so entirely in order to obtain these ends. At the beginning of my career, when I adopted a less responsible attitude towards literary work, it was no surprise that writing of mine which was aimed merely at pleasing others met with failure. From this it is clear that literature has no time for dilettantes and panderers. Literary creation expresses the soul of a people; it is work which needs to be approached in an extremely solemn manner and with a special sense of duty. A people's soul cannot be suffocated; it needs to breathe. And literature is none other than a vital means of expression of a people's soul.

Moved by this scene, a wave of pure emotion at once welled up in me. Unable to fall asleep that night, I got out of bed and wrote a piece which I submitted the following day to the *Guangming Daily*. Rather unexpectedly, it was published. Not long after that, I finished a short story entitled "A New Station Master", which, on the advice of one of my old colleagues in Gansu Province, I posted to the magazine *Gansu Literature*, and that was published too. From then on, I started writing in a variety of literary forms, including short stories, prose and reportage, and all of my pieces were carried by army and local newspapers.

I paid, however, a price for my achievements, in giving up my drafting, and in forfeiting prospects of further promotion. But I felt no regrets since literature and I had become mutually acquainted. Making use of my vacation time before reporting back for work at the factory, I took my demobilization pay (190 yuan in all) and made a trip through Xinjiang, Qinghai and Gansu. I had long wanted to see the great mountains and rivers of my country, to see what life was like in those regions. When I got to Xining Railway Station, however, I unfortunately lost all my money and grain coupons and was forced to return to my factory, taking up my old work once again.

In 1966, literary magazines closed down one after another and as a result manuscripts of five of my short stories and essays, most of which were already in the final proof stage, were all sent back. Nevertheless, since I had a special fondness for cultural work, I promptly joined the propaganda team of our factory, which kept me in touch with literature and which satisfied my craving for creative writing. In 1972, as soon as the magazine *Tianjin Literature* started publication, I staged a comeback and had my short story "Three Crane-workers" published there.

My account of how I happened to follow this particular path may seem a bit mundane and doesn't perhaps explain very much at all. I am convinced, though, that there are thousands of different ways of producing good literature.

I've been reluctant to part either with literature or with my previous work, so even now I remain hesitant about what move to make. However, whenever I suffer some sad experience, I become more and more involved with literature. As I see it, the lure of literature comes not from being called a writer, but from actual creation itself, from persisting in the effort to explore and temper oneself through life's tribulations.

In short, there is no ready-made path which one can follow; if you wish to have a path of your own, then you must break and explore it for yourself.

Jiang Zilong

Translated by Hu Zhihui

赤橙黄绿青蓝紫

蒋 子 龙

熊 猫 丛 书

＊

《中国文学》杂志社出版
（中国北京百万庄路24号）
中国国际书店发行
1983年（36开）第1版
编号：（英）2—916—18
00170
10—E—1753P